A THOUSAND
DEATHS
PLUS ONE

A THOUSAND
DEATHS
PLUS ONE

a novel by

SERGIO
RAMÍREZ

Translated from the Spanish by

LELAND H. CHAMBERS

McPherson & Company
KINGSTON, NEW YORK

A THOUSAND DEATHS PLUS ONE

Copyright © 2004 by Sergio Ramírez.
Translation copyright © 2009 by Leland H. Chambers.
All rights reserved.

Original title: Mil y una muertes
Published by Alfaguara, 2004

This edition published by McPherson & Company
Box 1126 Kingston, New York 12402,
with assistance from the Literature Program of the
New York State Council on the Arts, a state agency.
Book design by Bruce R. McPherson.
Jacket design by Paul Bacon.
Typeset in Carre Noir.
Printed on pH neutral paper.
Manufactured in the United States of America.

1 3 5 7 9 10 8 6 4 2   2009 2010 2011

LIBRARY OF CONGRESS CATALOGING-IN-PUBLICATION DATA
Ramírez, Sergio, 1942-
  [Mil y una muertes. English]
  A thousand deaths plus one : a novel / by Sergio Ramírez ; translated from
the Spanish by Leland H. Chambers.
    p. cm.
  ISBN 978-0-929701-87-5 (alk. paper)
  I. Chambers, Leland H., 1928-   II. Title.
  PQ7519.2.R25M5513 2009
  863'.64 -- dc22
                                             2009002415

The translator expresses particular gratitude to the following individuals

for help provided at various points in the process of translating this novel,

whose language touches in detail on such a broad selection of historical

and cultural themes: Sydney Chambers, Carolynne Myall, Javier Torre,

Zulema Lòpez, Oriol Casanas, and of course Sergio Ramírez.

for Antonia Kerrigan

It is a rule of refinement, when writing about and making use of the vicissitudes of our life, never to tell the truth.

SØREN KIERKEGAARD, *Diary* (1842-1844)

A man lies here, silent and ignored,
Who, living, lived a thousand deaths plus one;
Do not expect to learn about my days gone by.
To awaken is to die. Rouse me not!

XAVIER VILLAURRUTIA, *Epitafios*

Camera Obscura

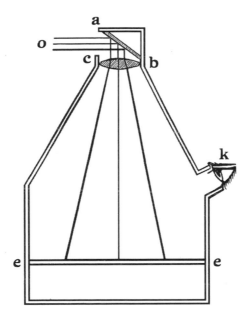

The Nomad Prince

by Rubén Darío

A MORNING OF SUMMER JUBILANCE this July Sunday, when I have come as far as the splendid Mallorcan paradise that for not a few years now has served as a lavish retreat for His Highness the Archduke Luis Salvador. You may be aware that Miramar, this princely estate halfway between Deyá and Valldemosa, was once the residence of Haddarán in times when the Arabs bestowed on these Balearic Islands their miracles of eastern civilization, some quite practical, like the terraces, irrigation canals, and cisterns for the benefit of the seeds, and others rather spiritual, such as the poetic writings inscribed on arches and walls to make the stones to speak.

The magnificent Richard-Brassier automobile which the painter Santiago Rusiñol has made available to me— together with his *chauffeur*, attired in a gray uniform with high boots like a police official—has made its way with the help of its strident claxon along the narrow, twisting road, blaring its warning alike for the *carretelas* drawn by dilatory Algerian burros, carrying peasants, and for the dray wagons transporting provincial gentlemen and pot-bellied priests on their Sunday excursions.

The fresh light shimmers over the heights and descends as if it were joined with the wind that is shaking the branches of the pines, while the sea with its changing face repeats the burnished solar reflections in the vapored distance where the plume of smoke from a steamer, appearing to the eye as a minuscule something, is dissolving. One can now breathe deeply and full of pleasure the balsamic air that spreads itself everywhere so prodigally, welcoming us, and then it seems as though you can hear the voice of the divine Virgil among the fronds rocked by light Aeolian gusts: *Hic arguta sacra pendebit fistula pinu.*

The royal landlord arrived here years ago while searching for a refuge, fleeing the rigors of court life. Ah, to have the courage to abandon forever the urban masses, those "rectangular abominations"! To understand the merits of solitude and the salubrious mingling of one's own spirit with that of wordless beings! To withdraw from what in religious terminology is called "the world" and come to a place such as this to finish out the task of earthly life!

From the crest of the escarpment, the landscape starts falling away in steep slopes until turning into the promontory of Na Cova Foradada, a tongue of rock stained with colorings of iron and copper that enters the sea foam like a colossal dragon, with its stone-like eye pierced through by the winds (and on the opposite side you can make out the cove of Sa Estaca, which serves as an anchorage) and where the wandering Archduke ordered to be placed on the heights a small palace cottage for a certain feminine personage who is still veiled in mystery. Her name was Catalina.

He carried her from the city to be the housekeeper for these precincts where once the nightingale of Raymond Lull, the Divine Anchorite, was heard to sing, and where now one sees in how flattering a fashion he honored her in his affections. But, persecuted by the Archduke's adverse destiny, she died of leprosy two years ago, having suffered the disfigurement of her elegant face together with the amputation of some fingers. It was an illness that she acquired, according to what I've been told, during a pilgrimage to Palestine.

In a small enclave in the garden stands a cage with iron bars, and behind them a vulture, making a show of its elegant boredom and gazing at us with some disregard and also a bit of asthmatic ferocity. There are small temples rising up from among the graceful pines, and one of those the Archduke has consecrated to Raymond Lull in the same spot where the author of the magic *Libro de Blanquerna* had his rustic chapel.

I have been told that this august personage happened to be absent on one of his frequent escapades around the Mediterranean, but that is not true because from Raymond's chapel, which also serves as a vantage point lookout, I see the *Nixe II*, his mighty three-masted yacht, anchored in the Sa Estaca cove. And now I catch sight of him and am amazed by a singular spectacle. Listen.

Along the road that goes down among the murmuring cypresses comes a strange procession, more resembling a band of acrobats painted by Goya than anything else, absurd figures of the kind so beloved of Valle Inclán, most of them bearing fresh armfuls of camellias, crocuses, peonies: a woman past her prime, thick-wasted and matronly, with a mantilla and back comb, sinking on her twisted heels as she walks; a peasant woman, hair now streaked with gray, one of those that dance the Mallorcan *boleras*; a turbaned

Hindu with the look of a fakir ravaged by the hunger of his fasts, his mouth dyed red from betel nut, and a wicker basket under his arm which might contain a deadly asp; a Turk with his fez, wearing embroidered slippers on his feet, with huge mustachios and his muscled torso naked, the very image of the executioner who would decapitate you painlessly with his gleaming scimitar; a "Miss" wearing a long skirt, with the air of an English governess, and a hat adorned with ragged tendrils, and impertinent eyes with which she seems to want to decipher the mysteries of the world by holding them up in front of her myopic vision; a chubby-cheeked little boy in a sailor suit that squeezes his flesh; a tonsured monk in a coarse-clothed brown habit, faded now, and wearing a pilgrim's sandals; a man in a tight frock coat and a bowler hat, the faithful image of a grave digger of the kind whose sight alone awakens a morbid terror in me.

At the tail of the procession, an elderly man, very fat and bearded, with a grimy blue jacket and visored cap, is carrying a Borneo monkey mounted crosslegged on his shoulders as if it were a little boy, and by his side a dog obviously of no known breed is leaping and running about, trying to get some attention from the monkey, who for his part just bares his teeth. It is the Archduke himself. And right behind him, a photographer painfully carryies his tripod, stopping periodically to rest with panting breath; he seems asthmatic. His wide-brimmed hat is thrown forward with a gesture that says, "Of course it's not out of nonchalance," his dark hair falls to his shoulders in Nazarine ringlets, his exhausted amber eyes are set in a face that one would say belonged to a maharajah or an Indian cacique, one of those mysterious faces that the tropic suns have baked in their implacable splendor; and all the while a little girl, whose straw hat is trimmed with colorful ribbons falling down her back, frolics about his feet.

Outrageously nonsensical in their appearance, but anointed with the devotion that you will only find in those hermetic cults which in their esoteric delirium worship Phoebus the golden or the pallid Selene. My presence goes unobserved by them, but I have no idea what they are up to, so it seems impertinent of me to follow after them. When once more in Palma I put the question to Rusiñol concerning this strange vision, he informs me that such creatures comprise the Archduke's entourage, and they always accompany him in his unforeseen peregrinations aboard the *Nixe II*. One might catch sight of them one day in Trieste, another day in Algiers, on yet another day in Palermo, or in Alexandria, or in Piraeus, and on not a few occasions they have been taken for the performers in a circus side show, or else for a *troup de comédiens*.

At the moment when I met them, they were, he informs me, on their way to throw those flowers into the sea, a ceremony that is held every year in memory of the Archduke's private secretary of old, Wenceslas Vyborny, a handsome boy from Bohemia who died of sunstroke after daring to sail on a clandestine trip from Sa Estaca to Palma to meet with a secret lover. He died there in a hotel, and the Archduke, unhinged by grief, purchased the bed where he had died, together with the rest of the furniture of the room, and brought it all here to be consumed in a kind of funeral pyre. The *Nixe II* carried back to his own country the remains of the young man so beloved of the Archduke, but before weighing anchor he ordered the cloth of each of the yacht's sails painted black.

Then he explained to me why, in a lower room of the Archducal palace, where visitors are permitted to go, and which exudes a monastic feeling because of its silence, the traveler is surprised by a marble monument signed by Tantardini in which the Angel of Supreme Justice is attempting to awaken, with the protesting clamor of his horn, a slim-looking Apollonian cadaver. What is that piece of mausoleum sculpture, I ask myself, doing here, looking as though it has been taken out of the Staglieno Cemetery in Genoa, which is considered the most beautiful in Europe, after the Père Lachaise in Paris? For, just like the funeral procession I have described, it commemorates the Archduke's singular relationship with Vyborny.

The wind of gossip, that *ventecello* which the immortal Rossini sets ruffling in *The Barber of Seville*, takes great delight in nibbling away at the opalescent oblation from Carrara that our imperial Pylades dedicated to his secretary Orestes. A simple case of ordinary pandering? Or could it be that the Archduke, exiled from mundane glory by his own will, sees nature as a whole and in consequence demonstrates a grand and extraordinary capacity for love that embraces equally female and male, animal and plant?

Dedicated to scientific research, his books and pamphlets on cartography, navigation, philology and history, on the flora and fauna of these environs, are learned and numerous, and the Royal Academy of Science in Madrid has honored him as a regular member for having discovered a rare specimen of buckthorn, baptized in his name as *Rahmanus ludovicus-salvatoris.*

Tragic, at any rate, is the appropriate appellation for his story and that of his illustrious family of Atreides, having suffered pursuit by the indefatigable Furies throughout the centuries. His fiancée, the Princess Matilde, daughter of his cousin Albert, died in a hydrostatic bed after going through two weeks of agony, the consequence of some serious burns she suffered when her clothing took fire; she had just finished putting on a diaphanous garment of tulle in her apartment in the Weilburg Castle when her father unexpectedly entered her bedroom, and the tragedy occurred either because in a fright she was trying to hide behind her back a cigarette she was smoking, or else because her progenitor had drawn too close to the sheer fabric while carrying a lit Havana cigar between his fingers.

And his brother Johan Salvator, the rebellious Johann Orth who lit such a fuse for the press when he renounced his heraldic surname to take that of a bourgeois citizen and then married the vaudeville dancer Milli Steubel? The two of them disappeared in the South Atlantic near Cape Horn when their merchant sailing ship the *Santa Margarita* was wrecked. And his cousin Maximilian, the Emperor of Mexico who was set up there by the ambitions of Napoleon III? He was executed on the Cerro de Las Campanas, as recently portrayed so admirably by Nargeot's lithograph, while Carlota, the fugitive Empress, lover of the cantatas and motets of Bach, and in her youth a devout reader of Plutarch's *Moralia: Customs and Mores*, today strolls around, out of her mind, through the rooms of Bouchout Castle in Belgium, the country of her birth.

His cousin Sophia, Duchess of Alençon, died consumed by a fire at La Charité in Paris, an event of which there are some astonishing photographs printed by Count Primoli. Another cousin of his, Rudolph, Crown Prince of Austria, true to a fatal pact with his lover, Baroness María Vetsera, killed her with one shot and afterward put another in his own head, in the solitude of their lodging at a hunting preserve in Mayerling. Still another, Archduke Wilhelm, died in a fall from his horse, after the noble animal suddenly shied and threw him violently from the saddle.

Shall we ever bring this tale to an end? His cousin Ludwig II of Bavaria, the fanciful king who, thoroughly saturated with Wagnerian melodies, spent his life building castles inspired by Teutonic mythologies, was capable of loving with equal passion both Wagner and his stableboy, rival of

Admetus (that *ventecello* once more), and died poetically by drowning in the Sternberger See.

And his cousin Elisabeth, Empress of Austria and Queen of Hungary, the mother of the unfortunate suicide Rudoph? Assassinated in Geneva by the dagger of that Luccheni, a fanatic anarchist who attacked her treacherously when she was strolling along the promenade by the lake, accompanied by a single *dame de compagnie*, such was her passion for anonymity. A strange and unsubmissive creature, she preferred the fortunate seclusion of the Gödöllö Palace in Budapest to the weariness of the ceremonial life of the Hofburg in Vienna. On her sumptuous yacht where she paraded her nervous hyperesthesia around the Mediterranean, she always carried two goats, one white and the other black, to be milked every morning so as to be able to give herself a cosmetic bath in milk.

Elisabeth, as nomadic as her cousin the Archduke, sometimes visited him incognito in Miramar, with no other companion than her hunchbacked confidant, the poet Cristomanos, who taught the queen to read the dactylic hexameters of Homer in classic Greek. That was when she and the mysterious Catalina met each other. When this poor unfortunate woman succumbed to Hansen's disease, Luis Salvador wrote a heartfelt pamphlet in tribute to her, of which Rusiñol keeps a copy among the rarities of his enviable library, and in which that encounter is described. I quote: "They got along as if they had known each other all their lives, since in both of them throbbed the same human feelings, very brightly. The sun went down on the horizon and the sea shone like gold, enveloping them in a glorious halo. It was like a transfiguration. Who would have dared suspect, at such a moment, that in a few years this earthly transfiguration would be turned into a celestial one for both?"

One must say that, Catalina being only a commoner, the

imperial court in Vienna with bureaucratic speed ordered all the copies of the obituary confiscated; a few copies were saved, and one of them came into Rusiñol's possession, as I said, purchased on the *rive gauche* from Père Bouchon, the most *intrigant* of the *bouquinistes* I know, capable of obtaining for you the original roll of the Torah, if that is what you were to request from him.

Given the incongruousness of his entourage, and the outrageousness of his habits, there are those who think that through the veins of Luis Salvador run the same miasmas of madness that muddied the mind of Ludwig of Bavaria, although he often has been heard to remark sarcastically, "In my family everyone is mad, but the one who is least so is myself." Judge for yourself.

A most pleasing solar glow burnishes the cupolas of the little temples when the eccentric procession becomes lost beyond the branches of the corpulent oaks that hold out the arabesques of their branches above the radiant blue of the sea. The Archduke turns his head for a moment, notices me, and gazes at me with definite curiosity. For my part, I contemplate him as if this were a matter of a photograph before turning over the page in an album. With his filthy jacket and visored cap, his little eyes imprisoned by the fleshy cheeks beneath the blond eyebrows, the bristles of his beard badly trimmed and graying, would he not look to you like the coach driver for a relay of post horses?

The traveler senses from afar his wheezing respiration, and afterwards watches him go off behind his procession with the monkey on his shoulder, stooped and clumsy in his obesity, taking air in with his snout down as if searching for acorns on the ground.

Published originally in *Orbe Latino*, Vol 3, No. 3, Madrid, August, 1907; included in *Pàginas desconocidas de Rubén Darío*, ed. Roberto Ibáñez, Biblioteca de Marcha, Montevideo, 1970.

1

And what is the worst? To be born

One body that is vile, the other one pure, virtues and vices all amount to the same thing: they turn into brothers when they are dead. Evidently, death is the best act of human beings. And what is the worst? To be born.

Chopin, *Notebook*, 1831

THE FIRST OF THE EPISODES I wish to tell about has to do with my stay in Warsaw at the beginning of autumn, 1987, when I went for an interview with General Jaruzelski. The Polish government put me up then in a residence for visiting officials on Klonowa Street, very close to the Belvedere Palace where the meeting was to take place.

Klonowa Street is very short, opening out beneath the ash trees and presenting an abundance of Neoclassical mansions with fences of gilded, sharpened rods standing in front of the gardens. The one they assigned to me had belonged to the merchant Karol Kumelski, a dealer in wheat and animal feed, and the double K of his improvised escutcheon could still be seen at the peak of the iron arch above the large portal door. They gave me a luxurious apartment at the back of the garden, while the rest of the delegation occupied the rooms in the principle section of the residence.

On that street were living now the dignitaries of the party, generals and ministers, as could be seen by the traffic of official cars that moved about noiselessly with their clusters of antennas, and by the guards armed with Kalashnikov rifles that were posted in the sentry boxes beside the front doors. I believe I recall, but this could be a fabrication of my memory, that the guards, squeezed into their gray wool overcoats, wore gaiters and white gloves, and that the sentry boxes were painted in stripes, as in the old comic strips of Tintin drawn by Hergé.

Those were the difficult days at the beginning of the transition that Jaruzelski, amid many tensions and in a rather enigmatic way, pushed through, garbed in his military wear and behind those smoked lenses with their heavy tortoise-shell frames. Because of his dark glasses, in Nicaragua those of us in the government used to refer to him, in the privacy of our jokes, as "José Feliciano," the name of the blind Puerto Rican singer who was all the rage then. Those glasses and his baldness, which had it not been for his uniform would very likely have caused us to confuse him with an inflexible professor of theology, did nothing for his charisma. But neither did they remove anything from his affability, interested as he was during that interview in listening to my stories of the far-off Nicaragua at war while the Soviet world was beginning to come apart like moth-chewed valances on an old curtain. Then he had me move into a salon surrounded by velvet drapes of Corinthian red, the sort that accumulate age and dust, and in a simple ceremony attended by only by some junior staff functionary, he fastened the Order of the Defenders of Warsaw on me, clumsily poking its none-too-sharp pin through my lapel.

We had arrived late the night before, coming from

Prague, but very early in the morning I got up to do my jogging. In those days I stuck firmly to my routine, knowing that the worst thing for keeping to the discipline of my exercises was these journeys, when I would be subject to schedules that usually begin with a working breakfast and end with a formal dinner lasting until well past midnight. That's why, to remove any excuses, I always brought my sweats and my running shoes with me. I thought of waking up Lieutenant Moisés Rivera, who accompanied me on my visits abroad at the head of a small escort of two men, more honorific than anything else, but in the end I decided to play a trick on him and go by myself, as long as the Polish bodyguards in any event were not going to lose the opportunity of following my footsteps. Nonetheless, when I went down to the garden there was only the one guard in gaiters and white gloves encased in his long, gray overcoat beside the sentry-box. He looked at me without saying anything, surely because he didn't recognize me, and then I decided to take off.

Trotting, I crossed the stripes of the pedestrian crossing at Avenue Ujadowskie. At that hour there was nothing moving except a trolleybus, half empty but with its lights on inside, and I passed in front of the Belvedere Palace, illuminated in the darkness of the early morning by discreet spotlights. When the caravan that brought us from the airport the night before had come in sight of the Palace, our official translator explained, with a serious countenance, that during the first half of the nineteenth century the Grand Duke Constantine had resided there. As representative of the Imperial Russian power, he was as hated by the Poles as his brother, Czar Alexander I. Beside me in the seat of the swank Chaika automobile, Josef Krajewska, who as president of the Planning Commission had been charged with receiving me, smiled without understanding the slightest thing about that spontaneous commentary.

The translator, the grandson of immigrants from Bohemia, was named Dominik Vyborny and was an Assistant Professor in the School of Arts and Letters at the University of Warsaw. Spirited and revealing a bony complexion with broad cheekbones, he must have been around fifty, and his coppery-colored hair was beginning to thin. Slovenly of dress, pompous in his gestures, he spoke Spanish with an appealing accent because he had learned it without ever having left Poland from an exiled republican from Sevilla, don Rafael Escuredo. He pronounced his lengthy sentences without a break, with guttural spasms, the thick veins of his neck standing out, and he would end them with a kind of sob, as if he were lifting his head out of water after a prolonged immersion. He didn't hide his sympathy with Walesa and the Solidarity Movement, and, of course, with the Pope Wojtyla; and as you can already see, neither did he hide his ill will toward the Russians of all epochs. Apart from that, he was a great admirer of Rubén Darìo, a respect passed on by his teacher Escuredo, and was the translator of several of Darìo's poems into Polish.

Beyond the Belvedere Palace I could make out beneath the motionless mist the woods of the Lazienki Royal Park. Soon I came to an esplanade where there stood several rows of iron chairs, and in front of them some five or six music stands dispersed around the damp grass, recent evidence of some open-air chamber music concert. Behind the music stands was a statue of Chopin in the act of seeking inspiration, a rock for his seat and his hands on his knees beneath a willow tree with a thick trunk, its bronze branches pushed in a motionless tide by the wind.

The night before, during the trip from the airport, I had been unable to get my host Krajewska, who was suffocating from the heat inside the Chaika and surely eager to get to sleep as soon as possible, to show some interest in the conversation topics I proposed. When I expressed my admiration for Chopin, he had merely smiled as he thanked me. Dominik, paying no attention to the limits of his job as translator, puffed up his mouth in a disdainful way and told me that Chopin, a very precocious genius and all that, had nonetheless accepted favors from the Grand Duke Constantine, even after the insurrection of 1831 against the Russian invaders, and that Czar Alexander himself had given him a ring loaded with diamonds that he not only accepted but kept in Paris among his sentimental treasures.

I began to run first down narrow sandy walkways and then on some paths covered by a jumble of dead leaves. The cold was pressing in, and I zipped up my sweats to the neck. Getting further away, I ran along now without a fixed plan beneath real grottoes of shade. I got onto an unknown path that started behind a thicket that suddenly burst apart, rustling with the sudden flight of a flock of partridges, and I crossed a small log bridge above the rippled current of an irrigation ditch that was sounding below me with a secret murmuring; and soon, as the master of this freedom that was like a gift, I was overcome by the joy of running cross-country through a place as unfamiliar and as beautiful as this one—and moreover, I was alone. I hadn't come across a single soul, no other runner, no passer-by, not even a park guard.

It was just at the break of day when I came out in a clearing and stopped to give myself a rest. In the center stood a summerhouse pavilion surrounded by a gallery of tubular columns topped by capitals without ornament. I mounted the flight of steps eager to get a look through the glass doors, dripping with dew, that calmly reflected the yellow and gold foliage of the trees in a light that remained diffuse. With my nose against the glass, I put my hands together before my face to form a kind of screen and thus managed to make out a long, double panel mounted at an angle on an easel, covered with photographs. I discovered the door was open because it gave way when the wind pushed it, and so I went in.

The exhibit was titled *Castellón the Photographer in Warsaw*. Paired off on the panels, the photographs with serrated edges, printed on glossy paper, and held up there with tacks, were divided into *Before the Nazi Occupation* and *During the Nazi Occupation*, and the legend beneath each one of them appeared in Polish and in French, carefully typed, all of which gave the whole thing an academic cast. *Before:* the crowded Chlodna Street with the Clock Building trimmed with neo-baroque decorations, the Panoptikum movie theater, the Amphitryon Theater, a huge silken slipper raised up above its slender heel at the door of a women's shoe store, a tailor shop with manikins of different heights showing in the window, for adults and children, wearing double-breasted suits and men's dress hats. At the intersection of Dluga and Naveliski streets, Simon's Arcades was a rather modern looking apparition of glass and concrete among the neoclassical edifices.

Then the camera visited interiors. La Fantaisie, a shop for gentlemen's wear. The cashier wearing a bakelite eyeshade proudly raises his glance behind a cash register decorated with ironwork, admiring the merchandise: umbrellas all open and suspended from the ceiling, bundles of canes in wicker displays, fans from Sevilla, ostrich feathers, necklaces of false pearls, brooches and cameos in glass showcases. The Blikle Café, where customers crowded in front of small, marble-topped tables are unfolding newspapers hung on shining rods, the waiters wearing their long aprons are poised with their empty trays, while an imposing porcelain samovar stands in the background.

The photos *During* were arranged on the lower part of the panel: the wooden bridge crossing over Chlodna Street at the intersection with Zelatna Street to connect the two sectors of the ghetto, and looking like a railway car suspended in mid air; at the steps leading up to the bridge German soldiers standing guard wearing their gleaming boots and long overcoats, sheathed in those flaring helmets that covered their ears, so familiar from the movies. At the entrance to the ghetto from Siena Street stood a long line of men with days-old beards and women with knotted babushkas on their heads waiting to climb into a military truck carrying their belongings: suitcases tied with rope, a painting with embossed moldings, and a table lamp dangling its plug on the ground, borne in the arms of a boy wearing an adult's hat, all bound for the siding yards at the Central Station on Jeroziolimskie Avenue. Little boys clutched at the grating over the tiny window of a horse-drawn carnival wagon, destined for the same place.

There was also Chopin's birthplace in Zelazowa Wola, *Before* and *During*. *Before:* the gable roof of slate straining under the snow that had accumulated also on the steps of the entryway, *Winter View*, February, 1934. *During:* being consumed by the flames of a fire that has left bare the framework of the roof, the beams smoldering. A swastika, painted with a wide brush, decorates one of the smoke-scorched walls: *A fire that was set on July 4, 1940, by attack forces of Nazi youths who charged Chopin with being decadent.*

The final pair of photos dealt with Szeroki Dunaj Street, very close to the Gate of the Butchers, in the old city. In the one below, *During*, the shuttered businesses have their windows nailed up with boards, and the snow is coming down like sperm over the streetlamps that look in relief like carnivorous flowers entrapped by tiny parasites at the tops of their iron stalks. A boy of some seven years stands in the foreground, with his back toward the door of a pharmacy, his hands above his head. The pharmacy's sign above the door says *Apteka Capharnaüm* on a ribbon held up by a pair of cupids. The boy is dark, his limp hair open in a pair of waves falling over his forehead, and he wears the Star of David sewn to his coat. A few steps away on the cobblestones lies a pair of bodies wrapped in overcoats, and between them and the boy is a trail of articles of clothing that have fallen out of a packed suitcase of cardboard that also is in the picture. The fallen man is corpulent, the woman quite slight, but their faces cannot be seen. Soldiers stand guard over the scene from alongside a motorcar, pointing their Schmeisser machine guns at the bodies, apparently waiting in expectation of the arrival of a superior officer. *The "chouette" couple from Mallorca comprised of Baltasar Bonnin, a butcher by trade, and his wife Teresa (Catholic Jews having immigrated from the Balearic Islands, Spain), murdered in the middle of the street on Christmas Day, 1940, by soldiers of the Gestapo, one of many criminal incidents occurring after the establishment of the Warsaw ghetto.*

The upper photo, *Before*, shows the same street on a spring morning. There are pots of geraniums on the balconies. In the upper floors the sun warms the glass of the open windows while the sendal curtains are flying. Baltasar Bonnin poses beside his wife in front of the butcher shop door. His temples are clean shaven, but he has a pair of handlebar mustaches, and his rascally eyes shine radiantly. His white apron, spotless, extends from his beltline to his gaiters. Teresa, with her abundant frizzy hair, wears a cameo on her lace blouse, and her flowered skirt covers her to the ankle. Above both their heads, in letters that stand out like a sudden blaze, are the words *Carnicería Balears*, and beside the doorway a hairless pig hangs on a hook, slit open from top to bottom. On the window glass is written in broad, white strokes, in Polish and German: *Just in: salt meat and sausage from Mallorca.* The whiteness of the pig stands out in the photograph, even whiter than Baltasar Bonnin's apron.

Who was that Castellón? A wandering photographer, an exile, an emigrant from somewhere? I carefully shut the door to the exhibit to make sure the lock was engaged and retraced my steps. Looking at my watch I saw it was getting close to seven. I started running then so as not to lose any more time, but after several turns I found it impossible to recognize any of the places I had passed by earlier. In the distance it was possible to make out the figure of a woman raking leaves on a path, and I went toward her. From behind the bifocal lenses of her frameless glasses she gave me a look of surprise as I was trying to ask her for the way out of the park; she answered me with something in Polish, surely to make me see that she didn't understand, but after I repeated the word "Chopin" several times she laughed, letting me see the rounded gold caps of her teeth, and pointed upward. For the sculpture was right there, on a plane a little higher than where we stood, and I only had to take a path that came out on the esplanade from which I had left.

I caught sight of police cars with their whirling lights flashing and then I saw the Polish bodyguards running toward me behind Lieutenant Rivera, full of concern. Dominik, standing next to the limousine, arms akimbo, watched the scene with a distant, mocking air as the wind blew at the flaps of his overcoat and the thin, coppery lock of hair that crowned his head.

Later that morning a female translator from the Council of Ministers accompanied me to the interview with Jaruzelski, so that Dominik had to wait in the opulent anteroom, persistent in his habit of never shedding his overcoat. When we left the palace he followed behind me in silence, until the members of my escort left me at the foot of the flight of stairs. Once seated inside the Chaika, he took between his fingers the medal so recently pinned to my lapel to get a better look at it, and without hiding his disdain he released it, as if abandoning it to its own fate. Back in the residence afterward—since we had a free moment before the next meeting, what in the official language is called "a transitional period"—he drew from the pocket of his overcoat a packet wrapped in onionskin paper, tied up with a fine thread, and he handed it to me with a deep bow.

Inside was a paperback volume of Chopin's letters, edited by Henryk Opienski and translated to English by E. L. Voynich in 1931, plus a thin leaflet that fell to the floor when the packet was being opened. It was an offprint from a magazine published in Madrid, *Orbe Latino*, with an article by Rubén Darío about the Archduke Luis Salvador, "The Nomad Prince," published in 1907. With a gesture like a prestidigitator, moving his long fingers rapidly as if he wanted to make the whole topic disappear, he forestalled any attempt to thank him.

"The offprint was a gift from my teacher Escuredo, and I have kept it because, as you will see, Darío mentions in passing the story of my ancestor, Wenceslas Vyborny, secretary to the Archduke," he said.

He became silent as a way of inviting me to question him more about that story, but I pushed it aside because what interested me most were that morning's photographs, and that Castellón, the one who had taken them. So I mentioned my furtive visit to the summerhouse in the park, and his reddish eyebrows arched in surprise. The Merlini Pavillion, so-called in honor of its builder, the Genoan architect Domenico Merlini, and dating from the year 1867, had been under repair for a long time now, and moreover it was located so deeply in the park that it would be useless to organize an exhibit there because no one would visit it.

I thought that probably he was joking, and adapting my tone accordingly, I responded that in such a case the word "chouette" written on the card at the foot of the photograph of the bodies of Baltasar Bonnin the butcher and his wife, a word that was unfamiliar to me up to that time, should not exist. And the photographer, that Castellón? Very seriously, and quite intrigued, he answered that the first *chueta* families who had emigrated to Poland established themselves in East Prussia, in the Danzig region, in 1823, and that hundreds of those Jewish "chouettes," or rather *chuetas*, had been subjected to trial by the Inquisition in Palma, Mallorca, accused of practicing their beliefs in secret while feigning a devout conversion to Catholicism. Many were sent to the fire after being tortured and stripped of their possessions.

As far as a photographer named Castellón was concerned, this was the first time he had ever heard that name. And immediately he dismissed the matter, as if in revenge for my lack of interest in the story of his relative Wenceslas Vyborny.

"I don't believe that medal was created in homage to the patriots of the rebellion of 1956 who challenged the Soviet tanks," he said, glancing meaningfully again at my Order of the Defenders of Warsaw.

Then he stretched his hairy hand toward the gift book he had brought, lying on the table where the waiter had just set down the tray with our coffee, and smacked it on its back a couple of times.

"Read it, when you can. Read what Chopin says about the resistance in 1831 against the troops of Czar Nicholas I," he added. "It wasn't only the Nazis that we fought against."

Chopin had just left for Vienna in November, 1830, when the revolt began, inspired by the uprisings in the streets of Paris in July of that same year. The rebels believed that when Russia found itself confronted by a war with the Ottoman Empire, it wasn't going to try to cover two fronts at the same time. But contrary to all the forecasts, the Czar sent an army of two hundred thousand men to snuff out the insurrection. The patriots, less numerous and poorly armed, sought refuge in Warsaw to put up a definitive battle behind barricades. The besieged city went into a panic, looting broke out, cholera struck, and the resistance was brutally crushed in September, 1831. In February of the following year, Poland received the punishment of being incorporated into the Russian Empire as simply another province.

"Look at the notes included among the letters," he said, striking the book again, and got to his feet; it was time for the meeting scheduled in the Ministry of Foreign Commerce.

My official duties ended that night with a dinner offered by the minister, Krajewska. I had a free day before going on to my next station on the itinerary, which was Vienna. As dessert was being served, my host announced with a broad smile that he had organized a visit for me to Chopin's birthplace in Zelazowa Wola, and I smiled too while thanking him, taking note of Dominik's hand in that courtesy.

"I have managed to prevent your being taken to the Church of the Holy Cross, where Chopin's heart is kept," he said. "You don't know how much that disgusts me, that cult of the viscera."

When we left for the excursion, I had already started reading Chopin's letters, and, following Dominik's recommendation, I also looked ahead to the section of notes.

News of the fall of Warsaw reached Chopin in Stuttgart, during the tragic first week of September, 1831, and his reaction became desperately anguished: *Oh, God, do you still exist? Are you there, and you do not avenge all this? How many more Russian crimes do you want? Or are you Russian, too?. . . Oh father, what a consolation for your old age! Mother, poor suffering mother, to have born a daughter so that even her bones should be violated! Mockery! Will my sister Emilia's tomb have been given its due respect? Thousands of other bodies have been piled up above her tomb. What can have happened to my beloved Konstancja? Where can she be? Poor child, probably in the hands of some Russian, a Russian who is choking her, killing her, murdering her! Ah, my life, and I alone here! Come, I will dry your tears and heal your wounds!*

"Why has it been doubted that Chopin wrote this, as it says in the prologue?" I asked Dominik, who was seated as always in the Chaika's folding seat, facing me.

"Because of the pathetic tone of the language," he responded. "They couldn't believe that a delicate soul would be capable of writing in that truculent way. For a long time they preferred to believe that his only reaction to the fall of Warsaw had been his Étude No. 12 for Piano, the "Revolutionary Étude.""

"But then," I said, "in neither of the two cases was this a question of his being a bad patriot."

"But you see, he accepted gifts from the invaders," he replied.

"A propos, I found in the book that Chopin was only ten years old when the Czar gave him that diamond ring," I said with a triumphant air. But he was unperturbed.

In May, 1825, Chopin was invited by the Grand Duke Constantine to play the Aelomelodikon for the very first time, and in the presence of Czar Alexander I. This was a machine that looked like an enormous copper samovar, a mixture of piano and organ, recently installed in the Grand Salon of the Warsaw Conservatory, and the boy performed a concerto by Moscheles on the keyboard of the instrument with such brilliance that he was given that ring as a prize. At that age, he still needed his mother's help when he wanted to use the urinal, and it was she, who always accompanied him to his concerts, who had to open the fly of his velvet trousers.

Chopin's birthplace in Zelazowa Wola is reached by a poplar-lined highway that runs through the broad Mazovia plain, sown with fields of oats and rye. On the edges of the fields stand trees that show the stumps of their shattered branches, and further on in the distance a few old barns under the authority of some huge towers holding up the high tension wires.

The modest building with the slate gable roof looks just like the one I saw in the *Before* photograph, the one taken by Castellón, except for the walls covered in places with ivy, possibly a matter of the season, so it certainly had been reconstructed faithfully. It must be approached on foot through a lovely forest of pines, maples, and birch trees, and then across a wooden bridge beneath which flows the Bzura River's gentle current. In a pool of dark water, the breeze seems to be pushing away a pair of black swans swimming along oblivious of themselves.

"I've already seen this house," I say to Dominik as we are about to climb the stairs.

"Oh, of course you have, at the exhibit at the Merlini summerhouse," he says, striking his forehead in reproach for his forgetfulness. "I found out the repairs have not begun yet; there's no budget, so I wish to offer you my heartfelt apologies. The exhibit you saw there was organized by the officials in charge of the park, but very unsuccessfully, as there wasn't a single review in the press. I spoke with the curator, Professor Henryk Rodaskowski. He is not retired, but for years he was the Director of Photography Archives at the Warsaw Library. I told him about your visit to the exhibit, and, very flattered, he gave me a letter for you, to-

gether with some documents. I will have to translate them
all before your departure."

"Did he tell you who this Castellón is?" I asked.

"I forgot to ask about him," he responded.

"The Nazis burned down this house," I said then. "That
also was in the exhibit."

"Despite the fact that Chopin was an anti-semite, at
least in his own words."

On going inside the house, where we are the only visitors, I say to him that it is the ideal place for growing up as
a musician. The piano notes played by a child practicing in
this silence would be heard for many miles, carried by the
wind from across the plain that sweeps the fields of oats.

"Chopin never lived in this museum; his parents took
him away from here a few months after he was born. All
of this is fake; nothing that is shown here ever belonged to
the family—" and filled with disdain Dominik points to the
furniture, the vases, the lamps placed around the room into
which the guide, who is dressed in a uniform rather like that
of railway inspectors, has first led us.

I am not going to remind him that it was he who organized this visit, and, if truth be told, everything here gives
the impression of being too tidy—the shiny furniture that
smells of wax, the recently cut roses in the vases. Not a bit
of dust on the curtains. Nothing ages on this artificial stage
set. I hear Dominik dismiss the guide, who retires, doffing
her kepi. He himself will be my guide.

"This is from the period, at least," his fingers draw near
the keyboard of the piano placed beside a window. "Back
then, 'pantaleones' is what pianos were called, in musicians'
slang."

Photographs and music scores are few in these rooms
because the curators had wanted to create the atmosphere
of a house to which the owners might return at any moment.

A drawing from 1829, by Miroszewski, shows Chopin's parents, Justyna and Nicholas, by now of a mature age, she in a hairnet and a night dress as if preparing to lie down, and he in a formal suit with a high neck. And there are oil portraits of their two grown daughters, Louise and Isabella, done by the same Miroszewski, plus an oval miniature by an unknown artist that shows the profile of little Emilia, dead of tuberculosis at an early age; it was a disease that ran in the family. And they all have the same long, prominent nose as the father.

Chopin always feared the solitude of death. He was afraid of dying among doctors who were really butchers and insensitive servants. When he felt his own end approaching he wrote his sister Louise asking her for help, and she made the trip from Warsaw to Paris in the disagreeable company of her husband Kalasanty Jedrzejewics, who hated Chopin because he was a constant reminder of his own mediocrity. After the funeral, when it was time to break up the apartment on the Place Vendôme and she wanted to keep his Pleyel piano, Kalasanty ordered her to sell absolutely everything. He would not permit a single scrap of anything from that consumptive to come into his house.

On a table there is also, in a silver frame, a portrait of Konstancja Gladkowska, fuzzy and distant, at the age of forty. This was the one for whom he had showed such fears and such rage at the time of the Russian invasion. She had been buried in the Père-Lachaise cemetery some time before Chopin was. They met in the Conservatory in Warsaw, where she was studying voice, and it is clear that he never loved her. Flattered by the memory of her devotion, he wrote to the friend in Paris who had informed him of her death, "She was too temperamental for me, her head was full of fantasies, not very reliable as a prospect for raising a family." As she gradually took on weight, no longer appearing on the stage, she used to sing occasionally for her husband's friends during their evenings at home. He was a dealer in fabrics.

A few steps away, in a small glass case, Chopin's left hand with its long fingers, modeled in the hours after his death, seems to pulse in the air as if he were accompanying Konstancja, just as on those tedious afternoons of her singing exercises, when she was practicing for her graduation examination the aria "E amore un ladroncello" from *Così fan tutte*.

And on a bare wall, copies of the portraits of Chopin and George Sand painted by Delacroix. Seen together that way, they appear to be what they really were, an incompatible couple. Chopin's is from the year before his death. Showing the thick bulk of his nose posed in semi-profile, he gives off an air of painful absence, of rebelliousness on the verge of being crushed; while she, at the age of thirty, looks like a vaudeville performer waiting for some lover at the stage door of the theater under the dirty light from a gas lamp.

"That tramp shouldn't be there," Dominik approaches the wall, unusually aggressive. "She was always tormenting that poor swan. Besides, as a writer, she was mediocre, if not just plain bad."

I am about to remind him that George Sand had the misfortune to have hung around Turgenev and Flaubert too much, and therefore she always seems somewhat diminished on being compared with them, but I have learned it is useless to try to convince Dominik, and instead I remind him that that very name, "swan," was given also to Darío, a swan equally unfortunate. On his own Pleyel piano, which was always under the threat of judicial seizure, he often played Chopin's Études.

"I know," he responded, "and he was tortured by another tramp."

"Rosario Murillo," I say. "But that one hardly knew how to read."

As we took our leave from each other the following day in the waiting room of the airport he handed me a manila envelope with the material he had promised, put together by Professor Rodaskowski. Unopened, the envelope accompanied me as far as Nicaragua, and it wasn't until days later, when I finished emptying out my suitcase, that I found it again.

On a separate sheet of paper, neatly typed, Dominik had translated the letter Professor Rodaskowski had addressed to me, and in the envelope there was a brochure about the exhibit, again in Polish and French, rather poorly printed, along with some photocopies of press clippings, all of this material translated into Spanish.

The professor lamented the circumstances of my visit to the exhibit, since he would have been honored to accompany me, and he told me that the photos belonged to the Graphics Collection of the Warsaw Library, and there were many more of them, enough to be able to organize a larger show sometime that would illustrate the passage of Castellón the artist through Poland. However (because of what he would get around to explaining to me later), an exhibit of this kind in a setting of true cultural importance might manage only after great difficulty to gain approval by the authorities of the party and the government. The letter continued:

> During the years of his youth lived in France, Castellón had a great influence on the development of the art of photography, above all through the medium of his contributions to the invention of the hand-held camera for taking snapshots; and likewise, he took portraits, for posterity, of famous people in literature and the sciences. His nudes, which were published in an album printed

in Barcelona, filled me with admiration when it came into my hands, and they convinced me that he was one of the greats of the century. I found out that he was living in Palma de Mallorca, and we established a correspondence. Although he always avoided the topic of his origins, I was under the impression that he was from Mallorca, since his facial features showed certain exotic traits that are sometimes peculiar to the people of the Balearics, given the racial influences from North Africa that those islands have been receiving for centuries.

Castellón had come to Warsaw by way of Barcelona in 1929, through measures taken by Rodaskowski himself, together with his daughter Teresa Segura and his son-in-law, the master butcher Baltasar Bonnin:

> I was working then as the social editor for the newspaper *Gazeta Warszawy*, and because of this I was in close communication with the organizers of the contest where for the first time a "Miss Poland" would be elected. They needed a photographer with an international reputation to take pictures of the contestants; I recommended Castellón and they accepted him. I doubted whether he would agree to the assignment when I proposed it to him, given the kinds of compromises that it assumed, but I was surprised to receive a telegram from him sent from Barcelona, advising me that he would be catching the train that same night.
>
> My letter had been forwarded to him in Barcelona. It turned out that his son-in-law had become involved in a serious difficulty in Palma, the nature of which he told me later on. He had been obliged to follow him to Barcelona, where the son-in-law had fled together with Teresa. That situation impelled him not only to take up the offer but to remain in Warsaw as an emigrant. The photographs of the contestants opened the doors of the great world to him; soon he had turned himself into the

photographer most in vogue, and he set up his studio on the bustling Nalewki Street.

I was in my twenties then, and despite our differences of age we frequented the cabarets and bars together. Castellón had a great love of alcoholic beverages, but his physical constitution was such that after a binge that lasted till dawn, he was always to be found at his establishment early in the morning, attending to the first clients of the day, cool and clean, as if he'd been sleeping like an angel the whole night long.

Once the German occupation had taken place, he ended up in the ghetto along with his grandson, Rubén Bonnin, after the murder of Baltasar and Teresa, an event that he witnessed and photographed, which you must have seen in the exhibit of his work. The boy holding his hands above his head, forced to do so by the soldiers, is Rubén. Inside the ghetto he installed himself on Karmelicka Street, and there he re-opened his studio, specializing now in social photography, pictures of high German officials and their families. In one of these pictures, published in a magazine a copy of which is preserved now in the archive collection next to the original, the Sturmführer Nikolaus von Dengler of the Gestapo is seen at the piano accompanying his wife, who, while wearing the costume of Cleopatra, is singing the aria "Da tempeste el legno infranto," from the opera Julius Caesar by Händel, according to what it says at the foot of the picture in the magazine.

Under assignment from the Gestapo, Castellón also took numerous pictures designed for the anti-Semite campaign, such as, for example, Jewish couples of the same sex being forced to copulate in front of the camera, or women of any age doing the same thing with mastiffs or greyhounds. But since on the other hand the Gestapo wanted to show images of a pleasant, normal life within the ghetto, he also took pictures of the concerts in the restaurants, of opera performances, like those that took place in the Femina Theater on Leszno Street, pictures that were later distributed both within and outside Germany, and he used his own grandson for the shots of the series "Das Glückskind," which became famous on the covers of the propaganda magazines of the Third Reich.

With makeup on and dressed in corduroy suits and lace collars, or wearing lederhosen and a Tyrolean hat, little Rubén appeared in front of tables loaded with cakes and fruits, gorging himself, or engaged in amusing himself alone while playing with all kinds of mechanical toys, as if that were the ordinary thing in the ghetto.

As you can see, it is for these distressing reasons that it would not be possible even to propose an exhibit of his work to the Polish authorities, something the artist really deserves, but the merit of the case simply clashes with the impropriety of his conduct.

That explains how Castellón would have been able to reach even the burning ruins of Zelazowa Wola with his camera. He traveled with the Nazis, who had murdered his daughter and son-in-law. I was perplexed, but Professor Rodasdowki came to my rescue.

Don't forget that under the moral decay provoked by the Nazis, the people went so far as to give themselves over to the worst sorts of abject behavior, the fruit also of fear and of the lack of possibility to choose. Castellón wasn't the only one. We never chanced to see each other during the course of those awful years, except once when I surprised him leaving the Gestapo headquarters in the Szuch Promenade. I was returning from having gotten some eggs at the home of a dealer in black market goods, and Castellón was coming down the stairs carrying a portfolio of large-sized photographs under his arm. We both pretended not to recognize each other.

In 1933 there had erupted the scandal of a lawsuit for adultery in which his daughter Teresa was involved. The clippings photocopied from the same *Gazeta Warszawy* which I found in the folder referred to the claim brought by the butcher Baltasar Bonnin against his wife Teresa Segura, accused of an illicit love affair with the Cavalry Lieutenant Jan Kumelski. In one of the clippings was a studio photograph of Lieutenant Kumelski in all his trappings, holding his shako with its shiny visor, and another of Teresa, taken as she was descending the steps of the courthouse in Dluga Square between two guards in their gray overcoats, with their long-barreled rifles on their backs, bayonets in place, and a crowd of gawkers surrounding them.

You can clearly see, beneath her coat, that she is quite pregnant, for she is expecting a child. And everyone, the prisoner, the guards, the gawkers are posed in front of the camera as if overwhelmed by a feeling of importance, staring at the camera lens with some kind of avid curiosity as if, instead of being seen, it was they who were doing the seeing. And in Teresa's case, she is a curiosity facing her own drama. An arrow in red ink cuts across the photograph and leads toward a legend in the margin, written in English, in Professor Rodaskowski's hand: "This picture taken by her father." The photograph of Lieutenant Kumelski is also marked by a red arrow: "Dishonorable discharge."

Lieutenant Kumelski, after getting her pregnant, had abandoned her. And it was her intolerable squandering of money spent on gifts for him that had ruined Bonnin without his even knowing it! In despair and faced with the imminent seizure of all the goods of his butcher shop, which had surreptitiously become so compromsed, one night he went in search of her lover at the Kumelski family chalet in Klonowa Street, where the Lieutenant had the use of an apartment with an outside entrance to the street. This was where they used to see each other. On Klonowa Street.

I push aside the pages with the translations of the texts,

and I don't stop thinking about all this for a long while. It was the very same apartment of the mansion where I had been lodged while in Warsaw. There is the picture taken from the street, when the newspapers took up the case. The old bed with its walnut headboard, set on a dais one step above the rest of the flooring, like a small stage—all this was surely the same. The lovers' bed.

That night Teresa had put on her black silk dress with arabesques embroidered in the same color, which she only wore to attend mass on Sundays and other solemn days of obligation. She and Bonnin, whether or not sincere, were practicing Catholics the same as they had been in Palma, and they never went near the synagogue. She asked Kumelski to lend her the sum of 3,000 zloty, and he told her "No!" emphatically, while attempting to slip away from her as soon as he could with the plea that his father would soon come into the apartment with some workmen to check on some gutters whose leaks were damaging the plaster on the soffit. Given the time of day, this was an obviously hollow excuse.

From the window Kumelski saw her running through the garden and going out to the street, ever more despairing, her skirt winnowing out behind her like a black flame that was scorching the trunks of the ash trees as it passed by them. Touched by a vague remorse, he saw her getting into the cab that waited for her while the meeting was taking place. After making the driver wander around for awhile with no particular goal, she returned to Szeroki Dunaj Street where her husband, having closed the butcher shop by that time of night, was waiting for her anxiously at the door that opened on the stairway leading to the floor immediately above, where they lived.

Castellón, who occupied a room in the back where he lived with his photography gear, and also concerned about his daughter's absence, had come to peer out to the street from one of the windows of the sitting room. And while Bonnin's footsteps resounded as he climbed the stairway, he put his face closer to the window glass on which the drizzle was coming down lightly, and he saw the taxicab stopping at a spot barely illuminated by the halo of the half-open corolla of the street lamp rising on its iron stalk. Just as Lieutenant Kumelski had seen her disappear behind the car door closing soundlessly in the distance, he saw his daughter emerge in her mourning dress, watched her standing still for a moment in the middle of the street as if she had become lost, and watched her walk with rapid steps toward the pharmacy followed by the cab driver pestering her for his fare, and then watched her pass through the illuminated door and go into the section where the restricted medicines were kept, which she reached without difficulty because the employees treated her as they always did. The rest Castellón could no longer see. Teresa pounced on the blue earthenware crock where the pharmacist kept tartar emetic and shoveled it into her mouth by the handful, as if she wanted to cure herself of a wild fit of hunger.

That was the story. They saved her life with a stomach pump at the Hospital of the Good Samaritan on Lezsno Street, where she was taken in the car belonging to the pharmacist, a Russian bachelor (and probably gay) named Serge Pestov. Once assured that she would not die, Bonnin determined to accuse her of adultery, despite her advanced pregnancy, and from the hospital she was sent to the women's section of the Pawiak Prison.

But Castellón understood that the only way to keep her out of jail was by saving Bonnin from ruin in his turn. He handed over all his savings and in addition sold his photography equipment, much of it expensive and then unknown in Poland, forcing him to close his studio on Nalewki street.

Bonnin then addressed a petition to the court vacating his claim, and just before the birth of the child took her back into his house, where Castellón had remained all this time, despite the litigation that involved his daughter, and where he would have to stay from then on as a dependent relative, for he was now without his own means of subsistence. The child was born, and they named him Rubén; they all lived in harmony until the day of the unhappy events through which both of them lost their lives.

Professor Rodaskowski wrote in conclusion:

> Take note of the admirable valor displayed by this old man, who by the date of the misfortune must have been more than 80 years of age, as old then as I am now, who from some hidden vantage point, perhaps from behind the glass window, scarcely moving aside the gauze curtains, was able with professional coldness and in spite of the emotions that undoubtedly were upsetting his nerves, to take a picture of the bodies of his daughter and his son-in-law stretched out on the pavement, meanwhile expecting that the soldiers would be coming upstairs for him, and without knowing how things would turn out for his grandson.

There is no doubt that Castellón was able to moderate his feelings when he brought his eye to the viewfinder of his camera, as he had done before when catching Teresa between her guards in front of the courthouse on Dluga Square. And if he hadn't taken her photograph when he saw her getting out of the taxicab to run toward the door of the pharmacy, that was surely because there wasn't enough light.

But on that morning in December, when he heard the menacing voice of the commander of the patrol ordering Bonnin to open up the suitcase, he did come to the window. He must have gone downstairs as well, in keeping with the instructions to go to the ghetto with the rest of the family, after the failure of all their petitions to the Nazi authorities during the previous days to avoid being treated as Jews since they were Roman Catholics. He was delayed precisely by his having forgotten his small hand camera, the only thing left to him after liquidating his studio. Bonnin had gotten befuddled, feeling around in the inside pocket of his overcoat for the little key to the suitcase without succeeding in coming up with it; and when he heard the dry sound of the machine guns as they were being brought to bear on him, plus some new threats, he became filled with panic and ran toward the opposite sidewalk, throwing the suitcase down on the cobblestone surface, where it sprang open with the shock. They machine-gunned him, and when Teresa screamed, they machine-gunned her as well. Castellón already had the little Eastman bellows camera in his hand. And he shot.

2

A country that does not exist

THERE IS SOMEONE who is on my trail but I don't know if we will ever run across each other. In the meantime I want to begin my story. Nicaragua, the extraordinary country where I was born. The Gran Lago Cocibolca, which the conquistadores called "The Sweetwater Sea" when for the first time they got a look at that gray, shoreless expanse, with fierce whitecaps cresting in the distance. Those ripples, however, were so gentle when the wind brought them closer only to let them melt away on the bank that the conquerors drove their mounts and pack animals right into the waters so they could satisfy their thirst, trampling down the coarse sand. A sea that seethed with bloodthirsty sharks without being an ocean, although it had an open door to the Caribbean, the San Juan River, down which my father traveled in his effort to get this so-called non-existent country to be recognized as real in the courts of Europe. A decisive trip for me, to the point that to it I owe my existence.

He departed from León followed by a train of mules with a quantity of baggage in which he was transporting a rich load of contraband indigo in bags, aside from the crates of idols, stone axes, censers, pots, and metates he had ordered dug up hastily from one of the indigenous cemeteries that were to be found in any empty field of the city and that he thought he would offer to Queen Victoria in order to get a sympathetic hearing in the matter that was taking him to London. Among his trunks was one that was well caulked, with maps and sketches exquisitely crafted on parchment, the work of Hermann Schulz, an engineer who had come from the Rhineland to look after improving the indigo industry on my father's properties but who, on his own, was also interested in the cartography of the New World and also in its archeology. It was he who had very neatly classified the exhumed objects. The maps and drawings sufficed to explain the advantages of building an interoceanic canal through Nicaragua, another of the concerns of my father's journey, the most over-arching though not the most urgent.

After painful leagues of riding on horseback he arrived in Granada to embark on a sailing barge that plowed through the Gran Lago and afterward down the river until it reached the seaport of San Juan del Norte, which the English had always coveted. They had even given it the name Greytown, there where the turbid fluvial current enters the Caribbean Sea, with waters the color of rust extending for miles beyond the sandbar in scattered billows, and which in flood times scatter clusters of water lilies over the emerald-colored surface, branches loaded with bananas, the wreckage of buildings, occasional uprooted trees bearing their tangles of roots, small boats pulled from their moorings, a cageful of monkeys, and once even the body of a jaguar, floating adrift.

The lands and waters through which he passed on his journey to Europe are the very ones into which I've seen my life divided, though at the same time joined together. I was born as a result of a journey and I turned out a wanderer, like Robin, the sailor of my own bloodline who inspired the character of Robinson Crusoe. His story was the basis of conversation in the meeting my father had with my uncle the King Frederick I one night during the month of February, 1844, the only occasion they met each other.

It was opposite those swampy, malaria-infected coasts —among which the kingdom of Mosquitia was to be established and entrusted to the dynasty of my uncle the King Frederick—where Admiral Cristóbal Colombo had dropped anchor at last in the course of his fourth and final voyage in September, 1502, upon getting free after having run aground opposite Cape Gracias a Dios, which he himself baptized with that name.

The Admiral must have kept his sense of humor, there is no doubt of that, despite the deep bitterness caused by the intrigues that beset him. A crossbowman had brought on board an animal with a prehensile tail, a mixture of a monkey and a cat, which he had knocked out of a tree and afterward broken one of its arms in order to subdue its fierce nature, as his son Hernando Colombo related the story. A captured wild pig, which previously had kept one of the Spaniards' dogs at bay, fled in fright after a single glimpse of this thing that appeared to be its enemy. The Admiral ordered them to catch it, whereupon the newly arrived animal wrapped its tale around the pig's snout and, using its one good arm, grabbed it by the bristles on the top of its head in order to bite down on it. When the pig screamed in terror, the Admiral laughed.

The one who is seeking me even now knows perfectly well what I am talking about—that this country my father was trying to get recognized as a real place has always been a remarkable country with a remarkable history, and that its history doesn't begin with that dialogue conducted with such admirably controlled nuances between Gil González the conquistador and Nicaragua the cacique, as some have insisted. According to Pedro Mártir de Anglería, Nicaragua proposed questions that caused astonishment among the conquistadores: about how the sky was made and the stars became lit, why the winds blow, about heat and cold, about the changes between the days and the nights, whether perhaps the Holy Pope is mortal, whether the King of Spain defecates and urinates. But no, this history was initiated with the struggle between a strange, mutilated animal—fierce as a jaguar, amusing as a monkey—and a wild pig crazed with terror.

My uncle Robert Charles Frederick was the fifth sovereign of the dynasty of *zambos*, the descendants of blacks and Indians, in the kingdom of Mosquitia. The Pacific coast creoles from among whom my father came scornfully called them "mosquito kings," made fun of them as illiterate puppets, and claimed over and over again that their essential function was to scrawl a dotted cross at the foot of the permits for felling trees of teak and other precious woods granted to English traders in exchange for casks of Jamaican rum and trinkets supplied by the Crown.

There is no question that they were a great deal more than that. My uncle the King Frederick, crowned at the age of 20 in the Anglican cathedral at Kingston on Sunday the 17th of July, 1842, had gone through the Greenwich Naval Academy; he had the rank of lieutenant-major in the Royal Navy, and though he was somewhat fatuous and vain, he was in command of an appreciable culture, extraordinary for his age, as my father was able to confirm firsthand. And he had a quick mind for daring ideas, the near relatives of ambition, and a spirit which, though some might call it ingenuous, I would judge to be rather dreamy. But although he was an idealistic *zambo*, a staunch supporter of progress and civilization, he was nevertheless capable of doing the most extravagant things, I must admit.

But it wasn't only the Mosquito Kings who had to put up with the British in those days. Perhaps the worst of it fell upon the very creoles of a liberal and rather arrogant Freemason stamp who ruled in León. That was precisely the reason for my father's voyage to London.

Her majesty Queen Victoria's consul, Frederick Chatfield, Esq., had presented himself in León at the beginning of 1844 to intervene in the dispute stirred up by two merchants, both of them English subjects based in Nicaragua, Thomas Manning and Wilson Glennon, who were being charged an inflated duty for supplying merchandise to the government. Coming from his headquarters in Guatemala, he arrived at the port of El Realejo on the frigate *Daphne*, with 14 guns aboard, 40-pounders, and then got himself terribly out of humor from the inconveniences suffered on horseback along the road between the seaport and León, the capital, what with the dust in his eyes and nose, plus the harsh sun on his head for hours on end. Scarcely down from his horse, he ordered a message sent to Colonel Pérez that he needed to see him immediately.

Colonel Manuel Pérez, ostensibly the chief of state, and Grand Marshal Casto Fonseca, possessor of the real power, occupied adjacent offices in the Casa del Cabildo, facing the Plaza del Laborio, where the hay grew high enough to hide the cattle who were grazing in the open. On receiving the communication from Chatfield, they had my father called, as Minister of General Affairs but also by order of the Grand Marshal charged with the portfolio of Foreign Relations, and he recommended as a matter of decorum that they postpone the meeting until the following day. But Chatfield gave them no time, and when they heard him shouting at the guards in the corridor, it was a frightened Colonel Pérez who went out to greet him while the Grand Marshal fled through the side door.

Colonel Pérez's office seemed much more like a sacristy than the office of a Freemason. Under the far clerestory window pierced through the shining whitewashed wall was hanging a Christ dripping with blood, and from under the table covered with a green cloth extended a mat decorating the floor of baked earth tiles. Colonel Pérez hastened to occupy the chair behind the table and invited Chatfield to be seated facing him, on one of the two leather stools. My father sat on the other.

It was with a great deal of hopeful enthusiasm that Chatfield had begun his consular career in the port of Memel in East Prussia, on the shores of the Baltic Sea, and there it was where his lifelong affliction first appeared, the boils that broke out in a perpetual flowering all over his face and neck, which by this time were already marked by the scars of his earlier pimples. A physician of the University of Berlin, Doctor Dieter Masuhr, had diagnosed a sluggish blood circulation in the region of his stomach and this in turn was the cause of an excessive affluence of blood in his head. That congestion was what was making those hateful boils erupt.

He recommended a course of treatment in the spa at Aachen, famous for its medicinal waters. Chatfield was not cured. He would never be cured, and since he had been afflicted with this misfortune ever since his youth, he remained a bachelor because women avoided him as if he were infected with the plague. But his summer residences at Aachen had allowed him to mingle with some high Prussian

officers, enough to turn him into a privileged spy. His dili-
gent reports to the Foreign Office earned him, years later,
the consulate in Central America, which was considered
more a political post than a commercial one.

He was now around forty years of age. Seated before
this Colonel Pérez who was smiling and so uselessly obsequious, and who seemed more like a cornered rat afraid of
a blow from a chunk of wood, Chatfield absentmindedly
raised his hand to his forehead where a new boil was coming out. Faced with his own misfortune he felt offended,
and now he would take it out on that mouse clothed in
such poor garb, in blue trousers with red stripes and a gray
flannel jacket which was suffocating him in the sticky heat
of the afternoon, while the vaseline which his hair was
greased with dripped down his neck. If Chatfield only knew
it, Colonel Pérez was more embarrassed by that reddish
protuberance which he didn't want to look at (as if to do
so were an act of impudence) than out of fear of anything
Chatfield might have come to tell him.

Chatfield didn't want to pay the slightest attention to my
father, though from time to time he glanced at him out of the
corner of his eye. He knew who he was and was aware of his
worth—as opposed to the Grand Marshal, who, he was certain, had his ear glued to the other side of the door during
this meeting. Unlike Chatfield, who decided to make his first
appearance while still wearing his traveling clothes, filthy
with dust, my father appeared neatly dressed, fragrant with
lavender, handsome of profile. His blue eyes were deep and
cordial, his mouth barely sketched in, and his brow generous. How Chatfield would have liked such a clean, polished,
attractive face for himself. He knew him as a gentleman and
a statesman. A rarity in this country of guerrilla fighters that
gave the impression of being a huge cattle ranch where flies
were always buzzing around, if not bullets.

He took a document out of his jacket pocket and spread it out across the table for Colonel Pérez. It was an ultimatum. The obligations the State of Nicaragua had incurred with the British subjects, the complainants, must be settled immediately or the Royal Navy had instructions to block its seaports to halt all commercial traffic. Colonel Pérez passed the document on to my father.

"An adequate period of time will be necessary to make a proper reply," he told Chatfield in an English that was correct and unhurried.

"That is simply a piece of sophistry," Chatfield responded in Spanish, addressing himself to Colonel Pérez and raising his voice loud enough so that the Grand Marshal could hear him from the other side of the door. "I must take with me a duly signed agreement to pay this note before I leave tomorrow morning at dawn."

"The claim is for four times the original debt because it adds in the delay besides the costs and damages," my father said in the same restrained tone, knowing also that the Grand Marshal was listening to him. "There wouldn't be enough left over to pay a single employee of the government for a year at least, not even the employees who collect the import duties."

"The Crown cannot meddle in the internal affairs of Nicaragua," said Chatfield, and now he was looking head on at my father, as if hoping to see himself in a mirror lost forever. "The manner in which the petition is satisfied is no business of ours."

Chatfield got to his feet, and my father held out his hand in a gesture that the other could not refuse to respond to. But he did not take his leave of Colonel Pérez, and he only gave a scornful glance toward the closed side door.

The Grand Marshal's head appeared the moment Chatfield had left and he made them come into his own office.

He was bony and wan looking, and the lid of his right eye wrinkled up over the sunken eye socket from which his eyeball had been removed by a saber stroke, not in battle but during an argument over fighting cocks. Barefoot, with his boots thrown in the corner, he had unbuttoned his tunic, and his undershirt, already the color of earth, showed large grease and sweat stains. A hammock of sailcloth hanging from two rings crossed the room where bundles of tobacco and demijohns of aguardiente confiscated from smugglers were piled up. On a table loaded with State papers, a rooster in yellow plumage stood guard, tied to one of the table legs by a length of Corinthian silk cord.

The bird, who was called Pericles, never failed to be present whenever the Grand Marshal, contemptuous of any bed, entertained himself in the hammock with one of the women encamped in the corridor who passed the time weaving hats of palm fibers for the foot soldiers or simply gave themselves over to napping, and who took their turns when he came out to mark his choice by removing his hat and placing it on the chosen one's head.

"Just a lot of fuss," he said, with a rapid stutter just as he was set to speak, a trait that made him seem rash. "The English don't have so many ships in these waters, and even if they did, they wouldn't waste gunpowder on a buzzard. We're too small."

My father thought the opposite. Rather than the size of its adversaries, for the great Albion there was no greater concern than never to appear the least bit weak or negligent. This he told the Grand Marshal but was not listened to. Chatfield returned to Guatemala without having gotten satisfaction, and a week later the frigates *Daphne* and *Chloris* were anchored in the bay at El Realejo, and opposite the sandbar at San Juan del Norte were two more, the *Scylla* and the *Charybdis*, every one of them with a displacement of six hundred tons and provided with twenty guns on each side.

The Grand Marshal, now really scared, revised his opinion. But he decided that he had nothing to work with in negotiating with that churlish, foul-tempered Chatfield, and so he gave instructions to my father to leave immediately for England to put the matter before Queen Victoria.

The cargo he was carrying with him would do to take care of the costs of the voyage, which he assumed for himself because the national treasury was indeed empty. It was not something he needed to pay attention to. He was rich enough. On his hacienda, Palmyra, where the purple mantle of indigo flowers extended for leagues to the sea, so close that the sea spray spattered their diminutive corollas, there were legions of peons toiling without cease, carrying the heaps of stalks to the troughs in the work sheds where they were to be undergo fermentation, and then the colorant would be boiled in pans and strained through the sieves, staining the workers all over their bodies depending on their part in the process, some with purple, others green, others blue, and finally the indigo violet of the cakes with which the leather bags were filled.

The *Prometheus*, a three-master out of New York, would arrive four times a year at San Juan del Norte to pick up and drop off cargo, mail, and passengers, so on the afternoon my father's sailing barge reached the port, to his joy he found it already anchored in the bay, alongside an old galleon with gilt adornments like a carnival float and gauze sails like the curtains of a bedroom suite. An impresario from Cartagena de Indias in Colombia, with rippled, wavy hair, a hairbrush mustachio, the manners of a prince, and fanciful notions in his head because he talked about wars that never had happened, used this old relic to mosey around among the seaports of the Caribbean transporting the paraphernalia of a circus in which he was the star because he used to put his head between the jaws of a white tiger from Borneo. And so, his anxieties relieved, my father was able to take a nap.

Because the *Prometheus* bore the flag of the United States, the commander of the English detachment, Major H.D.C. Douglas, knew that he would not be able to interfere with it. But he could prevent its passengers from getting into the boats that would carry them out to get on board, and that is what he did. At dawn on Tuesday, February 13, the day following my father's arrival, a contingent of Royal Light Infantry Marines took over the landing and confiscated the boats after disarming the local garrison under the command of Colonel Manuel Quijano, who was taken as a prisoner aboard the *Scylla*, the English flagship.

San Juan del Norte was not what it came to be a few years later when, after 1848, it served as a stepping stone for the gold seekers hurrying so feverishly toward California. With no trace of any street at all, the reed huts lived in by the fishermen, riverbank carpenters, coastal pilots, and sailors were all crammed along the river banks between the military headquarters—which was a slant-roofed, open shed lined with chicken wire that also housed the customs office, and from which one passed to the landing—and another larger shed built on piles punched into the mud, open on four sides and with a raised floor where travelers hung their hammocks from hooks or slept on the floor.

It was in this one and only lodging where my father had ended up that he was awakened by the news of the British disembarkation and the seizure of Colonel Quijano, who the previous night had honored him with a supper of turtle soup, plantains, and manioc boiled in coconut milk. But that was not the end of it. From his lodging, while dry shaving himself before a mirror being held up by one of the servants who was to accompany him on his journey, he caught sight of a small boat adorned with the flag of the Mosquito

King departing from the starboard side of the *Scylla*, in the direction of the north shore of the bay.

As it came closer he distinguished in the prow the figure of a young man who seemed quite blond, although with African features, and dressed in the uniform of a lieutenant major, his hand firmly grasping the helm. It was my uncle the King Frederick. Two children, a girl and a boy, accompanied him. The boy, perhaps ten years old, also in uniform and overflowing with arrogance, clutched his small sword by the hilt, and the girl, probably around eight or so, seated on some cushions, wore a frothy, sky-blue dress dotted with pink bows around the hem that billowed around her. These were his younger siblings, Francis Clement Patrick and Catherine Ann Elizabeth, my mother. Above the heads of all three a page in livery held the cupola of a brocaded sunshade with fringes around the edge.

Major Douglas had been warned by Chatfield of my father's intentions to board the *Prometheus* in San Juan del Norte. Moreover, he was ordered to prevent my father from doing so by obliging him to solicit a safe-conduct from the Mosquito King as a way of humbling him. On that basis, the *Scylla* had sailed into Bluefields three days before with orders to pick up my uncle the King, who came on board accompanied by his brother and sister.

To include them among his retinue was part of the secret design that had flashed through the royal mind like a bolt of lightning the moment Chatfield's wishes for him to cooperate in this bit of bravado had been communicated to him. And with a decisiveness that never accompanied any other act of his life, he had decided to put that plan into action.

My uncle the King was the first of the Mosquito sovereigns whom the English, though they had educated him in London, were unable to deceive. He knew himself to be the head of a kingdom of few subjects, hunters of manatees, alligators and monkeys, fishers of sea turtles, whose shells, useful for making combs and stays for chignons, letter openers and paperweights, were what most interested the colonial merchants based in Jamaica in those days, together with logs of teak and royal cedar. The territory, for the most part still unexplored and barely penetrated by Moravian missionaries, consisted of meandering watercourses, swamps and jungles. And because it was continually being beaten about by the death throes of Caribbean storms and was rained on incessantly the greatest part of the year, the coasts, which were too low, it remained constantly flooded and its rivers overflowing, which was why the riverbank villages, consisting of huts built on stilts, were constantly changing place.

He lived in Bluefields, his court comprising members of his lazy and selfish family. Encouraged by Chatfield, his relatives had taken among themselves the titles of dukes and admirals that gave them the right once a year around Christmas time to receive an allotment of gifts from the British Crown, which included, aside from the traditional casks of rum, some hats, patent leather boots and some linen shirts, bolts of calico and of poplin, and also razors and drums and cornets, crockery of enameled tin, cast iron pots, saucepans and washtubs, and a huge number of copies of the King James Bible, large quarto size.

Not even a well-educated man like my uncle the King Frederick was able to get himself into a position of advantage over a court in which ceremonies were few but intrigues abounded. The royal family had been arguing about its privileges since the year 1720 when the first of the dynasty, Jeremy I, received from the Duke of Albemarle, the Governor of Jamaica, a patent of recognition for his monarchy in exchange for supplying a corps of his subjects who were taken to Kingston in a sloop with the mission of pursuing and liquidating the last remnants of the black *cimarrones*, escaped slaves who had taken refuge in the Blue Mountains. Once their orders were fulfilled, the troop received rum and rice enough to last the return trip, plus a sum of forty shillings for the six months the expedition lasted.

The fact that my uncle the King Frederick had been given an elegant education is something that cannot be seen as purely gratuitous. In accordance with their plans to take over the Caribbean outlet of the inter-oceanic canal that had to run through Nicaraguan territory, England would have need of a competent king, not an illiterate one. On his ascending to the throne in 1842, he had to accept the arrangement with the Ministry of Colonies that turned the Kingdom of Mosquitia into a protectorate, and that was not gratuitous either. The British wanted to be certain that if they were dealing with somebody capable of negotiating the matter of the canal, the final word would rest with them.

The Royal House at Old Bank, built of unplaned cedar planks, did not have a single flush toilet like those in the cadet dormitory at the Greenwich Naval Academy, but instead a battery of latrines that emptied into the bay, and my uncle the King, just like the members of his court, had to bathe in the open beside the same well from which they drew brakish water with a bucket. In the rooms inside the building, divided off with chintz curtains, his relatives camped and did their cooking with the cast iron pots and saucepans received from Queen Victoria, and not even once had there been a fire from all that.

When he was not occupied with the sporadic matters of state in the Royal House, he was helping the fishermen to careen their boats and mend their nets, to gut porgies and take turtle shells apart. They always greeted him with, "God save you, King!" when they saw him coming near, that form of hailing him being offered as an affectionate sort of address or a family nickname.

My uncle the King was well aware of what his enemies were saying about him, those creoles on the other, distant Pacific coast of Nicaragua. But he himself felt his kingdom had a touch of something comical about it, and—abstemious as he was—he never ceased being amused by that story according to which he had been discovered one day sitting on top of a barrel, drunk and signing decrees with his dress coat open, bare belly showing and tricorn cocked askew, just like the characters who appeared in the engravings of the edition of *Tom Jones* that he owned and which was among the books that came to me by way of my mother, transported to León in a sailor's duffel bag. He knew as well what being a *zambo*, a descendant of black slaves and naked Indians, meant for the English as well as for the Spanish, although some kind of English or Dutch blood must also have strayed into his veins.

His lineage, and consequently mine too, was the result of a shipwreck. In 1652 an English schooner loaded with slaves hunted down in Guinea in order to be sold in Portobello had come apart among the rocks of the Tiburones reef opposite Cape Gracias a Dios, the same spot where Colombo's ship had nearly foundered. Those who escaped in spite of their shackles managed to swim to the chain of keys located to the south of the reef, established themselves there, and in time contrived to become friendly with the Carib Indians on shore, whom they later were able to dominate. Thus that new race of *zambos* came to be produced which the buccaneers and smugglers learned to understand, to the point of using them in their enterprises and, not a few times, their women as well, to let off steam.

If my father had seen my uncle the King beneath the fringed sunshade standing in the prow of the boat that was carrying the open-spread flag of the kingdom which had been sewn by my great-aunt Charlotte, he in his turn had been seen in shirt-sleeves shaving himself with long, sure strokes of a knife. He had his hat on, and a watch-chain crossed his waistcoat of white piqué with its double row of mother-of-pearl buttons. And every time the servant changed the position of his feet, made necessary by the task of holding up the mirror, the flash of the reflection reached as far as the boat, striking my uncle the King squarely in the eye.

If in accordance with Chatfield's plan, that gentleman who was giving himself a dry shave was to receive that very afternoon a note signed by Major Douglas ordering him to request from His Majesty the King of Mosquitia, formally and in writing, a safe-conduct in order to be able to embark, my uncle the King proposed, in contravention, to send the page with the sunshade, who was none other than his cousin James, bearing a polite invitation to make a visit to the Iron House, which from atop a bare hillock dominated the north bank of the bay, where he was now headed.

Transported in pieces from Bristol, the plate walls held together with rivets like the skin of a steam boiler, from the outside simulated a dressing of bricks. But once inside it, at no time could you find yourself comfortable, because in the morning the sun would start heating it up the moment the light touched it, and at night the heat would still linger in all the bedrooms, like that of glowing coals. The Iron House served to accommodate my uncle the King and his retinue during their stays in the port, when he was used to occupying the second floor, and also to hold the cages of ocelots, monkeys and pacas, the contraband turtle shells, the bundles of alligator skins, all property of the English traders (before being shipped to Kingston without passing through Nicaraguan customs) not to mention the saws, axes, chisels, chains, and other tools and provisions belonging to the owners of the logging concession in the jungle that extended as far as the channel of the Río Maíz and Monkey Point.

Douglas's note arrived just after midday, and after reading it my father returned it to the bearer, a seaman, as a sign that he rejected it, but the man was not sure he should take it back. A little later my father decided to send Douglas himself a note of protest not only because they were interfering with his movements within the sovereign territory of Nicaragua but above all because of the military occupation of the port and the seizure of Colonel Quijano. He did this without making the slightest reference to the safe-conduct. The proprietor of the inn, a mulatto from Martinique named Alphonse Benard, who gave himself the title of Viscount saying that he was a relative of the Empress Josephine and that he was a drinking companion of Quijano, offered to carry the letter to the military headquarters, occupied now by the English and serving as a jail.

The Viscount had just left when James presented himself in his role of emissary, bearing the invitation of my uncle the King written in his own hand, stamped with the royal seal and signed below with his given name only. It was now close to sundown. My father looked at the page, half offended and half amused; he read it again. And then, rather than feeling offended, his mind was overcome with curiosity. To meet that Mosquito who believed himself King represented a greater attraction than that of wrapping himself up in a blanket for the rest of the evening so as not to be eaten alive by the mosquitoes. And even though the arrangement had all the earmarks of being secret and confidential—because in the letter he had been asked for absolute discretion—instead of being concerned about being ambushed his state of mind suggested the attraction of an adventure, the likes of which had been few enough and far between in his life (except for the intrigues that took shape there in León every day and might be mistaken for such adventures when they developed into actual conspiracies).

James returned at nightfall and then my father let himself be poled along the edge of the bay in a small canoe, and it was not until they had stopped hugging the shore that James lit his carbide lamp to light their way along the narrow path that went up from the patch of scrub brush where the canoe remained beached. Beneath the soles of his patent leather shoes my father   felt crab shells being crushed at every step.

The iron edifice remained in shadow with the exception of a yellow glow, like an ember about to die out, that slipped through from a pair of transoms on the upper floor. They entered through the main door, which no one was guarding, and mounted a stairway of iron plates without handrails, with James's lantern shining ahead of them. Within this confined space it smelled of dried fish, and the sea breezes shook the metal sheets of the walls, making them sound in the blackness like the crackle of rifle fire.

My uncle the King was waiting in the depths of one of the rooms. He had not taken off his military uniform, and he held his kepi with its patent leather visor tucked beneath his arm. My father noted, however, that despite his attire he was far from projecting a martial impression. Although rather tall, he was not athletic but somewhat spongy, and his body tended to lean forward while his belly was beginning to be noticeable beneath the seams of his braided jacket. And he was actually a blond *zambo*, just as my father had concluded in that glimpse from his lodgings that morning. His hair, a pallid yellow as if discolored from the effect of those peroxide preparations which had just then come into use among women, had gotten all disarranged in loose folds, and his yellow-green eyes, struggling to appear insistent and lively, seemed half asleep inside the pouches of his eyelids.

There was a campaign cot in the room, quite low, and a couple of Viennese rocking chairs placed facing each other. On the table between them was a pile of books, bound in the Spanish style, plus a lamp. In one corner, in the darkness that the lamplight did not completely succeed in dispersing, there hung from the ceiling some bunches of bananas that were just about to turn ripe, and dangling from a line that crossed the room from one side to the other was a string of gaspar fish, salted down and gutted.

They sat down, and the silence stretched out, annoying, as if one more dimension to the sticky heat. My uncle the King was thinking, with his thumbs tight against his temples, in a pose that seemed very theatrical to my father.

"The conversation for which I have invited you has nothing to do with the safe-conduct. That, of course, is granted," he said as if at length suddenly awakened, and his deep voice resounded with powerful, sensual registers.

Now that he had finally broken the silence his eyes became animated and sincere, but my father, accustomed as he was to political comedies, thought that even the show of sincerity in the gaze of an adversary might be the fruit of some attempted ruse.

"I am grateful for your courtesy," he responded, barely inclining his head. He didn't want to exaggerate his demonstrations of respect and risk offending this young man who at heart could not be ignorant of the fact that his kingship was a lie. But my father knew that whether or not he was a buffoon, my uncle the King certainly had enough power to obstruct his journey. And quickly he saw where his decision lay. What was important was getting to London, not the annoyances of the journey. This was simply one more inconvenience.

"Do you wish to accept my safe-conduct?" my uncle the King asked.

"I have no alternative," responded my father, repressing his severity, as if instead of yielding to an act of kindness he would rather have remonstrated with the one who was offering it. But in any case it was a double-edged answer, a blend of defiance and submission, of insolence and conformity.

My uncle the King bent over the table with the books where the lamp stood and wrote out the safe-conduct. Twice he made some mistake and had to tear up the sheet of brown paper. He read it over to himself, finally satisfied, and removing the chimney from the lamp in order to melt the red sealing wax, placed his seal at the foot of the document.

The tide was coming in over the sand bar, and the booming of the waves seemed only to be pulling the screws out of the plates of those walls rusting out in the salt air.

Meanwhile, my father had been occupying his gaze with the pile of books he had before him, and he was able to read the titles inscribed on the spines: Montesquieu's *Persian Letters*, Rousseau's *Confessions*, the *Henriade* of Voltaire, Comte's *Course of Positive Philosophy*, Tocqueville's *Democracy in America*, every one of them in its own language. He couldn't stop thinking that those books had been put there to impress him.

Before closing up the envelope with the safe-conduct inside, my uncle the King, gratified by my father's curiosity, picked out one from the stack and handed it to him.

"Sometimes I manage to get some antique jewels sent me from London," he said.

It was an edition of the *New Voyage Around the World*. This was among the books I received as an inheritance from him.

"Dampier was a bloodthirsty buccaneer," said my father deliberately. "He made his entry over this very sandbar, sacked Granada, and put to the sword anyone who resisted. I didn't know he had the time nor the talent to write any books."

"He was also a geographer, and a map maker of the oceans," my uncle the King said, and the echoes of his deep voice resonated in his laughter.

"And what is there so interesting in this book?" My father was taking care once more to be polite.

"The mention that Dampier makes of a sailor who belonged to my race, picked up here in this kingdom." And my uncle the King stretched out his arm to signal the breadth of that territory of swamps and jungles submerged in the night.

The sailor was named Robin (this is the one I've already mentioned to that person who is seeking me) or that's what the English called him, ignoring his true name. Dampier brought him on board as a cabin boy on his schooner *Cinque Ports*. In 1681 he left him behind on the island of Juan Fernández, off the coast of Chile, with nothing but a knife, a musket, a small horn of powder, and a few bullets, for he had gone off chasing after a wild goat and took too long getting back, and there were three Spanish ships after them. Three years later, traveling the same route, Dampier ordered a boat lowered to search for him, and they found him. He had survived by first hunting seals and goats, and when he ran out of ammunition, he took to sawing off the musket barrel with his knife blade, heating pieces of the metal and shaping them by beating them with a rock in order to make harpoons and hooks. With pieces of braided sealskin he made fishing lines. He was totally naked when they found him because his clothing had fallen apart with the rot, and he was living in a hut lined with goatskins.

"Very interesting," my father commented.

"That's where Defoe got his Robinson character," said my uncle the King.

Sergio Ramírez

"So then Robinson is a 'Mosquito,'" my father said with a slight lilt of admiration that barely covered up his sarcasm.

"Whatever you most prefer, Mosquito or Nicaraguan," said my uncle the King. By this time he had closed up the packet with a brush smeared with starch and handed it to him.

My father took the safe-conduct somewhat too hastily, enough so that my uncle the King smiled sympathetically.

"Have you read *Robinson Crusoe*?" my father inquired, merely to disguise his discomfort as he hid the parcel in his jacket pocket. Immediately he regretted his stupidity, for if this *zambo* had been able to comment on it so precisely it was clear that he had read the book, and that furthermore as the owner of all those volumes he was used to finding consolation for his loneliness by reading.

For if he himself felt isolated in León among priests who enjoyed themselves in the brothels with their breviaries in their hands, one-eyed marshals who hung out with whores, learned lawyers who were skilled only in making use of the laws for their own ends, and dim-witted council delegates who scarcely knew how to sign their names, how would this young man feel here, among savages who were used to the stench of bits of peccary meat and lizards and slices of shark laid out to dry on racks inside their own wall-less huts and constantly under siege by the buzzards, as could be seen even from the shed of his lodgings?

"I had it as required reading in the Greenwich Naval School," my uncle the King responded, with calculated modesty.

My father had thought he would leave immediately once he had the safe-conduct in his hands, but now, quite certain that his voyage would not be thwarted, he allowed himself to gain something more through curiosity.

"This Robin of whom you speak seems closer to the

figure of Friday than that of Robinson Crusoe," he said, a bit petulantly.

"Why? Friday came from a tribe of cannibals, according to Defoe's novel, and here we don't eat anybody," responded my uncle the King, and he laughed with those same deep, calm tones.

"I didn't mean to say that," my father protested, moving his hands abruptly as if he were trying to erase his words from the air.

"In any event, the model turns out better than the character in the book," said my uncle the King, not ceasing his laughter. "Robinson is a European, who turns the fact of surviving on a desert island into a great feat. That's where the myth comes from. It is a European myth, that of the civilized man able to resist the harshest material conditions, not only the spiritual isolation. Robin, on the contrary, comes from a people for whom their Robinsons find nothing particularly unusual in surviving every single day, hunting and fishing, in perfect solitude. You may be sure that for Robin what happened to him during those three years on the island of Juan Fernández was no huge feat. Although in any event he didn't know how to write, it still would never have occurred to him to tell in a book what happened to him on a desert island because it was just too common a situation."

"Well, of course," my father managed to say, though he could not help but feel humbled when faced with the astuteness of that discourse, even though it seemed rather vain of my uncle the King.

"Very much to the contrary, you consider this meeting of ours not only most unusual but even extravagant, also worthy of being written about sometime," my uncle the King went on. "For you, I am Friday, the cannibal who reads Defoe. Don't tell me I'm not."

My father could say nothing. Suddenly he was being suffocated by the heat in that stifling room, the penetrating odor of the nearby string of fish hanging in the ristra. And he got to his feet, eager to leave.

"Don't be offended," my uncle the King said, taking my father by the arm to get him to sit down once more. "I have a somewhat English sense of humor, different from yours. I've heard that over there on that side of the country, it is the one who tells the coarsest jokes or laughs the loudest that ends up the winner. Certainly not the one who says the most ingenious and witty thing."

"I am not offended," my father said.

"Besides, I still have not gotten to my subject," said my uncle the King.

Then, as if produced by a magic spell, my mother, Catherine, appeared in the doorway. She bowed down in a full reverence, her hands pulling back the ruffles of her lace dress, and her tiny curls shining with coconut oil ointment. Right behind her came Francis, wearing the same uniform, and his heels clacked firmly as he raised his hand to his ear in a military salute. James came in behind them, loaded down with a bench that he placed in the corner underneath the string of salt fish; he left and the children went over to sit down on it in silence, their eyes fixed on the floor.

"These are my siblings, Catherine and Francis," said my uncle the King, pointing toward the bench in the corner. "As my parents died in a shipwreck while they were returning from Kingston, I inherited the throne when I was still studying in England. My Aunt Charlotte took on the role of Regent until the day of my coronation, and she remains in Bluefields to raise these children."

"I saw them this morning when they were coming with you in the small boat," my father said, his gaze set on them.

Catherine smiled at him from a distance, and then turned to fix her eyes on the floor once more. My uncle the King brought his head so close to him before speaking that my father heard him swallowing his saliva.

"You must marry Catherine when she grows up," he said, soberly, and placed his hand on his knee. "I brought her with me so you might be acquainted with her from now on."

On my father's face there appeared a look of bothersome surprise as if from the barely noticeable sting of an insect. But at the same time, it was an amused look.

"You must be thinking that is going too far," said my uncle the King. "Though perhaps you will change your mind if you hear my reasons."

A single country was necessary, from the Pacific to the Caribbean. Only a country like that, strong and united, would be respected at the time of constructing the canal through Nicaragua. That piece of work was a necessity for civilization. England very soon would be out of the game, if they wanted to go it alone. The United States was about to come on the stage, the new leading actor, and the fact is that it was going to be necessary to come to an understanding with them. England and France nonetheless should be considered important partners in the great enterprise. England would continue being a great mercantile power, while the best engineering for a work of that scope was had by the French.

My father, despite his growing eagerness to take his leave, listened with contrived courtesy to my uncle the King's statement, who while he was spinning his story was keeping himself rocking by pushing with his heels.

"I don't see the United States in that scenario," my father said, in spite of himself tempted by those arguments. "They are just Quakers. They only know how to contemplate their navels. The world doesn't interest them. The

English will show their teeth pretty soon, and the next step is they will occupy San Juan del Norte on a permanent basis so as not to be left out of their share of the control of the canal. The construction of it will fall to the French, that is for sure. Ever since Napoleon, they have been the masters of scientific development all over the world."

"You are mistaken about the United States," said my uncle the King. "My English protectors will yield to them in this part of the world. You are right about calling them Quakers, but don't forget that Quakers govern themselves by consensual mandate."

"In any event, I am not the king of anything in Nicaragua, and it is others who have the power," said my father with an amiable smile, trying to make a final point. "You are thinking of an alliance through marriage between two dynasties, the way they do in the European royal houses."

"What you have to conquer first is your fear," said my uncle the King. "Fear of what they will say there in León. The lord of indigo, wedded to a *zambo* woman!"

"I have grown up on ideas of equality and liberty," my father responded, seizing the hook, but immediately he realized that his declaration didn't ring true.

"We also hold prejudices against you," said my uncle the King, "but I am certain that Catherine, paying heed to my advice, will be ready to conquer them. Isn't that right, Catherine?"

My mother Catherine shrank back into herself, filled with embarrassment.

"You and I have the same color of skin," my father pointed out but without enthusiasm.

"I am a *zambo*, a descendent of Carib Indians and black slaves, the slaves who didn't drown when the ship wrecked that was transporting them like a herd of cattle." My uncle the King stood up and in his eyes an angry spark was glowing now. "The color white is nothing but an accident in my blood."

My father, upset, turned his gaze once more toward the girl who was half asleep in the corner, and he thought he'd better take care with what he said if he didn't want to risk being stripped of the safe-conduct he had in his pocket.

"When she reaches the right age, I am going to be too old, old and bald," he said, searching for a cordial note. "In my family we have a tendency to baldness."

"We are not talking about baldness but about affairs of state," my uncle the King said then. "Let us suppose you fail in England and you come back to Nicaragua defeated. Then my proposal doesn't make sense. But let us suppose you are successful. Suppose you gain many supporters over the prestige of having succeeded in arranging peace with the English. Suppose they elect you the Supreme Director."

"I'm not a career soldier, they will never elect me anything," my father laughed, unsure of himself.

"On that side there are no career soldiers at all, as you well know," said my uncle the King. "Once chosen Supreme Director you should proclaim yourself the Grand Marshal and pick out the flashiest uniform from some fashion magazine."

"That doesn't go with me," my father said.

"What doesn't go with you, the power or the uniform?" my uncle the King argued. "In my court I have admirals that go barefoot and field marshals without a second shirt who never take their tricorn off their heads. Over there where you're from those military ornaments are worth something, while here they're not."

"One can be in command without the uniform," my father said. "That is what I call civilization."

"Whatever you wish," said my uncle the King, "as long as you really are in command. Here, facing the English, I am the only one who is worth anything, because they need me. And you should manage to be the only one who is worth anything with the Americans. Work hard so that they need you as well."

My father was silent. He thought it a pity to waste such astuteness on a sermon that at all events wouldn't lead to anything anyway. But at the same time he tried to bury as deeply as possible the embarrassment of having been caught out in his ambitions. He would be the Supreme Director, he had thought this quite often, and he would grant himself the attributes of a Captain General, a rather more severe title that suited his republican convictions, not that of Grand Marshal. He would set all this chaos in order, he would bring all the factions together, he would open the country to the traffic of world commerce. The canal! A man of reason such as himself, with all the power in his hands, he would be the only one capable of succeeding with the canal's construction.

"You don't have ambitions?" he heard my uncle the King say in the deepest tones of his solemn voice.

"I do have ambitions," he stammered.

"It's the same thing. And you do want the canal?"

"Well, yes, I do want it."

"Then we will sign a treaty of incorporation of the two territories into a single one, under your command," said my uncle the King. "Only then you will offer to the United States the territorial rights to the canal."

"This conversation would be enough for the Grand Marshal to convict me of treason and have me shot," my father tried to be a little jovial.

He was beginning to be affected by drowsiness, but he knew that this sleepiness was not real. It always came over him when his ambition began to gain the upper hand, or his fear. He would be attacked by this desire to sleep.

"By the treaty of incorporation, I abdicate. There will be no more Mosquito Kings. You will name me governor of Mosquitia, and I will swear loyalty to you in a public ceremony. By that time, the Grand Marshal will be dead, he'll be assassinated by someone at a cockfight. Do you think there would be anyone else there from the other side capable of accusing you of treason when faced with a proposal like this one?" My uncle the King got to his feet and turned toward my father with his arms crossed.

"I promise you I will think about it," my father said, breathing deeply.

"Let us say then that we have arrived at an agreement of intentions?" my uncle the King said.

"Perhaps not quite so much as that," my father said, alarmed.

He wanted to look at this whole thing as a verbal game, a syllogism that was set up in an imaginary terrain without any problems, far away from any consequences, like the exercises in logic that his philosophy professor used to propose in scholastic fashion in the Jesuit school in León. Padre Gorostiaga, a rationalist Basque who was very nearly an atheist.

"Catherine will be waiting," said my uncle the King. "I will try to have her educated in London. When you are Supreme Head of State, she will manage to find you."

"That is, if I reach that level," said my father, without enthusiasm.

"You will be the Supreme Head, and for a long time," said my uncle the King. "In spite of Bishop Contreras, your sworn enemy, and despite the Grand Marshal, who wants you out of there, the longer the better. That is why they have given you this mission to England. That is what Chatfield thinks."

"Chatfield?" exploded my father. "He is not the least bit sympathetic to me."

"This is not a matter of sympathy," my uncle the King said, "but of reality. It is clear to him that if they let you, you'll bring together all the factions in this dispute, and you will have all the control."

For the Grand Marshal to fear him as a rival, he could have suspected that, and for the Bishop Pedro Mártir Contreras to have professed a hatred for him, that was also clear. On the morning of Holy Saturday two years before, beneath the doors of León there had appeared some verses which published in rhymed form the report about some illegitimate children from the relationship the Bishop had formed with the woman who had sewn the altar cloths. This offense was credited to a conspiracy of Freemasons whose leader was my father.

What he had been unaware of was that Chatfield valued him so highly, unless the Mosquito King were simply playing the cards of flattery in order to force him to take part in the comedy that he was putting together in his head. And although he continued to be prey to a kind of fear, or more properly, of repulsion, from the danger of getting entangled somehow in that deceitful game, the drowsiness was weighing on his eyes and he knew well that behind that fickle curtain of dream was hidden the thirst for power.

"We should begin by seeing how things go for me on this mission," my father said.

"That will not be an easy thing. Many humiliations and setbacks await you," said my uncle the King. "Chatfield will make sure of that. But remember at the same time that he fears you; he's afraid of your skills."

My father was silent, out of vanity. He would be able to open all the doors. He would get as far as Queen Victoria's chamber, if it came to that.

My uncle the King rummaged among the pile of books on the table and pulled out one, bound in red morocco, that my father had not noticed. The title, *Rêveries Politiques*, was inscribed in a arch on the cover.

"I offer you this in token of our friendship," my uncle the King said. "I hope it will serve as your reading material during your voyage. I admire the man who wrote it, the captive prince Louis Napoleon."

"I too admire him," my father said, taking the book. "What a pity that no one can free him from his prison, at least not during the reign of Louis Phillipe."

"He will get out of there, for he has many supporters, George Sand, for example," my uncle the King said, accompanying my father to the door, where James was waiting with the carbide lamp held high. "Don't forget that famous prisoners, if they are not destined for the gallows, are always candidates for a return to power."

My mother Catherine had now fallen asleep, bent over in Francisco's lap, who remained very composed in his military uniform, still making an effort to stay erect although his eyes too were half-closed from sleep. What I wouldn't have given to have been able to take that picture!

3

A champion hog at the agricultural fair

In the devastated cemetery were to be seen skeletons almost decayed while the trees above them dangled their golden fruits above our heads. Don't you feel the completeness of this poetry, and how it assumes a grand synthesis?

Flaubert to Louise Colet, March 27, 1853

THIS NEXT EPISODE took place toward the end of the spring of 1991. It was in Paris where I had gone, representing the Sandinista opposition, to attend the Conference of Donor Countries which had been convened by the World Bank for the reconstruction of Nicaragua after the war, with Doña Violeta Chamorro now in the Presidency. I was with Tulita, my wife. Peter Schulze-Kraft, the translator of my first stories to German, with whom I shared a friendship of some forty years, had come to meet us from Vienna, where he was an official in the Atomic Energy Agency of the UN.

The last Sunday before our return to Managua, Peter rented a car with the idea that we should make a visit to the Cathedral at Chartres. On the road we lunched in the Coq Hardi, a restaurant located in Haute-Seine, near Bougival, where he personally had made a reservation by telephone.

He is a methodical and romantic German in everything he does, like that Joachim von Pasenow in *The Sleepwalkers* by Hermann Broch. He bought a map of L'Île de France, handed it to me, and set me up beside him as his co-pilot. But we had scarcely left the ring road around Paris when we were already lost.

We left it by way of the Porte d'Auteuil instead of the Porte Maillot as we should have, and very soon the tangle of roads on the outskirts of Paris had become indecipherable on the map. Stuck as we were on these unexpected lanes and horsepaths, sometimes on a secondary expressway, and then on a narrow byway between walls of tall poplars that would suddenly vanish to reveal a barn or the belltower steeple marking a small village, we finally came to an obviously little used crossroad with a crumpled tin sign that pointed toward Bougival. After going down this new route for a while, when we stopped to look at the map once more—fearful of pushing our sudden stroke of luck too far with one more mistake—we caught a glimpse of another sign, shaped like an arrow, half obliterated by rust, that pointed toward La Frênes, the dacha of Ivan Turgenev.

We all agreed that this was an accident even more memorable than having followed precisely the signs along the road to our restaurant. We parked the car and, ambling down the gravel path indicated by the arrow, it wasn't long before we found the dacha, hidden in the haven of a stand of poplars and birch trees.

There were no other visitors than ourselves when we stepped into the foyer and bought our tickets from a girl in jeans who was listening to music on a small transmitter plugged into her ear. In a glass showcase next to the cash register some postcards showing the spot were on display, as well as a few books—translations of Turgenev's novels in the Gallimard Folio Series plus a leather-bound volume of letters exchanged between Turgenev, Flaubert, and George Sand, published by Flammarion.

According to the folded leaflet the girl handed us along with the tickets, the La Frênes farm, which includes a small eighteenth-century mansion, presently closed, was acquired by Turgenev for a price of 158,000 francs in the year 1874, and the following year he had the dacha built with the intention of spending the summers here, which he actually did until his death, which took place on these premises in 1883 in the bedroom on the second floor. The dacha was abandoned for nearly a century until it was reopened in 1983 by the Association des Amis d'Ivan Tourguéniev, Pauline Viardot, et Maria Malibran.

Going up the enclosed stairway, the visitor finds on both sides of the little hallway the double doors of the study and the bedroom respectively, each of them in turn opening onto a balcony of ornamental stonework which looks out over the countryside of Seine-et-Oise. Pushed up against a large window in the study there is an oak desk with a swivel chair like a bookkeeper's, and on top of the desk a blotter spotted with horrendous ink stains, a silver inkwell, and a pale marble penholder with a rusty nib, plus some papers with examples of the novelist's handwriting faded rather yellow by the sunlight, for they are photocopies, which makes one doubt the authenticity of the whole arrangement. A bookcase of leaded glass under lock and key faces the desk, and scattered throughout the room are other showcases with manuscripts, first editions, letters, music scores, sketches, and photographs.

On the walls, papered with a pattern of green ribbons, are seen more drawings and photos, portraits of family members of the soprano Pauline Viardot-García, Turgenev's mistress (a relationship of such renown secrecy that it bored everyone), beginning with her husband, the theatre impresario Louis Viardot, whose photo is hung very close to the desk. Viardot, who was forty when he married Pauline, then nineteen, is shown here in all the majesty of his old age, which he was able to carry off with rugged steadfastness, clutching the arms of the great chair in which he is seated like someone preparing himself for the final shock. He died a year before Turgenev.

Missing from this gallery are Pauline's children: Claudie, with whom Turgenev, already old by that time, fell in love when she was still a school girl, just as Chopin had become attached to Solange, the daughter of George Sand; and Paul, whose paternity, attributed to Turgenev, continues to be a rustling of old papers that yet stirs up the biographers of both lovers.

Pauline's father, the tenor Manuel García, the founder of a dynasty of lyric singers, occupies a principle place on the wall. The pastel drawing shows him already quite aged, dressed in the costume of Figaro as if it were his shroud. He donned that form of dress for the first time at the premiere of *The Barber of Seville* the night of the 20th of February, 1816, at the Teatro Argentina in Rome, personally chosen for the role by Rossini.

Next is Pauline's older sister, who was baptized María Felicia García but was better known by her stage name, Maria Malibran. Her death at age 28 cut short the surprising flight of her career, that of a prima donna of the European stage since she was sixteen. In the lithograph she is wearing the costume of Rosina, her backcomb in the shape of a fan stuck in her chignon, with her Andalucian mantle thrown carelessly about her shoulders, the way she looked on her debut in London (1825), also in *The Barber of Seville*, with her father then retired from the stage. Chopin saw her in Paris in 1832, in *Othello*, also by Rossini: "La Malibran took the role of Othello, and Shröder-Devrient that of

Desdemona. La Malibran is tiny, and the German actress
huge; it looked as though Desdemona were going to flatten
Othello. It was an expensive performance, 24 francs to see
her all daubed in black, and acting her part in a mediocre
way," he wrote his friend Tytus Wojciechowski.

Also missing from the gallery is Pauline's mother, Jose-
fina Siches, a native of Cádiz and also a prima donna in her
day, coached by Manuel García using the same intransigent
and sometimes brutal methods by which he trained his
daughters' voices. And then there is the other Manuel García, the brother of Pauline and La Malibran, a less celebrated singer but who on the other hand was the inventor of
the laryngoscope. One of those devices lies under the glass
of one of the showcases in the hallway, with an explanatory
note taken from one of his letters:

> I had very often thought of using a mirror to observe
> my larynx while singing but it always seemed to me an
> impossible thing. In September of 1854, during a trip to
> Paris, I decided to try it. I went to the well-known opti-
> cian, Charrière, and asked if he had a small mirror on
> a long handle; he did have one; actually it was a small
> dental mirror that he had sent to the London exhibition
> of 1851 but which had interested no one. I bought it
> and took it to my sister Pauline's house together with
> another pocket mirror, eager to begin my experiment. I
> warmed the mirror in water, dried it carefully, and leaned
> it against my tongue. When I directed toward it the light
> from the flame of an oil lamp, with the help of my pocket
> mirror I saw before my eyes the open larynx.

And now at last I move toward to the two photographs
of Pauline hanging close to the corner near which stands
a Pleyel piano that throws off its black reflections of the
splendor of the spring sunlight. On the piano's music
stand is spread the score, also a photocopy, of a song

which she composed, "Dolores No Son Candores."

In one of her pictures, she might well pass for a studious piano teacher, garbed severely in dark gray, with an ivory cameo closing her lace collar. In the other, she glitters in the costume of Rosina, just the way her sister La Malibran appears on the other side of the wall. Such was the weight of Rossini's influence on all the Garcías. These are the same garments in which Turgenev met Pauline in the autumn of 1843 when she opened the season at the Italian Opera House in Saint Petersburg. But the coquetry she attempts to show in this picture is pitiful, due to the mediocrity of her features that wholly lack inspiration; her eyes, too prominent beneath her narrow brow, give her the air of a frightened gazelle, while her prominent nose above those thick, almost swollen lips, plus her sunken chin, defeat the elegance of her face.

From that time on Turgenev no longer wanted to be separated from her and was her constant shadow for the next forty years, a circumspect bachelor cohabiting with an ugly diva possessing the allure of a gypsy. He put the dacha Les Frênes in her name, and besides that he left the eighteenth-century mansion to the Viardot family. For all his friends, as well as for visitors, it was a strange relationship, but he never felt unsatisfied with his part in that peaceful *ménage à trois*. At the end, old Viardot, undermined by his ailments, was hardly in the way, but this rival, twenty years younger—who was frequently forced to walk around in slippers because of the attacks of gout that he used to treat with salicylate of soda and also with the horse chestnut oil recommended by Flaubert according to his father's prescription—was unable to boast of any better health.

"Old age is a huge, opaque cloud that extends over the future, the present, and even the past, since it saddens one's memories," he wrote to Flaubert. But the worst side of that old age, as ominous as a cloud, was the role of clown that he played in the funny games he organized at Les Frênes on his own initiative every Saturday afternoon in order to amuse Pauline: "As odd as it is delightful is watching poor Turgenev interpret charades with the most extravagant disguises, adorned in old shawls, and crawling around on all fours. . ." writes Henry James to his father, after having witnessed one of those productions.

But if we must lend an ear to the insidious whisperings that are heard behind the doors of the past, he had a fearful rival, though perhaps an ephemeral one, in George Sand, who during the period she was Chopin's lover, decided to conquer La Viardot. A masculine whim in a feminine soul, Turgenev would think, but he was rather upset by the move because as an attractive specimen Pauline, we've already seen, was not a trophy animal.

In Turgenev's bedroom, on the other side of the hallway where the laryngoscope of the other Manuel García is on exhibit, there is a sober metallic bedstead with canopy, a Voltaire armchair, a washbasin of Sèvres porcelain, and a four-drawer commode made of ash with an oval mirror above its top—all of this furniture unlikely to be original either, as the commensurate card recognizes in the case of the Voltaire chair, but which ends up anyway belonging to the household thanks to the taste or the whims of the museographers, exactly the same as in Zelazowa Wola.

Concerning the authenticity of the canopied bedstead, however, there seems no possible doubt: a single photograph on the wall beside it shows Turgenev's body stretched out on that very bed, his white beard and hair like iridescent silk, and very well groomed, his black suit impeccable, with the soles of his useless shoes that touch the arabesques of the footboard, so tall was the man. And even the bedspread and the pillows seem to be the same.

He had died at two in the afternoon of a Monday, September 3rd, a victim of cancer of the medulla—which only came to be known after the autopsy, and which the physicians, including even the eminent Charcot, had all taken for a neuralgia of the stomach associated with his gout. His pain reached such a frightful state, despite the increasing dosages of morphine, that once he even tried to hang himself with a bell cord which, either the original or an imitation, can be seen hanging at the side of the headboard.

A hornet that has lost its way strikes insistently at the mirror, blinded by the sun, which also gilds the furniture and makes the room's waxed floor glitter. And this light in such torrents increases the sensation of grief, the very feeling that must have been manifest when the photographer, exhausted after mounting that narrow staircase carrying the brass case in which he kept the equipment for his job, was actually taking the photograph of the deceased Turgenev, even as a servant was heard nailing a crown of myrtles trimmed with black crepe to the door of the dacha, as instructed by Pauline Viardot.

Through the open window that opens out onto the balcony comes the sound of passing vehicles swiftly rolling along the expressway hidden behind the birch trees stretching away in dark waves. The framing of the photograph reveals that the camera's tripod must have been placed right there in front of the window, and as I look over at the empty bed from this point I imagine Turgenev lying opposite me, as in the picture on the wall, and I imagine myself in the photographer's place as he looked through the blurred lens to find close up the beading on the sole of the dead man's shoes. It was Pauline who had decided that Turgenev should take to the grave some brand new patent leather shoes, and it was she herself who watched to make sure his hair and beard were anointed with an aromatic pomade that gave off so intense a fragrance of orange blossoms macerated in aloe that the photographer's nose couldn't stand it. Meanwhile, that maddened hornet never stops buzzing around, insistent on trying to get into the white fire of the mirror.

Without the need of any written explanation, the photograph appears on the wall simply as a window on the past, a *Before* to go with the *After* that is the empty bed. A chambermaid is charged with making up that useless bed every once in a while with newly ironed sheets, different from the daily care that a bed for a living body would require. Or—to use the plural—living bodies, because this is where Turgenev made love with Pauline, with that deceitful splendor of the winter of their ages lighting their way.

The rubber stamp in the lower corner of the picture could only be read when you came up very close to it. *Castellón*, it said, inside an oval shape. And then I realized, with a joy that seemed like a form of anguish, that he had found me once more. He continued being a mystery to me, although I hadn't wanted it, and far from my exercising myself to mount a pursuit of him, it was he who was always coming to find me.

I still had not yet seen three other photographs of his on display in the dacha. Two of them are in the hallway that separates the study from the bedroom: the funeral service dedicated to Turgenev in the church of Saint Alexandre Nevski in the Rue Daru in Paris, and the send-off of the funeral bier on the platform at the Gare de l'Est, amid a sea of shiny top hats. And one more, in small format, that I discover on the way out in an awkward spot beside the upper end of the stairway.

The legend says: *The Champion in Good Company, Agricultural Fair, Rouen, 1873 (dry plate with gelatin bromide)*. Again his rubber stamp. A huge, white Yorkshire hog, so white he seems made of snow, is lying on a bed of straw beneath a wooden shelter with a triangle-shaped board across the front where the rosette for the First Prize is nailed. Turgenev, Flaubert, and George Sand are standing beside the champion hog, whose name is Hercules; and his owner, a rich farmer who was a neighbor of Flaubert in Croisset named Odilon Alegre, appears at one edge of the photograph, almost out of the picture. Everything is very clean and spotless in this shed which reminds one of a changing room at a seaside resort. From their slightly roguish air, you can see that the three friends have decided to get their picture taken as a result of some kind of joke, probably arranged by George Sand, who was quite knowledgeable about pigs, as is obvious from a reading of her *A Winter in Mallorca.*

Turgenev, thanks to his exquisitely combed beard, his greatcoat of black wool, and his medium-brimmed hat, and leaning on his cane, seems like a respectable judge of livestock contests, and he is like in height to the peak made by the triangle on the pig's shed, just as he was equal to the length of his deathbed. He was taller than Flaubert, and that already says a great deal. He was so tall that he had his own carriage made with a special body capable of allowing room for his knees and head.

"This colossus had the movements of a child, timid and repressed," Maupassant recalls. His figure seemed taken from the pages of Charles Perrault, where his role would be that of the old woodcutter, master of the beneficent secrets of the enchanted forest. Nevertheless, that old man with the simpering, flute-like voice, who would laugh with a nervous clucking sound totally unsuited to the majesty of his bearing, and who would get down on all fours to act out the comical skits designed for Pauline Viardot, never skimped on energy when tormenting Dostoevsky, like someone goading a captive insect, whom he treated like an insufferable rival after the success of his first novel, *Poor Folk*.

A colossus tormented in turn by his mother, Varvara Ivanovna, who was cruel and insensitive to the point of true madness, whom he never stopped being afraid of, even after her death, and who appears in his novels under different disguises, like an obsessive shadow. Widowed early, shut up in the gloomy rooms of her farm house at Spasskoye, she took a very young lover by whom she had a baby girl secretly, but that romance in no way tempered her bitter, despotic attitude.

In the photograph the cane on which Turgenev is supporting himself is due to the torments of his gout, exacerbated by the sausages they send him from Spasskoye, as well as the sturgeon caviar from the Volga that comes by rail to the Gare de l'Est in half-pint flasks all packed into long boxes lined with zinc, in a mixture of salt and ice. They are boxes large enough to fit a good-sized man into. From time to time he sends some of those flasks to Flaubert in Croisset, who eats them "in appetizing spoonfuls as if they were fruit preserves."

On the other hand, in the photo, Flaubert's head, which by this time has been despoiled of all his hair except for the scattered wisps above his ears, is bare. He is dressed carelessly, the sleeves of his jacket stained with ink, and his nankeen pants so creased and rumpled that he could well pass for a court clerk. If you look closely, the few teeth left to him seem blackened, and a spot of eczema (*gummata simple*) stands out in the middle of his forehead. Such eczemas are usually attributed, as a matter of decency, to the bromide of potassium he used as a sleeping potion, but in reality they demonstrate the ravages of syphilis, and the strong doses of mercury and silver that he has taken for years to hold back the advance of that disease have resulted in the loss of his hair and teeth.

His syphilis was the most unforgettable souvenir of his trip to the Middle East, undertaken at the end of 1849 in the company of his friend the photographer Maxime du Camp. In Beirut, already homeward-bound, he had picked it up from a Maronite whore, or perhaps a Turkish one, recalls du Camp. "And the chancres were only discovered in Rhodes, seven of them near his penis, a complete constellation, that ended up by merging into two, and finally into a single one. Every night and every morning he treated his poor cock."

The opposite of Turgenev, Flaubert is always showering attentions on his "poor mother," Anne-Caroline Fleuriot, a tyrant in her own way, and his impassioned filial love is never enrolled in the category of compromising sentiments, the ones that affect the neutrality of the artist: "You will never have a rival, do not fear. Neither my feelings nor the whim of the moment will occupy the place that lies locked within the depths of a triple sanctuary. Perhaps they may manage to shit on the threshold of the temple, but they will never get into it," he tells her from Constantinople at the end of that voyage.

George Sand, come from her retreat, Nohant, to make one of her rare visits to Flaubert, looks like an elderly bourgeois woman out for a day of shopping while her servants are waiting for her to get this photograph over and done with; long behind her are those days when she used to dress like a man. The little straw hat with its ribbon tied beneath her chin says nothing else, nor does the dowdy gray dress trimmed with edging partially concealed beneath her smock, and no one now would be able to see in her the possessive lover of Chopin that she once was. She had already abandoned him a quarter century earlier by the time he died vomiting blood in October, 1849, nor did she attend his funeral. Pauline García-Viardot, by Chopin's own desire, sang Mozart's *Requiem* at the memorial service held in the Church of the Madelaine. It was in this same month of October that Flaubert, still quite young, had departed for the Middle East in du Camp's company.

This is George Sand's final visit to Flaubert. Not that the photograph reveals any sign of the proximity of her approaching end, but the truth is, she has only three more years left before dying. And one continues to wonder what they are doing here together at the Agricultural Fair in Rouen, an organization that brings together the breeders of stud hogs, cart horses, and a variety of fowl, aside from the producers of cider or of honey and the dealers in fodder and grains, who, once the prizes have been announced, disperse to the taverns in the neighborhood of the site provided for the needs of the fair.

Since the trip from Croisset in a Berlin carriage takes very little time, and probably by then they have tired of literary conversations, they have been trying to amuse themselves for awhile wandering around the stalls and displays where this year, as a novelty, a sheep with two heads is being shown, which instead of looking monstrous demonstrates a redoubled mildness as it drinks from two baby bottles at once. They have already marveled at it, and the same with the pneumatic milking machine, an invention of a certain M. Picquart, that collects the milk in bottles connected by hoses to the rubber suction cups attached to the cow's teats. The details of this device Flaubert has put down in the little notebook he carries in the lower pocket of his jacket, for this is the period during which he is gathering information for *Bouvard et Pécuchet*, the unfinished novel destined to be his swan song to human stupidity.

In this new novel, besides a paragraph on the art of milking, there would be another on the breeding of pigs. Both of these are registered among the finicky interests of his two characters, the retired copyists, friends who are inclined to make of life an immense practical encyclopedia. At every step they quickly cast aside one idiosyncrasy for another with an avidness that is always suggestive of the fear of death, the only thing capable of parting them from the giddiness of attempting to devote themselves to all the arts as well as to all learning and to each of the trades, splashing about in methodical chaos.

And it was precisely his death that separated Flaubert from that exhausting occupation which consumed his last energies and from which he got relief by performing for his friends the Dance of the Bee, dressed as an odalisque in the image of Kuchiuk-Hanem, the dancer with the decaying teeth he had met in Esneb, in Upper Egypt.

Once in front of the exhibition stall, Flaubert, pushed by George Sand, proposes to M. Alegre that he get the official photographer of the Agricultural Fair take this shot of them next to Hercules, and the farmer accepts, more as a courtesy to a good neighbor than any recognition of the relevance of the three characters, whose literary works he is unaware of. The photographer, having been engaged in Paris, comes over escorted by M. Alegre. He is quite young. Flaubert greets him with surprising fondness, but he had met him several months before at an evening party at the home of Count Primoli; later he will receive from him a copy of this photograph that he has now come to take of them, plus another of the two-headed sheep, and one of the milking machine, which the novelist adds to the folder of the book in process.

Before posing, Flaubert, notebook in hand, has plied M. Alegre with questions about the animal's weight, the breed to which it belongs, how many pounds of manure (approximately) it excretes each day, how much he charges, in his capacity as owner, for a single service by the champion to cover a female. M. Alegre has given due replies to everything, moreover informing Flaubert on his own that at night Hercules has to sleep beneath the light of strong acetylene floodlights, something that stimulates his sexual potency. Flaubert notes down this final point, puts the notebook back in his pocket, and arranges himself to appear before the photographer who now makes his way to the spot where he has set up the tripod and camera, to put his head under the cloth of the black hood.

The photographer asks them to move forward a few steps, toward the camera. George Sand sees in the young man, in whose eyes an amber light seems to glow, much of the temper of those indigenous princes of the Amazon (like those shown in the engravings of Burnichon that illustrate her anthropologist friend Bonnard's book *Charmeur d'Indiens*), in whose veins now runs the blood of Dutch colonists come from Rotterdam to Manaus, preachers dressed in black or hired assassins with whips in their hands.

For Flaubert, on the other hand, the sight of the young man's hair in loose curls that shine as if moistened with aloe reminds him of Ahmed, the servant at the public baths in Cairo, as if that phantom from yesteryear, dissolving in sweat, had materialized once more amidst those same hot steam vapors, and he thinks: "If the scurvy hasn't killed him he must be around forty years old, already an old man in that poisonous climate that corrodes beauty under its scalding blasts."

"How old are you?" Turgenev asks him circumspectly.

In his figure there is something of a wild animal of the remote jungles where it smells of vegetal matter decomposing. Turgenev has never been in such a jungle, but he imagines burning eyes with that feline glimmer gazing at him through the thickets. The hog behind them grunts in his shelter. A hygienic, satisfied grunt.

"Nineteen, monsieur," responds the photographer without moving his head from under the hood.

From the window of the foyer I can make out Peter and Tulita waiting for me, seated on a stone bench at the edge of the terrace. Peter gets to his feet impatiently when he sees me appear, but then I still have to go back to purchase from the girl—engaged now in reading a movie magazine that has on its cover a shot of Alain Delon looking old and wearing dark glasses—that volume of the letters between those three standing beside Hercules' shed in the photo. While she makes out the receipt by hand I ask her what her name is and without raising her head she responds, "Pauline." "What a coincidence!" I tell her, and at that point she does glance up at me, surprised. Then, with unhurried movements, she goes in search of the guard to get some change for a one-hundred franc bill.

On the trip from Paris to Miami, en route to Managua, deep into reading those letters, I found two that I underlined with a yellow marker. They reveal certain domestic details not at all negligible for trying to shed light, even though with the scant help of a flickering match apparently soon to go out, on the pathway through that dark forest that is the human soul.

Flaubert to Turgenev, March 4, 1873:

> Are you acquainted with Mme. Ernesta Grisi, Theo's old mistress and the mother of his children? Probably not. But no matter. This is the favor I am asking you to do for me.
>
> Mme. Grisi came to see me Sunday to tell me that on the 19th of this month she will give a concert—in order to make some money, since she finds herself in a desperate situation—and she begs me to ask Mme. Viardot if she would agree to sing in it...

The "Theo" to whom Flaubert refers is Théophile Gautier, who had died the year before. Many years previously, in the course of his journey to the Middle East, Flaubert had sent a letter from Jerusalem in which he reminded him, as he was signing off, to "remember me to the lady of the house," who was none other than the Italian soprano Ernesta Grisi, at the time about to give birth to Judith, one of the three children she had with Gautier. The young Flaubert, besides telling the master that between Beirut and Jaifa he had seen an immense carpet of red oleanders stretched out so close to the sea that the foam was speckling their blooms, he informs him that he had witnessed the unusual spectacle of "a monkey that was masturbating a donkey" on a street in Cairo. "The donkey was discussing this, the monkey was gnashing its teeth, the people were staring. It was something dreadful."

Ernesta Grisi made her debut in the Théâtre Italien in the same season as La Viardot, who from that time on considered her a rival, with all the fury of those stage enmities. The competition was soon dispelled because La Grisi never managed to achieve the stature of the other, but despite all that, the rancor of that period seems never to have been extinguished in Pauline's soul, as you can see in this response from Turgenev dated in Paris, 48 Rue Douai, the nest they shared occasionally, and where he had had an acoustic tube installed the better to hear her from his study as she practiced on the floor below:

> I have spoken to Mme. Viardot about the wish expressed by Mme. E. Grisi. Unfortunately it is impossible. Mme. Viardot has a rule not to sing for private occasions. She has to do this because she has so many requests that if she consents even one time, she would be unable to refuse the others. She laments terribly that she can do nothing on this occasion. When she was younger, she would have been able to, but now she finds it necessary

to save her strength. And that, my dear friend, is the authentic truth.

It is not difficult to imagine Pauline, livid with rage over the memories, standing behind Turgenev's back, dictating these lines as he writes them with nervous care, while she takes a brief glance, corrects what he has written, and orders him to cross something out. She is a woman who does not forget so easily. One night, after she had sung *La Gazza Ladra* at the Comédie Italienne, she arrived at the Café Trianon with her entourage, and when they had made themselves comfortable at the table set up for them she heard the aggressive, teasing laughter of Ernesta, who was resplendent with joyousness while seated among her own followers. And she really was beautiful. That laughter offended Pauline as if it were directed at her lack of beauty. Evil-tongued backbiters, who traveled from one group to the other stirring up discord, had already warned her that Ernesta was in the habit of referring to her, sotto voce, as "the hunchback," because she usually held her shoulders thrust forward.

Turgenev crumples up the piece of paper and sets another clean one on the blotter. In the face of his compassionate insistence she has ordered him to cross out *she does not usually appear at charity affairs* and instead to write *she has a rule not to sing for private occasions*, a sentence that must not leave her totally satisfied although she says that it is all right, she accepts it, while she musses up his silky white hair with her bejeweled fingers, bending down afterward to kiss him on the cheek.

She is now forty-eight years old, and although her fame has not abandoned her as it has poor Ernesta, she is gradually beginning to be deserted by her voice, so supernatural that her public would hold their breath listening to her, unaware that this voice was the bitter fruit of fear and many tears, because the child used to practice between her sobs under the threat of the rod with which her father whipped her hands, the ones she was forced to place on the piano lid, every time she made a mistake.

Flaubert, who while pacing back and forth in the room is reading aloud a scene from *Le Candidat*, which he was just then occupied in writing, hears the click of the bolt on the garden gate, and moving aside the gauze curtains of the window he discerns Mme. Grisi who has mounted the steps and is just about to pull the cord of the little bell. Unannounced, she has come all the way from Paris looking for a reply, and he has just now received Turgenev's letter. Gesticulating urgently then before his niece Caroline, he warns her with silent words that she should tell Mme. Grisi he is not at home before he runs off to shut himself in his bedroom.

4

The prisoner in the fortress

A GOOD NUMBER of the archeological pieces classified by Schulz the engineer had been smashed to pieces during the hustle and bustle of the voyage, but enough remained to present Queen Victoria with a significant gift, so that the day following his arrival in London my father requested an audience with her "for the purpose of offering her in tribute a collection of pre-Colombian pottery of incalculable value and at the same time explaining to her certain delicate matters concerning the relationship between the British Empire and the Republic of Nicaragua." But even before getting a reply, he learned that the Queen was preparing to begin her summer retreat at Balmoral Castle to which she would travel with her family by train, thus inaugurating the rail line to Scotland, an event which everyone was talking about.

Sergio Ramírez

Once the summer was past, he reiterated his petition, and finally he received a brief note from the Lord Chamberlain of the Court in which he was asked to turn the pieces over to the British Museum and direct his request for an audience to the Foreign Office, since Lord Aberdeen had been commissioned by the Queen to hear him. He began then to present himself punctually in the antechamber of the minister's office, only to be turned away without success at the end of the day when the gas lights in the corridors were starting to be turned on and the employees were leaving, to the sound of distant doors slamming.

Since the money produced by the sale of indigo that he had negotiated with Pinter and Sons, his usual buyers, was running low, he decided to leave the expensive Hotel Brunswick in Jermyn Street and remove himself to a boarding house for traveling commercial representatives located in a bustling alleyway of florists and dealers in cutlery from the Covent Garden market. Dead tired like himself, the sales representatives would return at nightfall lugging their valises with samples of Chinese silks from the markets of Panyu bound in large quarto format albums, or tea from Ceylon and Bengal displayed in small drawers of portable cabinets, or tobacco leaves both Turkish and American, tied in small bundles with bows of different colors according to the aroma, or perhaps razors and barber's scissors gleaming in their plush cases as if they were surgical instruments.

One afternoon at the end of autumn, when he had already left his usual seat in the waiting room and was removing his overcoat from the coat rack, he heard his name being called in a loud voice by the usher dressed in a morning coat who had custody over the door to the office, and at last he was admitted. Lord Aberdeen apologized from a little way off in the reigning darkness, though in very cordial tones, saying that he suffered from an infection of the cor-

neas that made even artificial light unbearable, and then my
father heard him draw nearer with little bird-like footsteps
and felt him grasp his hand and squeeze it with a few short
jerks. He invited my father to be seated with him on the
same sofa and offered him some snuff, though only out of
politeness, because immediately after taking a few pinches
for himself he returned the silver box to his pocket.

It was an interview filled with trivialities, and every
time my father tried to get started on the matters that had
brought him there, he was cut off by a new banality. He attempted speaking to Lord Aberdeen about Chatfield, but
scarcely had he begun when the old man took care to dispel
his complaints with a dismissive brush of the hand: Chatfield was a little crude in his ways but at bottom he was an
excellent gentleman. At length, when the clock chimes in
the office struck six in the afternoon, Lord Aberdeen got to
his feet apologizing because he had to rush to the bedside
of a niece convalescing from scarlet fever whom he had
promised to visit, and he returned to his rather distant desk
to pick up a large box of chocolates that he was taking her
as a gift.

"Do you wish to know something?" asked Lord Aberdeen, the box of chocolates already beneath his arm. "The
territory of your country is too small to take its existence
seriously."

That was the sentence of civil death that my father had
crossed the ocean to prove wrong, uselessly, as anyone
can see. And after pronouncing those words, as if he had
done nothing more than come forth with another of those
platitudes he had so plentifully offered up during the conversation, Lord Aberdeen smiled innocently and put on his
violet-colored dark glasses to protect himself from the glow
of the gas lamps now lighting up the street.

Concerning his encounter with Lord Aberdeen my father sent a report to the Grand Marshal, who replied with a letter which, after having many times lost its way my father had received in Paris, told him, "About local matters, I must tell you that Chatfield, that leper, now insists that the accounts don't balance, that the income from alcohol and tobacco that we have given him as a deposit is not enough and he wants me to hand over the customs duties." That was how my father came to understand that the Grand Marshal had given in to Chatfield's demands without being concerned to let him know about it. And Lord Aberdeen of course had been kept up to date on the arrangement but had not bothered to take him into account either, not even to let him see that his mission no longer made any sense. If Nicaragua didn't exist, he existed even less.

He had decided to move to Paris thinking that there was still hope that the Emperor Louis Philippe might have some influence on Queen Victoria's opinion of Nicaragua in the matter of this dispute, but now that he had been stabbed in the back he decided to take advantage of the audience he had requested of the French Prime Minister, François Guizot, to inform him of the conclusions of Schulz the expert's report that proved the advantages of a canal through Nicaragua, which in a vengeful state of mind he had decided not to let England know about, not even if Lord Aberdeen should get down on his knees in the boardinghouse for commercial travelers in Covent Garden and implore him.

The New Year's festivities of 1846 went by without his receiving any response, but at the end of January Guizot sent to let him know that despite having caught a terrible cold he would receive him at his own home in the Boulevard des Capuchins. Even so, that was as far as politeness would take him. In the antechamber a very young secretary was waiting for him, smiling and playful, bereft of all formality as if he saw himself still in his high school recreation room. He led my father upstairs to a living room furnished with easy chairs and sofas upholstered in damask, so many of these that the place looked like a hotel vestibule. But despite the abundance of seats, Guizot did not offer him any. In a silk dressing gown, topped off by a Turkish cap, he was busy glancing through dossiers handed him solicitously by the same adolescent secretary, ignoring my father's presence as if, once more, like his country he didn't exist.

In the luggage rack of the rented carriage the trunk containing all of Schulz's reports and maps was waiting for the moment when the Prime Minister would order his lackeys to bring it up to his office. At length Guizot raised his eyes and, blowing his reddened nose into a cambric handkerchief, he gestured, inviting him to speak. My father, uncomfortable in his standing position, went astray right from the beginning, as if a prompter were dictating the wrongheaded lines of his speech. For as he sought to build up a rationale for offering France the route of the canal, he fell into allegations against the English, and Louis Philippe just then was the closest ally Queen Victoria had. Guizot stopped him, imperiously raising the hand that held the handkerchief.

"I am informed about your visit to the Foreign Office in London, and I share the point of view you heard from Lord Aberdeen's lips. So we do not need to lose time with accusations," he said.

"Nicaragua does not exist—that is the judgment you share?" said my father, his demeanor suddenly beyond repair, and at the same time his body was rocking back and forth like someone who had been drinking too much.

"I wish to tell you a story that illustrates my point of view," Guizot said, after blowing his nose once again, without paying any attention to the interruption. "The Baron de Menier, who owns some chocolate plantations in Nicaragua, tried to show me during a discussion after dinner at his castle on the Loire where that territory is which was completely unknown to me, and he took me over to a globe. He couldn't find it on that map because a fly had lit on the spot. He had to brush it off. That is why there is a good reason to share Lord Aberdeen's notion."

With another gesture Guizot brushed him off as well, the same as if he were the very fly his story had described, and went back to his papers, aided by his obsequious secretary who didn't even bother to accompany my father to the way out. Menier the chocolatier, he was starting to think as he descended the stairs. In a pastry shop on the Rue de Rivoli he had seen, displayed on top of a column of crystallized sugar, a box of chocolates as large as the one Lord Aberdeen had taken to his niece as a gift. In the colored print on the lid a woman wearing an explorer's helmet was climbing up a ladder to a turret lashed to the back of an elephant on a leash held by a black man wrapped in a tunic with a parrot resting on his arm. It was a box of Menier chocolates. The Baron de Menier had never paid a single peso in taxes for his plantations in Nandaime, beside the Great Lake of Nicaragua, nor would anyone dare to collect them, either. Elephants and parrots, ivory and chocolate, blacks in tunics and a Mosquito Indian with a crown—they were all the same!

The coach driver made his way toward the Pont Neuf under the snow that was falling in furious swirls. In the Seine a barge loaded with cattle with huge horns, squeezing themselves together with the cold, was ringing its bell in the thick fog. My father felt dejected, like an inveterate card player who gets the last hand of cards, after a whole night of failed persistence, and this one doesn't bring him anything either. When the carriage drew close to the Place de Saint Sulpice where his lodging was, and the coachman had to come to a halt to let a horse-drawn tram go past, he felt a puff of cold air mixed with icy water blowing in because a stealthy hand had opened the door suddenly to toss a flier inside. He hurried to close it again and picked up the damp paper from the floor. It was a lampoon signed by the clandestine "Bonaparte Committee for Manual Laborers and Soldiers," calling for the freedom of the Prince Louis Napoleon. On the reverse side, printed in small letters, was printed a public letter that the writer George Sand had written to the prisoner. My father succeeded in reading most of it although it was already beginning to fade away because of the water: "Speak to us every time you are able to, noble prisoner, speak to us of liberty and emancipation! The people find themselves in chains, just as you are; and the Napoleon of today, which is what you are, incarnates the sufferings of the people, just as that other Napoleon incarnated its glory."

The fact that this had been a year of poor harvests, that the Loire had overflowed the fields, that the infection which in Ireland was rotting the potatoes even before they came out of the ground must have arrived by flying through the dismal air—these were nothing but natural signs to announce a new revolution of justice, as was the starvation, "such that scurvy is already attacking the villages, bands of peasants are assaulting travelers along the roads, unemployment is beginning to be felt in Paris, Lyon, and Marseille as well upon the closing of the factories, while the bourgeoisie who govern us, and who aren't very clever except when it comes to foolishness, go on filling their chests with money." Guizot, my father sighed, was one of those.

He had seen George Sand once during a concert at the Salon Pleyel on Rue Cadet in which Chopin shared the program with Pauline Viardot-García and the cellist August Franchomme, an occasion that ended very badly. He had the opportunity to learn about the concert because, strolling along the Boulevard des Italiens, he had read a notice in the shop window of the Pagini music establishment. The ticket that he purchased there, which I found among his papers together with the program, cost him twenty francs. His hours of boredom, and there were many of these, he used to kill by giving equal attention to the brothels in the back alleys near the Place du Tertre and to the vaudeville theaters in Montmartre—and on one occasion to a spot with the sinister name Cabaret des Assassins, where he found himself looking on in shock as a comely young man with his cheeks heavily colored with rouge and wearing a ruffled skirt was attempting to dance atop a nearby table. When his inebriated state overwhelmed him and he crumpled to the floor, he was pounced upon by his companions, and what they tried to do with him then drew my offended father from his own chair, laying into them righteously with his cane until they retreated, tripping over each other and grumbling about how hard it was to have a good time. But other times were these musical evenings, and the night he saw George Sand she was dressed in a meticulous coat and tails with a starched shirtfront, and this masculine attire contrasted quite noticeably with her scarlet silk slippers plus that dark hair of hers parted in the middle and falling in waves on both sides of her face.

My father never failed to keep up with the chapters of her novel *Lucrezia Floriani* in the *Mercure de France* as they were published in daily installments, in which the central character, the jealous Prince Karol, a monarchist artist and extremely religious, obstinately unaware of the social agitation on the street, murders the freethinker Lucrezia, getting along in years, six years younger than he in fact but still beautiful, who is burdened with a long string of lovers behind her. The novel, the talk of every salon, was an exact record of the stormy sentimental relationship between Chopin and George Sand, as it was of their political differences, which were stormy as well, and the characters portrayed them both very closely, such that anyone could see it.

On the night of the concert it turned out that Chopin fainted as he was playing his Sonata No. 3 in B Minor, right at the end of the program, and as he swooned he struck his forehead against the piano keyboard which sounded with a moan of complaint. People ran to help him, Franchomme gave him some smelling salts, and when he came to and was helped to walk off the stage by Franchomme himself and by La Viardot, his shirt was spotted with blood because he had broken his nose or else perhaps he had vomited, and his face was a yellow color, like the ivory keys on the piano itself. But the oddest thing of all was that George Sand never moved from her first row seat, she just went on blowing out her stinking cigar smoke, sitting there with crossed legs, detached from the excitement brought on by the event, for which in the eyes of the public she was much reviled.

The name of Louis Napoleon however rang a bell in my father's mind concerning that book, *Revêries Politiques*, which he had gotten as a gift from my uncle the King at the time they bade each other goodbye, and which remained forgotten in one of the trunks of his luggage. That night, when he opened the book he discovered a dedication written in violet-colored ink on the title page: *In honor of our alliance, Frederick, King.* He couldn't help but smile, like someone who recalls in a kindly way a long past situation that had been embarrassing at the time, for the King felt himself so certain of that alliance that he had recorded it beforehand in this dedication. He snatched up the flier and amid the flames in the fireplace where he tossed it, all crumpled up, he thought he saw the face of that girl who later on was my mother, embroidered in gold.

He decided to get under the sheets as quickly as possible to begin reading. He dined quickly in the hotel's dining room, hardly paying attention to the company of a native of Arequipa in Peru, meticulous and taciturn, who was eating without neglecting his books and collections of notes, tenaciously occupied in investigating the ups and downs in the life of a female anarchist from his country who had died some years before and was destined to be the grandmother of the painter Gauguin. And at dawn when at length he shut the book with a soft, pleasant snap, the buzzing of those bees dressed out in all those ideas still remained in his head, ideas about artificial routes between the oceans, as much through the Isthmus of Panama as across the Suez peninsula, such as the Viscount de Lesseps was proposing, to the end of serving without impediment the commerce of all humankind, in the understanding that the nations who were the owners of those territories, whether powerful or weak, should be taken into account as worthy partners in the enterprise and be allowed to participate in its benefits.

My father felt dazed but also filled with alarm. Louis Napoleon had written about Panama but not about Nicaragua, surely because he had not had adequate information. It was necessary to get it to him. And in a corner of his memory another voice struggled to speak to him, like that night when he heard the voice of my uncle the King: "Famous prisoners, if they are not destined to the gallows, are always candidates for a return to power."

Now he didn't even try to go back to sleep. He got dressed quickly and went down to inquire of the coach drivers in the Place de Saint Sulpice the quickest way to get to Ham, in Picardy, where the Prince was fulfilling the conditions of his sentence, and they told him that the steamship *Ville de Monterau*, which went as far as Noyan, would leave at seven in the morning from the Saint Bernard jetty.

In Noyan he should take the mail boat to Saint Quentin which would drop him off in Ham. Then he had the trunk with all the reports and the maps put on one of the coaches waiting at the stand, and started off for the jetty.

After a whole day of travel he came to Ham and found lodging in the hostelry *Le lièvre rusé*, which was the best recommended. At dinner time, the young woman in charge of table service, filled with vanity, remarked as she picked up the plates, that she was the one who got the Prince's bedclothes ready and cleaned up his room every morning. Her name was Alexandrine, but they call her *la belle sabotière* because she wore wooden shoes, and they resounded like castanets on the tiles at her rapid, joyful step. Her air of familiarity with the Prince shocked my father at first, but very soon he saw how he might make use of the situation. He wrote a note addressed to the prisoner, warning him of his visit, and asked the girl to take it to him in exchange for a two-franc coin. She accepted the responsibility but refused the recompense, offended.

The following morning, confident that *la belle sabotière* had already delivered the note, he made his way to the fortress, followed by a porter carrying the trunk on his back. The mass of stone was reflected in the muddy waters of a canal no longer in use, and from the mire rose a mist that was starting to blend in with the storm clouds mounting up above the towers and battlements. The sentry standing guard over the entrance to the drawbridge sent him to the next sentry at the great door, and he was conducted to the operations patio through the vault that opened out beneath the keep, with the porter right behind him carrying the trunk.

On the ground floor of the castle, at the back of the patio, was located the office of the prison commander, Major Gaston Demarle, a room which from its meager size and the soot on the walls must at one time have been a coal bunker. After my father explained the reason for his visit, Major Demarle with no little ill will had the police inspector Hyppolyte Leras called, for he was the one actually in charge of the Prince's custody, since as a prisoner of the State he was entrusted directly to the authority of the Minister of the Interior, General Duchatel. Leras appeared, still buttoning up his long overcoat, and put my father through a banal interrogation, after which he warned him that the Prince was reluctant to deal with those who were unfamiliar to him, but at all events he did consent to go ask. In a little while he came back and without disguising his surprise he gave him the news that the Prince would receive him after noon, since all morning long he invariably was busy with his experiments.

"Yes, the experiments that *la belle sabotière* helps him with," said Demarle, and both men laughed.

At lunchtime it was the inn's hostess who attended to the table. Alexandrine never came out of the kitchen, and when my father tried to find her, she eluded him. Her eyes were reddened. Underneath the sink was the jumble of dirty clothes brought from the prison, and from among its folds escaped the edge of a sheet embroidered with the emblem of the imperial family of Napoleon. The woman came and went carrying the plates while she scolded the girl. Her intimacies with the prisoner of Ham would hurt them all, and who would pay to support the upbringing of that bastard child?

"She's already three months pregnant, monsieur, she's my niece and I just found out today," she said, addressing my father in hopes of consolation.

On the way back to the fortress, he felt upset by those revelations. He hadn't really given credit to Demarle's pointed allusion, but now it was clear that the Prince had let himself go in this affair with *la belle sabotière* to the point of getting her pregnant, and that evidence lowered him in my father's estimation. But he was not going to go back on his plan, not for that reason.

After an argument with Demarle, who didn't want to let the trunk into the Prince's apartment, my father did come to agree for it to be carefully checked over by Leras. When it came out that there were maps involved the matter became serious, because Leras, far from accepting the story about the canal, came to the suspicion that those sheets of paper contained some kind of military information, and Demarle had to agree with him, though in an ill humor because at that moment he too was trying to entertain a young lady of the neighborhood inside the coal bunker. They had already wasted two hours in these formalities, with the trunk in the middle of the patio, because Leras still did not understand that Nicaragua was not a French possession oversees where very likely some kind of rebellion against Louis Philippe was being hatched and therefore my father might be an agent entrusted with discussing those plans with the prisoner. Demarle suddenly found a resolution to the situation.

"The Prince, everyone knows he is crazy," he said. "And only another crazy nut would come from the ends of the world to propose digging a canal between the oceans. Let him go in with his trunk, but he has to carry it in by himself."

Then my father let the porter go and crossed the patio enclosed within the fortress dragging the trunk behind him. Leras, in front of him, led him to the entrance of the gallery, guarded by another sentry. At the other end of it a spiral staircase led to the apartments allotted to the prisoner, the only one in the whole castle. He began to climb up, and at the noise made by the trunk bumping against the steps, Thélin, the Prince's valet, came down from above to help him, but Leras blocked that.

At length my father reached the last step with his load, bathed in sweat and with his arms gone numb, and as he raised his eyes he discovered a figure whom he misidentified at first because he was dressed in a leather apron stained with grease and gluey residues. But it was the same pointed face as in the daguerreotypes, the same blue eyes with the exalted gaze, the same beard that left his cheeks free and adorned his chin like a brush, the same elegant mustache with its points, the same hair with its wavy locks in which there was always one or another stray curl standing up, and he was much taller in the trunk of his body than in his legs, as if he had been deformed by one of those mirrors at the fair, and when my father stood up with clumsy but hasty movements to offer him a bow, he felt that from his apron and clothing there came an intoxicating fragrance of turpentine.

My father apologized for his poor French, and the Prince reprimanded him with a look of cordial severity.

"Mine is much worse," he said. "Don't you hear that atrocious racket of Teutonic syllables dragging themselves around on my tongue? My tongue tasted only German milk, my dear friend, after I had to flee to Bavaria with my parents after the defeat of the emperor at Waterloo."

And taking him by the hand, he set out to show him the two rooms that he occupied, the one that was his laboratory, which is where they started, and the other his bedroom, with Leras sufficiently close so has not to lose a word, and Thélin just a few steps behind. Diagrams and sketches, luxuriously framed, were hanging from the walls as if they were paintings, leather tubes containing rolls of parchment standing in the corners, a pair of tables loaded with scale model structures in the center of the room, others in process on a carpenter's bench, books stacked up, papers in disorderly piles, magazines, the *Revue des Deux Mondes*.

The Prince picked up the latest issue, blew the dust off the cover, and, gesturing toward George Sand's name, "What a masculine writer George Sand is," he remarked in a show of praise. "A woman of the religion of progress." And my father started to tell him about the flier in the rain at the Place de Saint Sulpice, but the Prince was already showing him an abacus so huge it seemed like a musical instrument.

And still by the hand he took him now to his sleeping room, with a bust of Napoleon in a niche and, on a bare wall above the narrow bed, the portrait of his mother, Princess Hortensia; beside it was a bare nail where there should have been one of his father, Louis Bonaparte, exiled in Italy, and with whom he got along badly if at all, as he confessed now to my father while shaking his head slowly, somewhat distressed. There were more books and papers all jumbled together, and the black dress coat with gilded epaulets on the torso of a headless mannequin, and at its feet, the high military boots.

They went back to the laboratory, and while he turned over some papers he mentioned his treatise on electromagnetism, submitted for consideration to the Academy of Sciences in Paris, and the firearms manual in which he proposed a new method of fitting percussion caps to the rifles; and while explaining his most recent invention, which was a kite for military espionage, he picked up a notebook in oilskin covers covered with diagrams and read, "twenty kites connected together stimulate each other to rise, their separate energies joining together by means of a correlation of impulses, from which one is allowed to determine a considerable upward potency, capable of raising a basket with an adult crew member more than seventy meters high, and if the adult is slender and of little weight, to more than one hundred meters in altitude..." The Prince had been gradually lowering his voice and in order to dissemble in front of

Leras who had remained some distance away, without taking his eyes off the notebook he whispered, "I am happy. I will be blessed with a child."

"I know," my father quickly responded.

The Prince threw back his head, surprised, and seemed a little annoyed.

"I heard her mother scolding Alexandrine, Your Highness," my father said.

"Poor girl," the Prince sighed. "If I were only able to help her, give her a better life!"

But he regained his composure quickly enough and took my father over to a lectern on which rested a thick universal atlas open to a hydrographic map of the Isthmus of Panama, on which he had drawn a thick, crooked line in red ink which on being spread over the surface of Lake Gatún made it open out like a bloody flower.

"There is your country, the key to the future of humankind!" the Prince exclaimed.

Before my father could protest such a serious mistake, the Prince, his words spitting a shower of saliva that spotted the brush of his beard, took him to a scale model of a steamship with high-pressure boilers, capable of reaching a cruising speed of twenty knots, transporting in its holds the machines needed for excavating the canal in Panama. Then he took him over to the drawing of one of those machines that looked like a railway locomotive with its funnel-shaped chimney, except that the front end was set up with a kind of huge, pointed soup spoon like a guillotine.

Leras, leaning against the wall, clutched his hat in his hands and seemed not to be paying any attention to the explanations of the Prince, who was going along pointing out plates containing other inventions in sketch form, opening and shutting notebooks, with his finger tracing lines of text in different colored inks in his small, tight handwriting but with feathery tails, lines that overflowed the allotted spaces and climbed around on the margins, giving way sometimes to mathematical calculations and drawings of sections of equipment. Until, exhausted, he went over to sit down on a chair which he first had to sweep clean of papers, leaving my father standing, who was not irritated by this. He himself cleaned off piles of folders from another chair and took a seat.

"But where I come from is Nicaragua, Your Highness," he was finally able to get out. "And in my trunk I'm carrying the documents necessary to demonstrate that the canal ought to be built in my country's territory."

The Prince searched in his apron pocket for the note he had received this morning from *la belle sabotière* and studied it minutely, lifting his eyes more than once to look at my father as if to compare the resemblances between a portrait and the original.

"Thélin, bring that trunk here!" he called out into the hallway.

And when he had the trunk in front of him and my father started to open the closure, the Prince's impatience was so evident that he seemed ready to break the lock himself with one of the punches, hammers, or pairs of pliers they let him have for his work during the day but confiscated at curfew time.

In the first document that came into view, a tobacco-brown figure of Aeolus, adorned with a feather on his head, was puffing out his cheeks to blow the gentle trade winds, and the ships entering from the Caribbean ploughed calmly up the San Juan River on whose banks manatees were sunning themselves and came out upon the cobalt blue waters of the Great Lake of Nicaragua from which a joyous train of swordfish leapt out, then continued on toward the also blue waters of the Lake of Managua by means of the Tipitapa River, and, after traversing a modest stretch of about thirty miles of canal dug out from firm, flat land, they found themselves before long in the Pacific. Or vice versa.

My father had forced the hand of Schultz the engineer so that the line of the canal went through the center of León, and on a separate plate he now showed the Prince the new city, the formidable drawbridges, the tangle of railroad lines, the customs warehouses, the masses of the hotels, the towers of the commercial buildings, the banks, the financial exchange, the government buildings with their Graeco-Latin façades, the Great Temple of the Masonic Lodge, notable for its gilded dome like that on the Church of Santa Sophia, and built on a square toward which all the avenues filled with carriages converged. León would be the Constantinople of the Pacific.

The Prince sat back down again, and with his arms spread wide he set his eyes on the ceiling for a long while, my father's presence forgotten. So that when Leras made signs to retire, he was obliged to leave him in that state of self-abandon, prey to his anguish and wondering if he had failed in his mission. But when he returned the following day, under the pretext of reclaiming his trunk, there was not the slightest relic left of the Panama canal, and his own maps, plates, and sketches were now displayed everywhere.

"The canal is yours," said the Prince while embracing him forcefully.

"I have gone half way around the world just to hear those words," my father's response was colored with emotion.

"The hopes you have rested in me will be resolved when I manage to escape from this prison," the Prince said then, lowering his voice.

My father heard that remark without lending it any special importance, for he was a long way from imagining the decisive role he would have in the imminent plan for the prisoner's getaway. His defenders in Nicaragua, who still remain there, although really only a few are left these days, put that action in the balance while seeking a counterweight for the derision existing in the other, because if he is remembered at all today it is because of the unfortunate events that took place years later, which have left him for history as a traitor.

According to those who defended him, for buying off his guards he must have handed over to the Prince a bag of gold Louis hidden at the bottom of a pouch filled with cherries and a note, saying, "Try the ones at the bottom. They are the best." But the event, as a matter of fact, took place in a different way.

The Prince had requested that my father remain in Ham while he finished a memorandum about the canal through Nicaragua which he would send right away to the Viscount de Lesseps, then in Cairo, who was now the owner of a reputation sufficient to raise the funds needed to finance the enterprise. The sentries now permitted my father to get through at any time without challenging him, since the Prince received him even during the morning hours, and the only formality was to sign the visitors' book in Major Demarle's office, while Leras, convinced of the absolute extravagance of the conversations they maintained up above, didn't concern himself any more about watching over them. And if it was raining too much to set foot on the muddy path back to the inn, they would invite him in for a glass of brandy and perhaps to take part in a game of whist.

What my father heard on such occasions were complaints. The fortress of Ham was always a prison for them, although they hadn't deserved it. The dampness covering the walls with mould rendered unsuccessful their attempts to whitewash them with lime, it softened the official documents even though they used to keep them in canvas sacks caulked with pitch, and it was hard on their bones, which were deteriorating with swamp rheumatism.

One morning at the beginning of May my father presented himself at the fortress with a gift for the Prince. This was a map laboriously drawn in his own hands, where the canal figured now as the "Louis Napoleon Canal," according to the flowery letters inscribed along the line marking its course, and he thought this should be sent to the Viscount de Lesseps together with the memorandum. But hardly had he put it in the Prince's hands when the latter, paying no attention to the honor, informed him that there was a delicate matter to communicate to him, and he took my father by the arm on his daily stroll along the pathway connecting the battlements that he was permitted to take, when invariably he removed the leather apron and donned the uniform usually worn by the mannequin. When they saw him appear, the peasants working in the fields greeted him by raising their hoes and their scythes, while he, although this was forbidden him, responded by tipping his kepi.

The same thing would take place with the bricklayers who since the week before had been working on plastering the walls of the gallery that led to the spiral staircase. When the Prince went past them in his military harness, going and coming back from his stroll, they would stop their work on the scaffolding and remove their headgear, overcome with respect.

"Thélin has found out that they will complete their work in the space of the next two weeks," said the Prince as they climbed the ladders toward the parapet.

My father looked at him strangely. Was that the delicate matter? Once on the walkway up there, the Prince seized him by the arm once more, now so strongly that it was as if he were trying to lead him along a harsh and difficult path by main force. Had my father noticed that when the bricklayers went out to toss trash into the ravine beside the canal, the sentries paid them no attention, and they were able to cross the bridge with no control? If one of these days Thélin called in sick, he was sure no one would bother to come to inquire after his situation, leaving him by himself long enough to shave off his beard and mustaches, put on a wig, and get dressed in a bricklayer's clothes. He could also put on some wooden shoes in order to raise his height, and put a clay pipe between his teeth so as to look like a real bricklayer. In that disguise, he would go down the ladders and once in the hall below he would pick up a piece of board from the scaffolding (Thélin would take care to make sure one of these would be at hand). When he went past the sentry on the way to the operations patio, he would cover his face with the board and would do the same thing to evade the other sentries when he left the prison on the way to the ravine as if to toss out the board as no longer useful.

My father was not even sure whether the Prince was speaking seriously, but that still gave him no time to ponder over the plan.

"That day," said the Prince, "you will come to see me early in the morning. You will come to the foot of the spiral staircase and there Thélin will tell you, in a loud voice, so the sentry can hear it, that I was ill when I awoke, with fever and pain in my bones, just as Thélin will already have reported to the prison authorities. But I will already be disguised behind Thélin, standing in that area at the base of the staircase. You will say, also out loud, that in that case you will leave and ask him to transmit to me your greetings and wishes for me to get better. You stop to ask him something, anything to distract him, while I pick up the board and go outside beside you. You wait then until I can cross the drawbridge and follow me to the ravine."

"And if the bricklayers discover the trick?" my father asked, his voice a mere thread.

"I'm certain they wouldn't say a word, but in any case that is a risk we have to run," responded the Prince.

"And then?" my father asked again.

Afterward the Prince would go into the thickets next to the ravine to take off the bricklayer's clothing, having kept his own things on underneath. My father would wait for him on the path. They would walk, the two of them, like unconcerned folks out for a stroll, as far as the cemetery, where the road to Saint Quentin splits off, and there they would find a cabriolet, which Thélin would have arranged for in Ham.

"And the disguise?" my father asked.

Alexandrine was going to take care of obtaining the bricklayer's outfit, the wooden shoes, and the wig.

"*La belle sabotière*, will she be coming with you?" my father asked. It was an idle question and incompatible with the serious matter they were dealing with, but he was not able to avoid it.

"No," responded the prince categorically. "She will make her way to Paris, where she will have the baby. I have friends there who have agreed to take care of her. I beg you to accompany me all the rest of the way. In Saint Quentin we will take the mail coach to Valenciannes, and from there the new rail line runs to the Belgian border. Afterward, we will go to London."

My father grew silent. They had already gone around the perimeter no less than ten times. The Prince, hands behind his back, also became quiet, but from time to time he looked at my father, expecting a reply.

"And if we fail, Your Highness?" my father asked.

"I have calculated the dangers," said the Prince. "Don't worry about that."

"I'm not worried," said my father. But the Prince saw that this was not true.

"For you, as a foreigner, they will only have to deport you," said the Prince, and with a pleasant laugh sought to calm him. "But I, on the other hand, must be prepared to take my own life with a dose of cyanide I have here in a little bottle hanging around my neck."

"That will not be necessary," my father said.

"Then you agree to help me?" asked the Prince, gazing at him now with grateful eyes.

The fortress of Ham found itself so well safeguarded for dealing with prisoners like this that a plan of escape like the Prince had described could only be seen as a foolish blunder. But the fact is that my father agreed to it, though biting his lips.

"There is another matter that I can hardly bring myself to share with you," the Prince said then.

"Your concerns are my concerns, Your Highness," my father responded gallantly.

"It does me no good to escape to London if I must live there like a beggar, because no one in France will believe in my future undertakings," the Prince sighed, and in his eyes there was now a gleam of insinuation that shamed my father.

"Give me the name of a trustworthy banker in London, and I will negotiate with him my indigo harvests for the coming years," he said and was not surprised at his own imprudence.

The Prince received the offer with no show of emotion, as if he were only placing an artillery piece on the mock-up of a field of battle. "In Paris you can turn to the Count de Orsi. He has just finished complying with the conditions of his sentence for the military uprising at Boulogne, in which he accompanied me. Now he finds himself bankrupt, but he maintains excellent relations with the English bank."

"There is very little time left before the bricklayers leave," my father said.

"Two weeks are enough," the Prince said. "The Count de Orsi will tell you to whom to apply for getting a false passport that allows me to cross the frontier."

The fog was now beginning to rise as high as the parapet from beside the canal, as if someone must have lit a fire in the weeds along the bank and it was enveloping the silhouettes of the two while they were descending to the enclosed patio.

"I have always known that I would only leave this place bound either for the Tuileries Palace or else headed to my tomb," said the prince, coming to a halt for a moment halfway down the ladder. "And the idea that I am bound for the Tuileries distresses me most. My destiny distresses me. I'm distressed over the glory."

Soon my father was on the way back from London with the documents that certified a loan in the amount of 150,000 francs, negotiated with the Kerrigan firm through the good offices of the Count de Orsi, with an interest rate of five percent guaranteed by his indigo harvests for the next five years, valued according to the documents of previous arrangements. The securities had already been issued in the Prince's name as the only holder and the only one to sign them. My father carried them with him, together with a falsified passport in the name of one Jacques Fontaine, dealer in brandy.

"It was his cousin, Princess Matilde, who obtained the passport," my father said, handing them over to the Prince. "Count de Orsi sent me to her."

With a quick motion, the Prince brought the envelope containing the passport to his nose. "Ah, the same perfume," he said, mostly to himself.

Then he confided to my father that Matilde was his frustrated love. Her father, his Uncle Jérôme, who during the period of the Empire had been set up as the King of Westphalia, vetoed the marriage after the prince's first defeat in the insurrection at Strasbourg, and he married her instead to the Prince Demidoff, a Russian both alcoholic and libertine. It was an unfortunate life Matilde suffered in Moscow. To be able to obtain a legal separation she presented herself before Czar Nicholas I dressed in a very low-cut dress so that the bruises and contusions that barbarian had caused her were visible; he had tried to drag her toward a window with the idea of throwing her into the void. Now that she had returned to Paris, the Prince was aware of her relationship with Count Emilien Niewerkerke, a sculptor who had gotten commissions for decorating the public fountains with naiads and tritons.

The escape was set for Saturday the 23rd of May, 1846. It was a very good choice because the garrison's discipline was quite relaxed, for usually on that day boots and military garb were shined and spiffed up, the carts laden with relief provisions arrived in the enclosed patio, the soldiers received visits from the lovers they had acquired in Ham, and those whose turn it was to receive passes were going out. As for the bewildered bricklayers, who worked only half a day on Saturdays, they would wander around glumly in the middle that fair-like crowd.

But it was necessary to put it off due to an unforeseen complication. Before the Prince would have had the opportunity to claim he was sick and, fortunately, before he could manage to get his beard and mustaches shaved off, a large delegation of citizens from Ecuador arrived, loaded into three large carriages. In the first came the Archbishop of Quito and in the others there were five deputies from the National Assembly and five generals from the army, all of them on a mission to offer the Prince the Presidency for life of the Republic. And together with the offer, they brought a letter signed by the hand of the Emperor Louis Philippe in which he undertook to pardon him if he decided to leave for Ecuador forever.

Forced by circumstances, my father was present during the interview that took place amid the disorder of all the trash and papers in the laboratory, since to cover up the escape better everything was going to remain in its usual place, even the maps and the drawings from the trunk. The visitors spoke one by one, and the Prince listened to them with complete serenity. The project that animated them, a remedy for anarchy and the key to progress, would barely have begun with the Presidency for life, because the larger design was to build a great Republic of the Andes, bringing together the neighboring territories, always with Louis Napoleon as its head. Republic or Empire, however he managed to decide it.

They retired with the promise that he would think about the matter and would give them a reply a week later. They could inform the Emperor Louis Philippe of that.

"My God! I've never heard a wilder blunder!" the Prince exclaimed, bringing his hands to his brows, when the sound of the visitors' footsteps had just barely begun to be lost as they descended the staircase.

My father, when he heard him call that proposal a "blunder," sketched on his own face a worried smile, thinking that their escape plan was a similar blunder, rivaled by that of the Republic of the Andes only in its size.

Everything had to be postponed until Monday, the worst choice imaginable but the only possible choice since that very afternoon the bricklayers would be gone. The situation in the prison that day was altogether the opposite from Saturday. Demarle, generally in a bad humor anyway, because he was looking at one more week here without hope of relief, ordered the garrison to muster early for review in the patio, and he checked over the rifles personally as well as the supply of ammunition for each soldier, while he gave a severe reprimand for a missing button or a belt badly tightened. The whole matter took at least an hour, and now there was the risk that the sentries might refuse to allow my father's entry until after the review had been completed.

The troop was just dispersing at the order to break ranks when he presented himself at the great door, and there was no obstacle to his proceeding on through the vault, nor getting through the patio nor entering the gallery, where a few of the bricklayers were at work taking down the scaffolding. But he couldn't find Thélin. He was filled with panic at first, assuming that the plan had been discovered and he had fallen into a trap. Then, noticing that nothing was taking place around him, he simply felt alone, useless, and abandoned, convinced that the Prince had already escaped without his help.

He went up the spiral staircase with cautious steps and upon entering the bedroom he encountered a wholly peaceful scene. The Prince was being shaved by Thélin. The mustache had disappeared and now the valet was working on shaving that brush of a beard. On the table was a sheet of newspaper where the jumble of soap and whiskers fell after leaving the razor blade.

On feeling the presence of my father the Prince looked at him out of the corner of his eye, and with the movement, a bit of blood sprouted amid the lather beneath his chin.

"Keep your hand steady," he spoke firmly to Thélin.

My father could not get over his astonishment. By this time the Prince should now be carrying his board out the great door.

"We must wait until the review is finished," the Prince said, noticing the uneasiness in my father's face. "The brick-layers right now are confined to a single corner, at the foot of one of the towers of the ramparts. They will remain there until the soldiers break ranks."

"The review has finished, Your Highness," my father said, his voice filled with restrained urgency.

"So soon? Then let's get to work!" responded the Prince, quickly wiping off the remainder of his soap with a towel.

With all possible calm he went to open a package that *la belle sabotière* had brought him on Wednesday afternoon as if it were a matter of the recently ironed bedclothes. There he found the pants and rough-woven shirt, carefully dirtied with blobs of mortar; the wig, cut from the head of the inn's hostess, which she had allowed her niece to work on after being convinced that her hair was full of lice; the wooden shoes, with rather high heels, and the clay pipe. In the package there was also a letter from *la belle sabotière*, who was already on her way to Paris, written in an ungainly hand, and which the Prince scarcely glanced at before tossing it into the fire in the stove.

To the sound of his wooden shoes, the Prince drew close to the mirror to adjust the wig of curls that gave a theatrical look to his beardless face. There was no way that anyone would believe that this personage was on his way to toss a useless wooden plank into the ravine outside the prison walls, and not to a pre-Lenten festival.

"Wait!" my father heard at his back when he was starting to occupy his post at the foot of the spiral staircase, in accordance with the plan. "Where did I put my head? My God! It won't do any good now to hear from Thélin that I'm sick if the sentry has just seen him come up here a little while ago."

He looked around on all sides, as if among the objects remaining in such disorder in the bedroom he were hoping to discover a solution. Thélin, for his part, had rounded off the heap of pillows and pieces of clothing on the Prince's bed in order to pretend there was a body on its back lying beneath the sheets, and now he was occupied in hiding, underneath that very bed, the piece of newspaper dirtied with whiskers and shaving soap.

"The two of you go down and stop to talk in the gallery, where the sentry can hear you, talk about my feeling so ill, you know, the same as before, rheumatism..." the Prince was suddenly giving instructions to Thélin and my father. "Say you are going out to get Bouzy the pharmacist, he is always the one who prepares my medications. When you hear me coming close, get into a conversation with him about any old thing. Just then I'll be passing by you, very close, and then you come along right behind me. Once we get over the bridge, everything will go according to the original plan. And Thélin will go to the pharmacy for the medications and come back here immediately."

Thélin stared at him, filled with alarm.

"That's what we agreed on," the Prince sounded harsh. "Why is it so strange now? You can't accompany me. I have ordered that your wife will receive enough money while your imprisonment lasts. At most a year, more likely it'll be just months. But you have to return with the medications. No one should suspect anything until we have reached the Belgian border."

My father and Thélin descended. They were talking animatedly with the sentry about the rheumatism pains that had been troubling the Prince ever since dawn when they heard down the hall the sound of loose-fitting wooden shoes coming nearer, almost seeming to be in too much of a rush. Despite the fact that smoking while on duty was forbidden, the sentry, almost a young kid, had accepted from Thélin the gift of a black cigarette and was at this very moment getting a light from him as well. The Prince passed them with the plank on his shoulder, heading for the patio.

The majority of the bricklayers, after having finished the job in the gallery, were working on the front wall of the building, and you could hear the sound of the trowels as they stirred the mortar in the tubs, and the whirring of the pulley as it was lifting a bucket of slaked lime up to the scaffolding. The Prince was already going toward the exit, and Thélin and my father got ready to follow him.

"Halt! You with the wooden board!" shouted the sentry.

The Prince stopped without turning around.

"Come here!" he was ordered.

Thélin and my father found themselves halfway between the sentry and the Prince and they didn't know whether to stop too. The Prince signaled them to go on ahead as he took advantage of having to shift the plank to his other shoulder so as to remain behind it. They obeyed, although measuring their steps to give themselves time to hear what was happening behind their backs.

"Where are you going?" they heard the sentry ask.

"The boss ordered me to toss this thing from the scaffolding into the ravine," they heard the Prince respond.

"You're sure you haven't stolen anything from the Prince's rooms?" The sentry was examining him close up now, almost as if he were smelling him. "The Prince isn't feeling well, and you're capable of having taken advantage of it."

"God keep me from doing anything like that!" the Prince responded. "I have mouths to feed, but I gain my bread honestly."

"It's bad manners not to show your face while the authorities are talking to you! Come on, let's see. Put that board on the ground!" the sentry said.

"Search my pockets if you think I have stolen anything," said the Prince. "If not, let me go on!"

"All right. Go on, then," the sentry said. "But this will be the last time you forget to show me any respect, you swine!"

"What's wrong?" Demarle was heard to shout, appearing at the door of the coal bunker.

"Nothing, sir," responded the sentry, who had thrown the cigarette butt hastily to the ground and was grinding it in with the sole of his boot. "It's a bricklayer going to toss some trash in the ravine."

"Thank God we're getting rid of this plague of bricklayers today," Demarle said, and turned back inside.

5

The knife that cuts both ways

I seem to be crossing an endless waste, going some place
I know not where. I am at once the desert, the traveler,
and the camel.

Flaubert to George Sand, July 20, 1873

AT THE BEGINNING of October, 1992, I found myself in
Madrid attending the final meeting of the Betancourt Commission which was preparing a document on the theme,
Iberoamerican Identity: Perspectives Toward the New Century.
The Commission, organized by the Casa de America as part
of the celebrations of the fifth centenary of the Discovery,
was headed by the ex-President of Colombia Belisario Betancourt, who had asked me to serve as secretary, with the
result that, as usually happens in these situations, we ended
up writing the document between us.

While the war was going on in Central America, it had
fallen to me to make numerous confidential visits to Bogotá
to talk with don Belisario about the complex schemes for
the peace process. On those occasions we would also talk
about literature as well as painting—he had had a splendid

exhibition of paintings by Colombian painters mounted on the formerly bare walls of the Nariño palace—and I usually returned to Nicaragua with a cargo of books that his generous hand had placed on the private jet formerly belonging to Somoza which I used for these trips. And we always joked around on those occasions, putting me to the test in the difficult art of competing with his wit.

Among many other things, then, we were bound together by our passion for books, and that afternoon in Madrid we had agreed, as if this were a matter of one of those plots in a time of war, to escape the rigors of a formal cocktail hour at the Círculo de Bellas Artes by running off to investigate the kiosks at the Old Book Fair in the Paseo de los Recoletos, which happened to be very close by, in front of the old palace of the Marqués de Linares, where the Casa de America was located.

The crowd was quite thin at that hour of the afternoon, and thus we were able to snoop around among the book stalls to our hearts' content. According to don Belisario, the best way to come across bibliographic treasures is to stop talking, because words scare off your luck, and to plunge your hand into the boxfuls of books without looking. It wasn't long before he discovered a biography of Manuelita Rodríguez that way, written in Italian, and absolutely unknown to him, which he bought at the price they asked. He occupied himself talking about Bolívar's women with the bookseller, who was from the Canary Islands and had lived in Caracas, and meanwhile I went on browsing and moving along until I came to the stall belonging to the Raymundo Lulio Bookstore, among the last stands in the direction away from the Cibeles fountain. I became attracted by a collection of loose numbers of *Life* in Spanish.

One of these from the year 1959 had a photograph of Hemingway on the cover, and inside it was the first installment of a long account of the rivalry between the matadors Luis Miguel Dominguín and Antonio Ordóñez, his somewhat younger brother-in-law. These stories were published the following year in a book, *The Dangerous Summer*, Hemingway's last important literary enterprise before he took his own life, terrified by the irreversible progress of his bouts of paranoid delirium, by putting the barrel of a hunting shotgun in his mouth.

I was leafing through the story beneath the vigilant eyes of the bookseller, half surly and half bored, wearing his myopic glasses and a Basque beret and smoking Ducados one after the other, drowning the butts in a huge water-filled ashtray ornamented with the logo of the Osborne bull. Hemingway told of his arrival in Madrid to watch Ordóñez performing in a bullfight at the San Isidro bullring, and of his stay at the recently opened Hotel Suecia on La Calle Marqués de Casa Riera, and—surprise!—the very place where I usually stay. Among the photographs which illustrated the story was one in which Hemingway appears with his legendary friend Juanito Quintana, taken in the bar of that hotel, which I knew very well, and so I decided to buy this magazine to take back to Felipe, the bartender on the night shift.

I was waiting to pay the bookseller, who was busy with moving around a pile of unbound atlas pages, medical pamphlets, notebooks, and circulars, when fate beat its invisible wings about my head once more. The pile made such a huge armful that some of the pieces slipped from the man's hands and fell to the counter and down to the ground, where I happened to see in plain view on the cover of one of them the very same photograph of Turgenev lying on the bed that I had seen at Les Frênes. I picked it up. *The Master's Eye: Castellón*, it said above the picture, and below it, *Maucci's Books, Barcelona, 1915*.

I flipped through the pages, printed on very good quality glossy paper that in spite of its age retained its original whiteness and its sheen. These pictures consisted overwhelmingly of feminine nudes, and then I realized that I was looking at the album to which Professor Rodakowski had referred. As a frontispiece, there was a biographical account of Castellón, unsigned, illustrated by a self-portrait. This was the first time we found ourselves face to face. He had taken the picture in front of a mirror toward which he was gazing disdainfully, in one hand the bulb that actuated the camera's shutter, as if it were an atomizer for asthmatics; behind his back glittered the glass panes of the half-open balcony door, and beyond the balcony appeared the gray masses of some slate roofs. The way he looked in the photo, in shirt sleeves, skin dark as if having passed through fire, his rebellious hair in waves tamed by hair cream, his mustachios sharp as stilettos, he gave off the air of a timid, lonely savage, but at the same time proud, haughty, with the whole light of the room concentrated in those eyes that must have been, just as George Sand had seen them, the color of yellow amber.

After paying for the magazine, I asked the bookseller for the price of this album, with the absurd fear that he was going to tell me it was not for sale. He took it out of my hands, gave it a quick once-over with his eyes and returned it to me, saying that it was five thousand pesetas. I gave it to him without haggling, from that moment on deprived of any authority in the future to criticize don Belisario for buying at just any price, and then, with the careful attention of an owner, I began to read the biographical notes. A new excuse for astonishment then jumped out at me at the start: Castellón was a Nicaraguan! "Our renowned artist of the camera was born in the year of our grace 1854 in León, the old capital of the Central American Republic of Nicaragua, and at a very early age, in 1870, he arrived in Paris under the sponsorship of Napoleon III, a few months before the collapse of the Empire, to undertake medical studies."

At that point no other customers had drifted as far down as this book stall, and I leaned my elbows on the showcase to go on reading in the album. The bookseller, after confirming to himself that his pack of Ducados was now empty, looked all around him as if in appeal for aid, and then, since no help was forthcoming, he crumpled up the old pack and tossed it at his feet into a packing box that served as a trash bin.

The biographical account mentioned the friendships Castellón had with Maxime du Camp and Count Giuseppe Primoli, who were introduced to him by the Princess Matilde, the Emperor's cousin, early in the month of August, 1870—very close to the start of the military campaign against Prussia—during one those famous "evenings" at her residence in the Rue de Berri. Primoli, a Roman aristocrat, was a devotee of literature and of photography, and his obsession over the possibilities of the snapshot image succeeded in being transmitted to Castellón, who was little moved by Du Camp's "frozen scenarios"—dunes, cliffs, ancient monuments—but very much excited by Primoli's "moving scenarios"—horse races, foxhunts, railway stations, charity balls—that entailed freedom of movement and that were impossible for the fixed devices of delayed exposition.

Primoli's ambition was to obtain a hand camera provided with flexible film and capable of standing up to those "moving scenarios," and therefore sufficiently small to take everywhere and introduce anywhere. With one of those, constructed of oak wood and which looked more like a jewelry box with a leather handle, he was able to take pictures of the moment when the Duchess d'Alençon was fatally burned in the fire at the La Charité bazaar in Paris, as Darío mentions in his piece "The Nomad Prince."

Castellón's role in the development of the invention, mentioned by Professor Rodaskowski, was explained next. He soon became Primoli's helper, and between them they managed to provide the little box with a means of pulling a roll of paper negative through, impregnated with a jelly-like coat of silver bromide, and with ten squares of two inches across on each roll. The camera never reached the market, nor was it patented. The difficulty was that the handler would have to send the camera back to the manufacturer each time the roll needed to be extracted and developed, which made commercial exploitation impossible.

Looking at the nudes reproduced in the album, I realized that Castellón had demonstrated very well the advantages of the little box, since it allowed him to move himself around the bodies, to get closer to them in search of the best angle or detail, for he was able to move the shutter in a way unnoticed by the model. Those nudes are amazing because they lack the ostentatious lasciviousness that the photographs of the time so often brought out, those spongy bodies like hastily ripened fruits, a whole erotica of gluttony.

On the contrary, Castellón's figures are rather osseous, with gothic lines, or if you wish, they seem related to art nouveau, blacks and whites rubbed out to ash and snow, like the Satanic inks of Beardsley. He knows how to render tribute to the bone, bringing out the grace of the polished shoulder blade or a barely insinuated rib cage, and he knows the charm of gaunt breasts like the meager teats on a goat, of an angular face without cosmetics, of his models' hair lopped off with a pocketknife, giving his women the air of quarrelsome youths.

None of the notes in Princess Matilde's diary for the month of August of 1870 mentions that party at which Castellón was introduced by her to Primoli and Du Camp, who were regular attendees at her evenings. She tells, of course, of the preparations for war, and notes that it was a torrid month like few in recent years, having been responsible for several cases of fatal sunstrokes in public view because of the heat, as well as for the forest fires in Auvergne and Languedoc-Roussillon. She also tells of a runaway carriage having crashed, horses and all, into a haberdasher's shop on the Rue de Babilone, killing one of the attendants by pinning her against the wall with a broken axle, while the front wheels, having gotten loose, smashed up some fruit and vegetable stands on the sidewalk outside.

The summer sun still has not gone down, and it bathes the city in a light like that of a theater's footlights, which must seem supernatural to Castellón. Thin and shy, his hair in a tumble and with his badly cut suit hanging loosely on his body, he stays on his feet close to one of the windows without anyone paying any attention to him, nor does he want them to, but it's not for that reason that he stops trying to make sense of the din of all the conversations that die back when the Princess Matilde requests their attention because she wishes to squeeze a little of the juice of humor from the tensions of the moment and so reads to the people gathered around her a letter from Flaubert she had just received that afternoon, in which he describes himself in the uniform of a lieutenant in the National Guard, since he has been called to service and is now an officer with soldiers under his command, for whom he would allow a ration of cider at breakfast, if he had the power.

After that is when the Princess must have gone over to him bringing Primoli and Du Camp by the arms, one on each side. The Emperor has decided for our friend to be a physician at the Sorbonne, she tells them, but until he goes to get acquainted with those in charge of the dissection chambers, it is your task to give him something amusing to

do. It seems to me that photography, that mysterious invention that fascinates you both so much, would suit him very
well. Du Camp at that time is forty-eight and his manner is
unhurried and distant, while Primoli, about twenty, is brimming over with enthusiasm.

"Does photography attract you?" asks Du Camp.

"I don't know, sir," he responds. "Photographic cameras
are unknown in Nicaragua. But I saw one yesterday in the front
window of Charrière's shop in the Place de Saint Honoré."

"Voilà le bon sauvage," Du Camp is smiling. He didn't
want this "good savage" to think he was disliked; after all,
Castellón was the Emperor's protégé, for reasons unknown,
and immediately he set about praising his skill with French.
And when he left the salon, he invited him for a drink, and
Primoli as well, at his study close to the Passage du Prince,
where they arrived shortly before midnight.

As Castellón raises to his lips the glass of absinthe he has
been served—a liqueur he is trying for the first time, and it
tastes like a medicine—on the mantle over the fireplace he
notices a photograph in small format and goes closer to examine it, closely followed by Du Camp as Primoli, smoking,
stands in the soft light of the Japanese lamp hanging from
the ceiling, where the remains of a fresco inspired by Delacroix's *The Death of Sardanapolis* can just be made out.

"That is Flaubert in Cairo, photographed by me," he
hears Du Camp tell him. *House and garden in the French
quarter, Cairo, 1850: plate wet with collodion.*

Taken from a distance, Flaubert is walking through the
garden of the Hôtel du Nil, dressed in a Nubian cloak, wearing a beard, his shaven head covered by a red tarboosh.

"Who is Flaubert?" Castellón inquires.

"Definitely *le bon sauvage!*" Du Camp is smiling again.

"He is the author of *Madame Bovary*, a novel about an
unhappy woman who in order to end her life bursts into

the back room of a pharmacy, pounces upon a blue piece of pottery where the tartar emetic is kept and shoves fistfuls of it into her mouth, as she were trying to cure herself of a savage hunger," says Primoli while he watches his smoke rings disintegrating. "Some reading for pharmacist's wives."

Meanwhile, Du Camp has come over to stand by Castellón's side.

"Pay no attention," he says. "In the novel Emma Bovary is a beautiful woman, beautiful and tragic, imagined by a stubborn and fussy author. But notice what a contrast: the character's name was suggested to this fussy writer by that of Madame Bouvaret, one of the owners of the Hotel du Nil, who was ugly and had a glass eye of a color that was different from the real one, after a fateful attack by a pigeon that had left her blind in that eye."

"What should one photograph?" Primoli asks. "Desirable eyes that change from black to violet according to the light, or the blind eye dressed up with a glass prosthesis?"

"I stopped doing photography long ago," Du Camp responds, "but nothing happens by itself. Beauty will always be contaminated."

"The eye of the artist is neutral," says Primoli.

"That is the same old theme song by Flaubert the fussy writer, that you can only paint wine, love, women, and glory on the condition that you are not drunk, nor a lover, nor a husband, nor a buck private in the army—that is, that you don't get your life mixed up in it," Du Camp says, returning to his place. "Notwithstanding, that neutral hypocrite didn't care a fig that he was passing his syphilis on to a poor prostitute from the Galata district of Alexandria. Was he not only compromising himself with sin but also with crime? Because that was a premeditated crime."

Weeks before reaching Alexandria they had gotten on a boat while it was tied up on a swampy bank of the

Nile; it was engaged in transporting some black women kidnapped in Abyssinia. Some of the women were grinding wheat while bent down over the grinding stones, with their hair hanging down over their faces like horses' manes. One old woman with teeth like a porcupine was fixing the hair of one of the youngest girls with an ivory comb. Eager for some amusement, the men haggled over the price of an Abyssinian girl, and when the boat bearing its slaves departed, very slowly, they were still hearing the women's laughter, and that was the strangest thing, to be reminded of the sound of laughter issuing from that mournful boat moving off with its merchandise of foul-smelling and toothless women. It was fate, implacable and untouchable, that was departing.

"Is it not true that it is necessary to have been cruel once just for a prank in order to know what cruelty is like?" Du Camp asks at last.

"You keep on hating Flaubert, you have never pardoned him," Primoli says, who has come around behind Castellón and begun to lean his head on his back as if he were really trying to rest there.

"Stop that. Don't you touch him," Du Camp demands angrily.

Darkness had now fallen and I was obliged to move closer to the fluorescent tube installed under the bookstall's eaves, when I discovered a snapshot of a nude which was not feminine in the least, and which was the *Before* to the *Afterward* of the cover photograph that showed Turgenev's body on his bed at Les Frênes. One explained the other, and their relevance was mutual. At the foot of this other one was this description: *The Russian writer Ivan Turgenev after being embalmed (flexible negative treated with gelatin).*

The body rests on what looks like a joiner's work bench, enveloped in a troubled light that comes from a clerestory window above. This doesn't look like the dissection room of a hospital but rather one of the shed-like service buildings at Les Frênes, a stable perhaps, or an equipment room, with stucco walls blackened by candle smoke. There is a pail at the foot of the bench that might be used for milking, or might be there to receive the viscera from the cadaver. But that isn't all. At one side, barely offering her profile to the camera, Pauline García-Viardot is staring at the body with religious fervor, her shoulders thrown forward—don't forget that Ernesta Grisi found consolation in calling her "the hunchback"—and dressed severely in mourning, with a veil thrown over her face.

This is a furtive visit by Pauline to that shed after the embalmer has finished his work, as furtive as the presence of the photographer, who took the snapshot from outside, through the window. He would have been carrying his brass suitcases full of equipment along the path among the ash trees and had sat down on one of them to rest near the shed when his attention was caught by the banging of the shutters loose in the wind, and he looked in. There was Turgenev, naked on the work bench, and Pauline in her pose of motionless contemplation. He hastened to get his portable camera out of its bag, took the picture while scarcely poking his head in, and disappeared immediately from the window frame, fearful of having been betrayed by the sound of the camera's shutter. Then he went on his way carrying his equipment cases toward the dacha to wait there for the body, now dressed, to be moved to the bed, and to go ahead with fulfilling the assignment from the *Revue des Deux Mondes* that had brought him to Les Frênes.

The naked body, which in the contrast of the dimly illuminated snapshot looks as white as if it were a leper's cadaver, barely fits on the work bench where it lies exposed, just as in that other one, fully dressed, it scarcely fits on the bed. And the feet jut out in the foreground of this one too, freed of those seven-league-boots and looking as though they belong to the old Slavic king placidly asleep after a wild night of feverish love, his beard and hair in disarray, his legs still firm, his broad chest covered with a light snow-colored down, the two dark nipples like eyes still alert, and the abdomen flat without a hint of that senile obscenity that is a flaccid belly, swollen with fat. The Slavic monarch seems to be enjoying the majesty of his repose, unaware of his nakedness, and Pauline could be taken for the servant girl who doesn't dare to wake him, her protuberant eyes fixed on his sex that rises from the furry mat of his pubic region like the pestle belonging to a pharmacist's mortar.

But all this serene harmony is shattered by the clumsy seam that is marked by long stitches from sternum to stomach. After performing a radical evisceration, necessary because a long journey by train all the way to St. Petersburg awaits the body, the embalmer has injected two liters of formol into his veins and has filled with tow the cavities that used to hold his soft organs before concluding by sewing up the lengthy incision with horse hair.

Flaubert's hypocritical rule asserts that one should not become involved, Du Camp says again after Primoli separates himself from Castellón, raising his arms as if asking for peace. Thirsty for new experiences, you can go off to Upper Egypt to observe the hunting expeditions for blacks and elephants, but only as an observer whose emotions cannot deflect you from your mission to see. The blacks, the elephants are simply motifs, pretexts of a nature that is rich in varieties of cruelty and the marvelous, destined for the eye. A ten-year-old slave, for example, whose owners, a pair of Christian merchants about to board ship in Beirut, have put her into the water to scrub her skin with sand until she begins to bleed. In the dawn's light, all that is visible among the waves is the girl's naked body and the thick copper ring around her neck, scarlet blood on ebony black. But the fact is, Primoli argues, that the artist is a pathologist who must preserve the dried-up pieces in the formol-filled flasks of his memory; any other way would be to take on the role of redeemer. They can be stripping the skin off your own mother, your own daughter, but your duty is to register the fact.

Perhaps (Castellón would probably say now) after having taken the photograph of the naked body, being neutral consists in seeing one's own self as an object, even at the moment when the syphilitic digs around in the vagina of a prostitute before penetrating her, fingers that are moved only in order to learn about the sensations of the touching but as if they were not one's own, this artist who may infect another body with his own but does not infect the page nor the negative.

And the knife that cuts both ways, one way for beauty, the other for repulsiveness, the ornament and the ulcer, the fragrance of orange blossoms together with the stench of cadavers, the caterpillar on the flowered branch—but the two edges are in harmony within the whole that is the knife itself, a single instrument that serves to flay flesh and cut out viscera and at the same time to pry the precious stone from its mounting, to separate the pearl from the oyster, to cut the rose from its stalk. Beauty is always contaminated; nothing occurs separately.

Don Belisario approached in good humor after completing a successful hunt. He had picked up some good pieces in addition to that biography of Manuelita Rodríguez, and he came loaded down with bags of books. We strolled towards Cibeles, looking for a taxi to take him to the Palace Hotel, and meanwhile I mentioned my discovery of that issue of *Life*, hoping to surprise him with the news of Hemingway's stays in the Hotel Suecia.

"Of course," he told me, "and the bullfighters would stay at the Hotel Wellington on Calle Velásquez, because that put them close to the Plaza de Las Ventas. Matadors are afraid of getting stuck in traffic on the way to the bullring because it makes them irritated."

It was impossible to find a taxi at that hour, and we decided it would be better to walk to the Palace, and I would help don Belisario with part of his load. And then, thinking this would be of no interest to him because Castellón is my secret obsession, I told him about the album.

"Hombre!" he said. "That's the Nicaraguan photographer who shot your poet Rubén Darío dressed as a Carthusian monk in the Palacio del Rey Sancho, on Mallorca."

"How do you know that?" I asked, stopped dead on the sidewalk.

"From José María Vargas Vila," was the answer. "Your poet and your photographer got dead drunk several nights running and scared the life out of their host, don Juan Sureda. You can find Vargas Vila's story about all that in his book of literary miscellanies, *Conversations After Dinner.*"

"What good can Vargas Vila have to say about Darío? He hated him," I said.

"You don't have to love Darío to tell a story of how he got drunk," don Belisario said.

We were now at the door of the Hotel Palace. "The moment I get back to Bogotá I'll send you a photocopy of the book," he promised me as we bade each other goodbye.

As I was crossing in front of the Teatro de la Zarzuela on the way to my hotel, I thought, a little discouraged, that I still had a long way to go in my search for Castellón. He was getting further away but going in a circle, and as long as I continued in a straight line, we would end up meeting at last in the solitude of the endless desert. And both of us, moreover, were at once the desert, the traveler, and the camel.

Camera Lucida

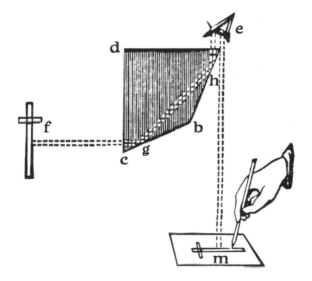

The Drunken Faun

by José María Vargas Vila

IT IS SO UNJUST the silence now beginning to spread its lethargic wings above the tomb of Rubén Darío. His laurels were becoming wilted along the quiet footpaths.

So let us speak then about our eminent friend, the one with the golden lyre trimmed with chrysanthemums. About what his jinxed, hapless life was like, the life of a wretched worshipper of Dionysus. The eternal seafarer ever making for the island of Cythera.

A memorial...

In the autumn of 1913 we both set foot on the divine Mallorca. We were honoring the gracious invitation of don Juan Sureda, a Catholic ascetic, who lived as if he were still in a convent, and his wife, Pilar Montaner. She is the painter of olive trees with their supplicant branches and of snowy almonds, to wit, her lovely *Ametllers florits*. She was putting the finishing touches on this canvas, so splendid on its easel, the day of our arrival in Valldemosa.

We had embarked in Marseille, the only passengers in first class, on a steamer belonging to the Compañía Isleña Marítima, very clean and very well maintained. One noticed, nevertheless, "a vague, very mother-country smell," as Rubén said, that came from the inner retreats of the galley and the toilets so futilely disinfected with creosote.

He was the one who had received the invitation, but he requested of Sureda that I should accompany him. According to him, my proximity would serve as an alleviation for his melancholic failings. That gentleman, brimming over with kindness, was very agreeable.

As a patron of the arts, he never stinted him during our Mediterranean jaunt. But Rubén was ignorant, and I too, of the fact that this Maecenas was nearly bankrupt. He could not much longer keep up his Palacio del Rey Sancho as the setting where he enjoyed playing host (his genteel obsession) to literary figures of renown.

Rubén did not bring his wife Francisca Sánchez along, that campesina from Navalsauz to whom he was not really married. And it wasn't only that the very Catholic Sureda couple wouldn't have permitted it. By that time he really wanted to get well away from the poor woman, and he had left her behind in Paris with the intention of forging a rupture forever.

He had convinced himself that she was too common and ignorant for his taste and his reputation, which was then at its peak. And as free as he hoped to feel in that palace, in an ambience where lineage and artistic refinement would count, the return to conjugal life, carried off in very dramatic form during the recent years, seemed to him a horror. It was that frame of mind that brought forth what I heard him say on deck in the middle of the crossing: "That poor woman used to be my wife, and whether it was my fault, or hers, or just fate, my life was a hell."

Moreover, he showed himself quite jealous of some fellow named Huertas, a peasant from Aragón who was paying court to Francisca's younger sister, María. Those of us who frequented the apartment in the Rue Michel Ange, where he lived with the two of them, maintained the belief that Rubén was at the very least the secret and stubborn suitor of the ignorant María. As for anything beyond that, let the tomb keep its silence.

Sureda himself came to the port in Palma to meet us with his carriage on that splendid morning in the last days of October, and we started the trip back to Valldemosa occupied in pleasant conversation.

Hours later, one of the curves on that difficult road that opens out above the cliffs revealed to us, as a propitious manifestation that we were nearing our goal, the tiled cupola of the new church of the La Cartuja monastery. Illuminated by the solar fires, it sparkled sometimes with bluish hues, like lapis lazuli, and sometimes with green ones, like malachite.

The gate at Santa María was dressed out with branches of pine and the flagstones were carpeted with myrtle leaves, in sign of welcome. The whole staff of servants awaited us at the entrance to the mansion.

Rubén had a regal apartment. Through its windows, the slopes of the mountains with their staggered stone terraces. Vineyards, a profusion of fig trees, pomegranates, cacti and palm trees, aside from the mysterious pine groves that are so captivating.

Inside the apartment, a bed for a bishop, with a canopy supported by wreathed columns, plus a prie-dieu near the head. To one side was a study with bookcases, a desk, a chair of embossed leather, and abundant paper and pens.

I was given the Tower of Honor, or the New Tower,

The Drunken Faun

very nicely remodeled and comfortable. Godoy, the Prime Minister of Charles III, and lover of the scarcely attractive and very Goya-esque Queen María Luisa, held don Gaspar Melchor de Jovellanos a prisoner here...

In such a withdrawn atmosphere Rubén wanted to write another novel, *Mallorca's Gold*. The first one, which was *The Island of Gold*, begun during his first Balearic visit, was a failure. He never found an end for it, fickle as he was with respect to labors requiring a long wind...

And his intentions would turn out to be futile once more, since he didn't succeed in getting past the first chapters of *Mallorca's Gold*, which *La Nación* of Buenos Aires published. Equally futile was his resolution to break forever with Francisca, "Princess Franny," as that poetaster Juan Ramón Jiménez called her.

Shortly before leaving the palace toward the end of December, Rubén showed himself already sorry: "What is one to do, one usually gets accustomed even to animals, and eventually one usually feels pity together with affection," he used to say to me.

Regret-filled recollections of deceitfulness in the throes of his first love affairs back in his own land, plus the mishaps of the present, these must have turned his opinions about the opposite sex sour. On recalling the wretched Chopin at the hands of "that terrible George Sand," he tells us in *Mallorca's Gold*:

> A woman, whether uneducated or intellectual, is a hindrance and a hostile enemy element for a man of thought and meditation, for the artist.

And he grants no judgment of benevolence to Margarita, his character, who is a sculptress. Not in the slightest, despite the love she manages to awaken in the already tired and skeptical heart of Istaspes, the novel's hero, who is a portrait of the author himself:

She is missing something, that 'something' short which one quickly notices in the productions of feminine talents. What is missing? Some people wondered about that. And the more extreme ones among them repeated a funny remark by Jaime de Flor: 'She lacks. . ., well, just what all women lack.' A sentence that they discussed with innumerable examples and supporting assertions, all with the approval of Benjamin, who considered any situation in which a woman intellectualizes as teratological.

Ah, le charmant Rubén! "Teratological" is a word that refers to the study of abnormalities and monstrosities among animal and vegetal organisms. . . .

That Margarita of the novel, the sculptress, was none other than Pilar Montaner, the painter, our hostess, whom he took as a model. And for Jaime de Flor, the Catalan painter Santiago Rusiñol.

My traveling companion began to show signs of neurasthenia soon after our arrival. Instead of enjoying the landscape and the good food, his mind was occupied with lucubrations. Serious illnesses he thought he was suffering. From there to the bottle, his old enemy, it hurts to say so, was only a step.

Our hosts deceived themselves with the idea that by submitting to a strict regimen of spring water he would forget the drinking. What happened, as was to be expected, was just the opposite. . . .

On the 6th of November we went on an excursion with Sureda to Pollensa to visit the painter Anglada Camarasa. We stopped at the inn El Loro, next to the Pi de la Posada. At meal time, as if he hadn't a worry in the world, he began to try the wine. He went on drinking, seriously now, until midnight, paying no attention to our entreaties that it was necessary to go to bed.

The following day, Anglada Camarasa invited us for an

outing to the ocean at Formentor. Rubén dedicated himself to drinking whisky to excess, to the irritation of the artist and all the rest of us.

That night, having returned to the inn, he continued to be given over to the whisky. And then he got away from us. "Go search for him, José María, he'll pay attention to you," Sureda begged me.

He had come upon a house where they were holding a wake. He tried to pull the corpse out of the coffin to climb into it himself. He only managed to get beaten up by the man's relatives, from whose hands I rescued him.

Lying on a bed of straw in a wagon that was designed for various agricultural tasks, he returned to Valldemosa. Then, sober for a few days, he undertook to pay no attention to how he was behaving.

One day, halfway through the morning, the photographer Castellón appeared. He had a studio in the *chueta* neighborhood in Palma. He arrived in answer to the summons of the lady of the house for the purpose of arranging how to photograph the paintings to appear in the catalogue of an exhibition Pilar was just then in the process of preparing.

Castellón revealed that he was Nicaraguan, which didn't seem to interest Rubén all that much. Nor when he strove to remind him, with great eagerness, of a piece he had written during his first visit to Mallorca in 1907, which was reproduced in the magazine *Caras y Caretas*, of Barcelona. The article described the photographer as a member of the Archduke Luis Salvador's crowd of followers but without naming him.

But when Castellón inquired as to his health, he came back with a long speech which went far beyond the visitor's polite intentions: "There was a minor crisis over a dinner moistened with wines in Pollensa. I no longer have any need for W & S (whisky and soda), no doubt about that. The incident at Pollensa was just by chance, and that crisis was visited upon me because of what Lugones calls 'intersections,' little things and inconsequential worries that my mind views as great ones. This spring water that my inquisitor gives me will push me toward the purification that I seek." And gratefully he pressed Sureda's hand. Our host was touched.

Nevertheless, in spite of his optimism, there would be a relapse.

One afternoon, as Sureda and I were returning from an excursion to the Deyá stream, Pilar informed us that he had bribed a servant to go purchase wine for him.

We found him seated on a stool, motionless as a marble statue. With his finger he pointed to a page in the Bible that lay open in his lap. At his feet, lying every which way, were numerous empty bottles.

The passage he had pointed out was the one in the Gospels where Jesus changes the water into wine.

Sureda, always graceful, understood the allusion. He tried to go look for a stock of wine that he kept in the pantry under lock and key. But I got him to see that wine would no longer do in a situation of this kind. It would be necessary to send to Palma for whisky.

Rubén heard. He abandoned his stationary pose. Drawing near to Sureda, he requested that the whisky be of the McCullay brand. And also that the steward should bring back Castellón as well, given the fact that since they were compatriots he would be a great consolation.

An odd request to bring Castellón along, since the connection between the two of them was totally new. But Sureda gave in. The steward got on the road, and he returned in the company of the photographer, bringing a sufficient consignment of the whisky. Three bottles. Rubén was supplied with as much as he wanted.

Castellón's arrival, unfortunately, caused a major upheaval. In place of one drunk there were now two of them kicking up a racket until the morning's light.

That first night, as he ran around from room to room wrapped in a coverlet from one of the beds that in his imagination was a bishop's cope, Rubén would yell, *"Ad Deum qui laetificat juventutem meam, judica me!"* and then he would jangle a cowbell which they had provided him with for calling the servants.

The photographer, running after him as if he were the bishop's coadjutor, would respond, *"Ad veniat regnum tuum!"*

Sureda tried to convince Castellón to contain himself with the use of alcohol, since he was asthmatic and his health might find itself impaired. When faced with his reluctance to do so, he determined to throw him out. Rubén took offense and threatened to leave as well.

I intervened then, seeking a way to throw oil on those waters. Both of them promised they would stop their drinking. But that night came to be the most frightful of all.

At about one in the morning, along the dark and icily silent hallways of the palace, the two of them started running again, just the way that God brought them into this world.

Rubén, shaking his cowbell, got as far as my door. I determined not to respond to him, but he shouted, "Get up, get up, they've put you to bed on top of the sepulchers of the Knights of San Roque! In times past, you dumbbell, there was a cemetery located there beneath your room!"

I leaped up when I heard this and opened the door immediately. I followed him to his room, and there he went on drinking. By dawn he was in the middle of a fit of bacchic saturation, stretched out on his bed. Castellón was on his knees, weeping, as if this drunken sot were already in the final throes.

As Christmas neared, he got himself together again. While walking with him one day through the corridors of La Cartuja, Pilar told him the story of a relative of the Suredas,

Antonio Llabrés, a holy man who lived a hermit's life in Bini-salem. Rubén, rather pensively, said, "Oh, why could I not have been a hermit?"

She recalled then an old chest in which they kept a habit belonging to a Carthusian monk. On their wedding trip, her husband had bought it in Chamonix with the idea that it would do for his shroud.

After the meal she went to look for the outfit. She made Rubén put it on. But he took it all very seriously. He raised the hood over his head and began to strut around with his hands concealed in the broad sleeves. Then he didn't want to take it off.

Castellón, who had brought his equipment with him, proposed to shoot him with the habit on. Rubén took a seat and posed on a monastic chair.

Afterwards, we all had our pictures taken with him by turns, our hosts first.

Sureda placed himself, standing, with his hand over his breast, like a knight in a painting by El Greco. Pilar, seated to the left, put on a gentle smile. Both of them were in a very solemn mood, as if they knew that because of this closeness to their guest posterity would make a fuss about them as well.

Yet another disaster took place. Quite early on the morning of December 24th, Rubén started wandering around terribly upset. He was thinking about the Christmas Eve parties in his native Nicaragua, in which Castellón seconded him.

Together they went out to buy some bottles of rum and also some champagne, which was of dubious quality. As our own celebration went on they would go out rather frequently to drink the rum on the sly. But the storm was not ready to break out just yet.

There was much pleasant conversation about art, especially about painting and photography. Rubén agreed to

write a laudatory piece for the catalogue of Pilar's show.

After midnight the Suredas returned from the midnight mass celebrated in the new church at La Cartuja which they had attended along with their full staff. They found Rubén more agitated than before, and now the signs of inebriation were obvious.

He came forth with his resolution to leave the next day and go to Barcelona, in the company of Castellón. It was very urgent for him to meet General Zelaya, the recently overthrown president of Nicaragua, said he.

Sureda gave his consent, of course. If that was his guest's desire, he could not oppose him. Rubén responded triumphantly, "And now that I am leaving, you cannot object to my having a drink, you inquisitor!" As if this peaceful gentleman had impeded him before! Right away he sent Castellón out in search of champagne.

They greeted the dawn's light under the influence of the extravagancies of their inebriated state. Sureda, fearful of not being able to handle them alone, asked me if we could travel together to drop them off in Palma.

On the way they were singing snatches of the Christmas songs of their childhood, although they were unable to recall any of them in their entirety. Before the carriage got into Palma, Rubén wanted for them both to offer the Lord's Prayer, to which Castellón agreed. They knelt down in the middle of the road. Sureda, so fulsomely entrenched in his religious faith, did not know whether to be uncomfortable or to marvel at them.

At the office of the Port we discovered that because this was Christmas day there would be no boat leaving in the afternoon, not until the following day.

Sureda, a little disappointed, took us to the Grand Hotel, where he secured lodging for Rubén and me. He then went off to eat with some friends at the Círculo de Palma, leaving me to care for the two carousers. Quickly they took possession of the bar, not without Castellón having first handed his photographic equipment over to the concierge.

I tried to persuade Rubén to take the steamship and return to Marseille, for it was also leaving the following day. I well knew he had no business at all with General Zelaya in Barcelona, and there would be even less point to it if Castellón were to come along. If he accepted, I would then ask Sureda to send to Valldemosa for my luggage.

Rubén insulted me. Castellón, to my surprise, leapt to my defense. After a bitter, spirited argument, he declared he would no longer accompany Rubén on the trip. Instead he would return to his own house, where his daughter was waiting for him.

Rubén begged him, weeping, that he not abandon him. They embraced, and Castellón backed down. They were a hopeless case.

They decided to follow after Sureda's footsteps. Unable to hold them back I was forced to go after them. At the door of the Círculo they were prevented from entering, and that set off a row. Sureda arrived then, having been called by the attendants.

The moment he saw Sureda approaching, Rubén broke out with a complaint, vehemently stated, about his never having done anything to get the principal street in Palma baptized with the name of George Sand. That seemed a little unusual, since he was never a saint in her church.

Anxious, though, to avoid the scandal, Sureda went to excuse himself before his friends and then accompanied us to the home of the mayor, don Felipe Puigfordila, a close friend of his, in order to present the petition.

After the conversation with the mayor, rather point-less and disorganized, Sureda went back to his dinner and deposited the two drunks in my care once more. They tried to escape, but I managed to bring them around to return to the Grand Hotel.

They installed themselves in the bar again. From there, Rubén sent a note to Antonio Piñas, a reporter for *La Tribuna*. He quickly arrived. He was received with huge embraces and invited to drink champagne.

"Amigo," Rubén told him, "I feel myself as much of an Israelite as you are, for you belong to the sacred race by blood—so now you see, it's for good reason my name is Rubén." Piña, in his booming voice, responded in Mallorquín, "Well, you've really tied one on. That's a good one!"

Meanwhile, Castellón asserted that he also felt himself an Israelite through his deceased wife, a *chueta* of Mallorca, though now dead. So much an Israelite did he feel that he was one of the citizens living on Call Menor, in the Palmas barrio inhabited by Jews who had converted to Christianity.

Piña, by now nice and drunk, said he considered himself fortunate as a *chueta* to be able to share a toast with another *chueta*, even though it was by adoption. It was enough to make one ill.

Sureda decided to return to Valldemosa. He asked me to continue taking care of Rubén until he boarded ship, leaving me money equivalent to the value of the ticket. If Castellón insisted on accompanying him, he warned me that he would have to defray the cost of his passage himself.

My first arrangement was to instruct Mister Palmer of the Grand Hotel to cut off their drinks. That way I succeeded in getting Rubén finally to go up to his bedroom, not without conceding that Castellón would sleep with him on the sofa. I didn't want him to think he would be alone with his terrors if he awoke before dawn.

On the following morning I got ready to leave the hotel in order to buy the ticket for the steamship which was to raise anchor at six that afternoon. Mister Palmer then came to meet me, fuming and indignant.

If great men are like this, he said, he would prefer to deal with ordinary folks. And furthermore, he didn't want to have anything to do with Rubén again whether he was sober or drunk. Nor with that photographer, his sidekick.

What had happened was that once I was asleep, they went downstairs again. And when faced with the waiter's negative response to their request for more alcohol, Rubén really hit the roof. They had words, and he threatened to give the hotel a bad name in an article he would ask Piña to publish in *La Tribuna*.

They went out on the street and started knocking at the door of a pharmacy nearby to get someone to sell them some *vino de quina*. The "bartender" said he had just one, rather old, that had lost some strength. Rubén found the wine exquisite, for it was mature. And Castellón was of the same opinion. But, Mr. Palmer informed me, they had not yet returned to the hotel.

Quite worried, I looked for them everywhere. I found out that on the way to the Plaza del Mercado they had been taunted by some ruffians. A doctor named Planas, anxious to look in on a sick patient, had noticed the shouting and the gibes by the unruly crowd. He called a policeman to take them to the Casa de Socorro.

Rubén fell asleep there for nearly an hour, looked after by Castellón. Apparently the photographer never got tired.

I found them finally when they were getting out of a car in front of Piña's house. They were about to knock on the front door to speak to him about the article concerning the Grand Hotel. After a lot of effort I dissuaded them from interrupting the sleep of the residents at such an early hour. Then by stages I got them into the cafés of the Port, given over now to drinking anise, as I prayed for the moment to come when I would be able to put Rubén on board *El Balear*.

Sureda came back then, convinced by Pilar, who came with him, to go through with the courteous formality of bidding their guest goodbye. We all went to eat at the C'an Per'Antoni.

Once at the table, after more libations and without having swallowed a bite of nourishing food, Rubén ended by falling deeply asleep. And asleep Castellón left him, saying goodbye to us.

The photographer appeared to be completely sober. When I reminded him that he should collect his equipment at the Grand Hotel, he smiled in an understanding way. He had not forgotten a thing.

At four in the afternoon we finally left Rubén, prostrate in his bunk, on board *El Balear*. We advised the captain about him.

At six the steamship had already raised its anchors...

Sureda shook his head dolefully and burst out, standing on the dock, "What a shame for this man! He is killing himself and bringing dishonor upon himself as well before he dies! His life will end badly, very badly, if he doesn't have some friendly hands to help him. That wasn't Verlaine's fate. I hope he doesn't end up ill, turned into a mummy like the ones covered with dust that are on show in those glass showcases in Vich."

My poor brother poet who has departed, gone ahead of me down the path toward the immeasurable mystery!

He is not dead, he has merely just ceased living.

But he was already a dead man who bore upon his shoulders the corpse of his genius.

And he knew the Soul of Pain, when the others have never gotten to know the Pain of the Soul...

(Published originally in the magazine *Cromos*, second epoch, No. 23, Bogotá, September, 1918; included in *Conversaciones de sobremesa*, Tipografía Ariel, Bogotá, 1934.)

6

The filibuster and the princess

My MOTHER CATHERINE arrived in León with her retinue on the afternoon of Friday, June 15th, 1855, when the drought which that year had prolonged the summer season was still merciless, the oxcarts finally came to a halt in the middle of the Plaza del Laborio after many months at a sluggish pace, and after so many catastrophes suffered along the route marked out by my uncle the King Frederick on the map spread out before the eyes of his cousin James, who now had the rank of brigadier and had been put in command of an escort of twelve grenadiers for this journey. Six women in the role of ladies-in-waiting comprised the original entourage, besides my great-aunt Charlotte, the former regent, who had undertaken to accompany her niece on her nuptial journey despite the fact that it amounted to an onerous charge, since she was already blind and crippled. She was to die as they were beating their way through the dense jungles of Mulukukú.

All the grenadiers except two had been murdered or had fallen in the skirmishes against the gangs of deserters from the civil war that ambushed the procession every so often along the way, and three of the women of the entourage ended up having been kidnapped. Of the original train of six carts purchased in San Pedro del Norte when they left their bongos at the end of the portion of the route that led up the Río Grande de Matagalpa, four had been captured by their attackers, with which the bride's trousseau had also been lost.

The deadly plague of cholera, brought to León by the bands of defeated soldiers who were returning already ill, had taken hold in the city and was running loose in the streets. The stench of the swollen bodies not yet retrieved from their rooms, along with the smell of the carbolic acid that had been spread on the sidewalks like a thick milk, was carried on the rotten air in which clouds of steel-blue flies were buzzing.

The pennant of the Kingdom of Mosquitia was fastened to a bark-covered stick on the first oxcart, the one that carried my mother Catherine, and the yokes worn by the oxen were decorated with garlands of flowers plucked from the edge of the road. "Arrange for wreathes of flowers on the yokes and for martial music to be heard at the moment of arrival," was recorded in the orders dictated by my uncle the King, and before the oxcarts could begin their entrance into the city, James had to scout ahead in search of musicians. In the barrio of San Sebastián he ran across a clarinet, a trombone, and a bass drum, plus a kid with some cymbals, and that was the music heard by the sentries all of a sudden from the height of the parapet above the Casa de Cabildo when the oxcarts entered the plaza, a military fanfare that sounded more like a polka with the chords all out of tune.

My mother Catherine finally arrived at her destination having just turned seventeen years of age, accustomed since childhood to the idea of that marriage which my uncle the King had instilled in her as if it were simply one more of the lessons in the *Little Pilgrim Book*. He himself, having become her tutor because she was unable now to study in London or in Kingston like the rest of her line, had taught her the four rules of arithmetic, fractions, and decimals, and how to write with clear letters using the Palmer method. The English these days listened to the demands of my uncle the King only with boredom, and it was only possible to order her bridal trousseau from Bristol after taking up a collection from among the members of the royal family: half a dozen sets of patterned sheets, three cambric nightgowns with caps decorated in lace, a canopied brass bed, two porcelain chamber pots, a set of saucepans for the kitchen, frying pans and ladles, a pitcher for milk, a meat grinder, a washbasin with pitcher, a tiled vessel of a size sufficient to bathe in.

The bongos had been sent off with a prolonged drum roll, pushed away from a sandy bank into the greenish waters of the Río Grande de Matagalpa assisted by the *zambo* fishermen from the small village of Kara, and in the early morning light of the dawn, my uncle the King saw the craft glide leisurely toward the open river, with James holding the fringed sunshade over the bride's head. He would never see her again.

An old man at thirty, suffering from dropsy to the point where he had to leave the top buttons on his pants unfastened, he had finally accepted the lot of his ancestors on the throne by yielding to the lure of rum. In one of the letters that James carried in his document case for official correspondence, he told my father with an aching aftertaste of irony that he finally was accepting the annual ration of rum that the Governor of Jamaica dispensed every year to the Mosquito Kings but that never had he ceased to demand his ration of books. Those he liked best among those from his library, he added, were his legacy to the first male heir to be born of this arranged marriage, and Catherine was to bring them with her. No one had bothered to rob them of that legacy during the attacks on the oxcart caravan.

Months afterward, at midday under a burning sun, he would be assassinated when he left the communal latrine of the Royal House. He didn't even have time to close the belt on his pants. One of his great-uncles with the rank of admiral who had come once again from Sandy Bay, a settlement on the coast south of Bluefields, to claim his share of the provisions that the members of the royal family used to receive, sliced him deeply across the gut. It was a period of uncertainty and misunderstandings. So it had not been difficult for other restless relatives to convince the old man to commit such a crime, and also provide him with the razor he used to rip out my uncle the King's intestines, of which the latter was still holding a section in both hands when he collapsed on the street where not a soul was to be seen.

Since he died without an heir, another uncle, Francis Clement Patrick, was consecrated as a new sovereign in the Moravian Church at Bluefields, a long way from the pomp that had marked the ascent of his elders to the throne, all of them having been crowned in the Anglican Cathedral in Jamaica or else in the one in Belize.

My uncle the King had always kept himself informed about the changes in my father's life, and so he knew the latter had finally become Supreme Director and that he remained celibate. And now that England had abandoned him, he said in one of the letters entrusted to James, it was time to move. The great event of the century had taken place—the discovery of gold in California (and here his tiny, clear handwriting went off on its own until it became difficult to decipher)—and Commodore Vanderbilt, associated with the Morgan bank, had established the Transit Accessory Company, the proprietor of all steamship traffic on the Río San Juan and the Great Lake of Nicaragua, and ships proceeding from New York were setting down legions of adventurers in Greytown en route to San Francisco by way of the Isthmus of Rivas. Vanderbilt, then, was the indispensable partner for the future enterprise of the canal.

In that almost abandoned port where they had met, a cosmopolitan trade center had sprung up out of nothing. On coming into the bay, travelers would get a view—through a tangle of masts and rigging belonging to schooners and brigantines—of the cupola of the Transit Accessory Building crowned by a Mercury with winged feet, and next to it another cupola above the offices of the Morgan Trust Company, its concave interior surfaces painted with fat cherubs emptying cornucopias over the heads of the cashiers. They seemed close together here perhaps, but Morgan and Vanderbilt were battling each other in a war to the death. A horse-drawn streetcar ran from the dock on Victoria Square all the way up Shepherd Street, which was paved, no less, with blocks of mahogany, and there were gaslights on the sidewalks, every fifty feet, on standards of bronze. Viscount Benard now had, in place of his former lodging, a hotel with wrought iron balconies, and in each of its rooms a bronze clawfoot bathtub. In among the palm trees there were slate-roofed mansions with weathervanes in the shapes of fish and skylarks. Other mansions displayed oval-shaped façades like a ship's quarterdeck, with iridescent stained-glass windows that showed hunting scenes. Meanwhile, toward the northern coast of the bay, where the Iron House was rusting away helplessly, were the monuments belonging to a Sephardic cemetery, an Irish one, and also one for Free-masons, all behind spiked gratings.

My uncle the King was certain the United States would not be long in trying to snatch Greytown from English hands. The Accessory Transit Company was already the actual owner of everything, the ships, the docks, and all the shops, and if he needed to come to an understanding with Vanderbilt as soon as possible, it was because Morgan would cave in fatally before the merciless genius of this "bull shark" with spats and possessed of a triple row of well-polished fangs.

Moreover, said my uncle the King, there had come into his possession the declaration published in London by Napoleon III after his flight from prison, *The Constantinople of the Pacific*, in which he breathlessly defended the building of the canal through Nicaragua, already baptized with his name, and recommended it thus to the Viscount de Lesseps. That made it necessary therefore that my father should settle the civil war in his favor in order to take advantage of his invaluable friendship with the Emperor (which he was entitled to because the latter owed his freedom to him)—a situation which my uncle the King took for granted even though Chatfield saw it as a hare-brained notion—and thus assure the backing of France in the whole enterprise.

When my father finally read those letters, so long after they had been written, his hopes of receiving some help from Napoleon III, even to support him in his role as Supreme Director, had already come to an end, overwhelmed by that nostalgic impotence which intimacies with the great ones of the earth always come to, for they are gained in the first place during equivocal times when the golden glitter of power has not yet begun to shine on them. Once he was back in León, they kept up a heavy correspondence for quite a time, but one which began to thin out according as the events that led to the fall of the Empire of Louis Philipe accelerated, and which ceased completely when the Prince left his exile in London to return to Paris in 1848, already destined for the Imperial crown.

Now my father finally had the power, but in the event it was actually miserly. From León, with the title of Supreme Director and backed by the liberal party, he governed only half of Nicaragua, while in Granada there was another government of the conservative party. The two bands were still at war, and the two cities were in ruins and wracked by cholera. There were no harvests, no customs duties, and both forces were chasing down ordinary campesinos to press them into service under the red flag of the liberals or the white one of the conservatives.

Then at the end of 1854 he had received an offer for the contract of a company of soldiers of fortune in California, on behalf of one Byron Cole, the editor of a third-class newspaper in San Francisco, who happened to be passing through León on his way to Honduras, where a company in which he had extensive investments was proposing to work the deposits of gold along the Río Patuca. His situation was so in jeopardy that he didn't hesitate to accept the agreement. Each soldier of the company would receive, besides his pay in gold pesos, five hundred acres of arable land and the officers three times that.

A precarious power, that of my father the dreamer, and much more so than it used to be for that other dreamer, my uncle the King Frederick, now that his Kingdom of Mosquitia was dissolving in the vapors of the chill night air of the Caribbean coast, amid the muffled noise of its rain showers. But of the two, my father's dream was the one that smelled the worst, for it was decomposing right under his nose like a body swollen by the plague. The seductions of power, no matter how precarious it is, never cease to attract mistakes that then turn out to be real misfortunes. That is when the most disconcerting illusions take shape before men's souls.

The very moment at which the oxcarts came to a halt in the middle of the plaza, that was also when Byron Cole entered on horseback at the head of a small troop, since he was on his way back, bringing the first sixty men of the Phalanx who were waiting in the port of Realejo. It was he whom my father went out to receive in the hall, in a getup that was foreign to his nature, a military uniform of gray wool with red stripes and high leggings, and high up on his right sleeve was a black ribbon of mourning because a week earlier the cholera had killed his sister Engracia together with her husband and their two children.

Then he became aware of that music of festive desolation sounding on the plaza, drowning out the tattoo of the cornet that the sentry was obliged to play in his honor every time he went outside and made himself visible, and he saw the oxcarts with their drum-shaped leather sunshades, the ox yokes blooming with roadside flowers, and the royal pennant, the same one that had fluttered above the stern of my uncle the King Frederick's boat that mid-day so many years ago in the bay of San Juan del Norte.

Cole and his companions had already gotten off their horses which their orderlies were holding by the reins, and before mounting the steps they removed their masks of gauze soaked in alcohol with which they protected themselves from the fumes of the plague. The music, sounding sometimes like a mockery and other times a lament, did not stop, and my father's eyes remained glued to the flag of the Kingdom of Mosquitia while a vision flashed inside his head, like a dark lightning bolt, the image of the Iron House. Now Cole, with the manners of a Lutheran minister, was introducing him to the two companions who also had mounted the stairs. One of them raised his hand to the brim of his Kossuth hat and clicked his heels together, rattling the spurs. He heard his name vaguely, William Walker. And he also heard, just as vaguely, that the other man was his brother, Norvell Walker.

He paid little attention to them because just as he asked them to come in to what used to be Colonel Pérez's office but now had been turned into the reception room (while he occupied that of the Grand Marshall), he had been staring at the figure of that *zambo* dressed in a brigadier's uniform, completely dirty and tattered, who was crossing the plaza, drawing nearer. He did not recall James's face as the latter tried to maintain himself erect while climbing the steps, and only much later, that night, was he able to recover it from among his most fleeting memories. James, who had now stopped short with his hand raised to his ear, searched in his leather knapsack and handed him a bundle of letters. My father took them and asked him to wait. The riotous music had ceased and now one could hear the cornet's transparent call, saluting the Supreme Director because he was about to go inside. The mercenaries of the escort did not alter their demeanor as a matter of respect for the cornet's call to attention; their amused glances remained fastened on the *zambo* in a brigadier's uniform as he sat down to wait on the top step.

My father went to his table, broke the seal on the envelopes, and looked over the letters, altogether too hastily, for his other visitors were waiting. Through the door still ajar he saw Walker striding back and forth impatiently, striking at his thigh with his riding crop.

I have already mentioned the charitable judgments about my father made by the few historians who wished to express their support. But those of his enemies, who have always been legion, go much further, like this one that was published immediately after his death in *El Centinela*, a clerical broadside under the watchful eye of Bishop Contreras:

> In order to maintain the luxuries of his house he needed the nation's money, having succeeded in becoming accustomed to it while vegetating in ministries and diplomatic missions. Since he had thus acquired the habit of comfort and affluence, there came the day when he fixed his ambitions on a higher public destiny, so that his style of life might attract even more gifts, and he didn't care a fig that when he insisted on proclaiming himself Supreme Director he provoked a copious shedding of blood among the citizens. He led others into similar outrages when he called foreign adventurers to his side, with the abominable consequences that we still lament. Excessive in his vanity, he allowed himself to be ruled by pride, and when he felt his self-love had been hurt he responded with passion, or he hatched crimes that perhaps are not worth the trouble to recall now, in the face of the majesty of death.

In referring to these so-called crimes, the libel alludes to the accusations circulated against my father that he had plotted the bishop's death by ordering the turkey innards prepared for his lunch one Palm Sunday to be sprinkled with glass that had been finely ground in a mortar, for which he made use of a coachman who was the lover of the cook in the bishop's household. The bishop's greatest pleasure was in eating, the proof of which was that dewlap of his which trembled like a slice of bacon; but he also was extravagant in offering the first morsels to his pack of cats, which for that reason soon found themselves prey to the agonies of the death rattle at the very table where they had received their snacks. The only one of the cats to survive the massacre, a splendid Herculean specimen with a black coat, appears on Bishop Contreras's lap in the painting that may be seen in the back of the choir in the Cathedral of León among the portraits of the other bishops, and it was this cat who years later buried his claws in his jugular vein while being petted, in an inexplicable access of madness.

The truth is that my father did not take his living from the public treasury as suggested so maliciously by the bishop, the true author of that gossip column, but the treasury lived because of him. Besides having committed his fortune to honor the debt contracted on behalf of the then-prisoner Napoleon III, he spent his last resources paying the wages of the Phalanx, determined to win this war which, as a frustrating side effect, had brought about the abandoning of the indigo workshops of his hacienda Palmyra, in whose big house, in worse repair every day, he lived. In short, he was altogether a ruined man. And so his luxuries could not have amounted to much more than the liter-sized flagons of the Three Crowns brand of lavender water that he ordered from New York. And in his despairing letters to Napoleon III appealing for war provisions and food, he always was tactful enough not to remind him of the little matter of the debt.

But I ought not to hold back any longer. Walker went on impatiently beating himself on the leg with his riding crop, and the jingling of his spurs was now more insistent. When my father approached the connecting door to have them enter his office, Cole advanced smiling, took him by the arm and leaned into his ear. The man smelled like filthy underwear. He explained, and my father found it difficult to understand him well, that he had had to endorse the expedition's contract over to this gentleman, and he gestured for Walker to come closer, this gentleman with impeccable credentials who had covered himself with glory in the campaign for the independence of Sonora.

Now my father could observe Walker thoroughly. He was wearing a blue greatcoat, riding boots, belt and sword, plus the Kossuth hat with its excessively broad brim that he had not remembered to remove in my father's presence. And in the garish light of an old thunderbolt flash that breaks out suddenly with its dirty glitter, he recognized him. He was the young man who had needed to be defended from his own student friends in Paris years ago, in that *Cabaret des Assassins*, where my father had gone on one of those lonely nights while he was waiting for the audience he had requested from the minister Guizot.

Yes, this was the same fellow. He had fallen down drunk from the table on which he had been dancing to the sound of an accordion, his face bedaubed with rouge and wearing over his pants a ruffled skirt belonging to one of the ladies accompanying the group, who was left in her petticoats. Seeing him on the floor, the young men in the party jumped on him and began stripping off his clothes in the spirit of festive riotousness of the crowd, and when they had succeeded in pulling down his pants, after pulling off the skirt, they raised him up in the air and one of them brought over a oil lamp to illuminate his posterior, which in spite of his slimness was surprisingly abundant, like that of a woman. That shocked my father. He had just come in and had barely gotten himself seated on a sofa apart, but he came to his aid, attacked the merry band with his cane, and the fellow with the lamp, who was behaving insolently, was dispatched with a blow to the head. When they finally released him, with much mockery and whistling, he brought him over to his sofa, helped him put on his pants again, and with his handkerchief wiped the rouge from his face. He tried to get him out of the place, making him lean on him, but when the others called to him from their table, he went back to them, stumbling.

My father had not remembered his reddish hair, which he sees now that he has finally removed the hat, after some elbowing by Cole, and he thought that a hair color of that sort took away from his trustworthiness. But on the other hand, there were his eyes. In this face with its feminine lines, free of facial hair and mustaches, with prominent cheekbones and narrow brow, those steely eyes, without luster, were staring at him with obstinate impertinence. They had lost the desolate bewilderment of that night in Paris. "An experienced soldier," Cole whispered in his ear. "A lawyer and a doctor. An excellent litigant and a good surgeon, having studied at the Sorbonne in Paris. Moreover, a fiery journalist." Walker gave no sign of having recognized my father.

"Mr. Cole tells me that you speak English correctly, and that facilitates things," Walker smiled slightly and now his disdainfulness turned into cordiality. "I understand the situation in which your forces find themselves, but we should utilize two elements immediately: speed and surprise. The one depends on the other. I am completely at your orders."

"Señor Walker. . ." my father began, very much despite himself, since his mind was leaning toward "Señorita Walker."

"Colonel Walker," Walker corrected him gently.

"Colonel Walker," my father continued, "this is something new for me that the contract has changed hands, and I must think about the matter once I have examined your credentials."

My father spoke in a courteous voice, searching for the most formal turns of speech, and he had stepped back to sit at his table while his visitors remained standing, a little put off, especially Cole. Fury was building up in Walker's cutting eyes. It was a strange contrast. On his womanish face, anger appeared like a threat of tears.

"Take a seat, please," my father said.

"Listen," Norvell spoke up then, Walker's brother. He came forward and placed his huge hands, covered by a reddish down, on the table. "You are not being very nice and letting us speak. We have used our own money to get this far. We come from a long way away on a ship because we want to keep you from the military disaster facing you, and you sit there talking about credentials."

"You, are you perhaps a professional soldier?" my father asked Norvell indulgently.

"Lieutenant, Third Regiment, Tennessee Volunteers, in the war against Mexico," Norvell responded. He smelled of cheap rum and looked as though he were sweating it off.

"Excuse him," Walker shoved his brother aside, "but you should understand that we have spent a good many days traveling under miserable conditions, squeezed into tiny cabins on an ancient, uncomfortable schooner. And what we need is action."

"You shall have it," my father responded, "once I examine your credentials. And since I expect I will find nothing bad, at this moment I foresee that your first duty will be to defend the plaza in León against any surprise attack."

"You are mistaken," Walker unfolded a map that he pulled out of his coat pocket. "To defend yourself is to perish. You have to put the Phalanx on the offensive, take the enemy by surprise. Attack the Plaza de Rivas and then use the ships of the Transit Accessory Company at La Virgen in order to capture Granada. . ." and with his finger he struck the map held in his other hand.

"Vanderbilt's ships?" my father smiled disdainfully. "It would be madness, taking on Vanderbilt like that."

"Just a loan," said Walker. "He'll come around later on, when we return his ships to him, for the best thing about his business is to have you as the only one he talks to, under a new contract. That will help him get rid of Morgan once and for all."

My father remained silent and blinking, starry-eyed. Vanderbilt would have to understand. Just one person to talk with. One command. Just one firm hand, at last.

"D'ya see?" Norvell advanced triumphantly.

"Shut up!" Walker ordered his brother. "If you dare speak a word again without asking me first, I'll have you arrested."

"How many men do you need on my part for that operation?" my father asked, still blinking. "The Phalanx can't do it alone."

"Just a few; what I need more is horses," Walker replied and put the map in his pocket. "And I don't want any of the troops of your chief of the army, General Muñoz. I don't trust him."

"Why not?" my father asked, astonished.

"He already talked to me, before I got here, on his own hook."

My father couldn't avoid getting to his feet, although he did so slowly. "How was that?"

"He set up a road block on the way and gave orders to take us to where he was," Walker went on. "Do you know what he proposed to me? To divide my men into groups of ten in order to reinforce his own columns. As they say, hand him the rope with which to hang us, and he will hang you."

"I won't permit it," my father was resolute.

"You need to give me the autonomy for my work," Walker said. "The American legion will have no other superior than you yourself."

"You shall have autonomy, and you'll have the rank of General," my father showed determination now.

"At your orders," Walker responded, and the fingers of his right hand lightly brushed against the brim of his hat.

When the visitors had gone, my father rang the little bell, and when the orderly appeared he gave orders for the oxcarts, with all their passengers, to be conducted to Palmyra. Then he noted down in the big accountant's ledger that he used for registering the events of every day, "I have to trust this man whom I once saw dancing on top of a table, painted like a prostitute, although I don't take to him at all. But I like Muñoz even less. He made me laugh while taking his leave when he said that Muñoz is arrogant and pretentious. The pot and the kettle. But I also need Muñoz."

In those weighty volumes with their covers lined with sailcloth, he always wrote down the laundry list he gave the laundrywoman every week, the list of workers at the hacienda, calculations regarding the price of indigo in London, and inventories of gunpowder in the government arsenals; one of them contains the liquidation of fees he owed to Schulz the engineer before his return to the Rhineland, afraid because of the war. Moreover, between the pages of those books, he kept clippings from foreign newspapers that spoke of the canal through Nicaragua and the Accessory Transit Company. Thus there are also some clippings about Commodore Vanderbilt's European tour aboard his transatlantic steamship *Centurion*, which was provided with a luxurious ball room and another room for banquets, because it was his desire to overwhelm the nobility there with attention, although they scorned his invitations because they considered him a *parvenu*; and later on, other clippings with the news that Morgan, his partner, had stolen the company by means of a stock exchange maneuver during his absence, because of which he had to return to New York at full speed, swearing revenge.

"Whether Vanderbilt comes out ahead in this dispute or Morgan does, either of them will have to deal with me," he wrote in the margin of the entry concerning Walker. Then comes the concise notation about my mother Catherine. And finally, another hand added the obituaries that announced his funeral ceremonies, plus the judgments I have mentioned about his person.

In his book of memoirs, Walker also tells of that first meeting with my father:

> It did not require many minutes to see that he was not the man to control a revolutionary movement, or to conduct it to a successful issue. There was a certain indecision, not merely in his words and features, but even in his walk and the general motions of his body; and this trait of character seemed to be aggravated by the circumstances about him, extremely peculiar to any observer. He did his business in a building that might serve as a stable or a shed for storing farm tools or gunpowder in any public installation in the United States. The only decoration visible on the wall, aside from the country's coat-of-arms, was a portrait of the Emperor Napoleon III of France, taken from an illustrated magazine, I believe *Harper's Weekly*.
>
> As we went in for the interview a couple of oxcarts had just arrived at the plaza, covered with hides tanned by the sun, accompanied by an outlandish orchestra, and as we left they were still there, as well as a *zambo* individual waiting in the corridor, strangely dressed in the uniform of a brigadier in the army of Her Majesty the Queen of England. One of the oxcarts carried a pennant that, according to Colonel Henningsen, the chief of our spy unit, belongs to a so-called native kingdom on the Caribbean coast of Nicaragua, invented by our perfidious cousins to give support to their moribund interests in this part of the world. The brave boys under Henningsen's command also found out that in one of the carts was a young woman, also of the *zambo* race, or black, which comes to the same thing. Our conclusion, as we rode back to the port of Realejo to get the American Phalanx moving toward Rivas, was that don Francisco gets his women by bringing them from a long distance away, and he doesn't care what color skin they have, bless him.

Notwithstanding, pages later Walker writes benignly about my father when he puts in the notice of his death which took place on September 6, 1855: "Much as his friends and neighbors loved and respected him, their estimate of his character will rise yet higher if they live long enough to see in maturity the fruits of the policy he inaugurated and which open the doors of his country to the civilization of the southern United States." It was precisely the opening of those doors that earned my father the reputation as a traitor; and Walker himself, after the repeated failure in his adventure of trying to take over Nicaragua and the rest of Central America, harvested no other fruit than that of ending his life before a firing squad.

In the solitude of the Casa de Cabildo when it was dark, my father decided that this time he should not put off his return to Palmyra to find out if the travelers had been properly treated. But he himself knew that this was nothing but a pretext. He went back again to the letter in which my uncle the King described my mother's attributes; she was loyal and compliant, with a peaceful temperament and blessed with innocence, since her only reading had been the *Young Woman's Friend (Or the Duties, Trials, Loves and Hopes of Women)* by the Reverend Styron, the best compendium of edifying stories and moral advice that a young woman ought to be familiar with. And thus he would swear to him that no man had ever known her as a woman.

That was what stirred my father—a seventeen-year-old virgin, far from her family—and he started thinking about that while he was riding along the main road, a servant trotting along on foot before him to light his way with a good-sized torch of ocote pine, and the lancers of his escort riding behind. And when it occurred to him suddenly that it could only be disgraceful of him to overwhelm by trickery or by force the virtue of an unknown child whom the kindness of a madman had left in his hands, he drove away his lingering fastidiousness by whipping the horse's crupper with his hat to the point that he nearly ran down the servant trotting in front of him.

The escort invaded the rooms with a great show of noise, and when he himself entered the room destined for my mother the soldiers were already there clutching torches that lifted their splendor up to a ceiling lined with bamboo. He discovered her cowering in a corner, on some burlap sacks stretched out on the floor, in the care of her ladies-in-waiting, fearful and disheveled and sobbing quietly in plain sight of the troop.

She had lain down in brassiere and bloomers, the same ones she had been wearing underneath her clothes for weeks, ever since they had been robbed of everything else, and as she got to her feet, wrapped in one of those burlap sacks, she told her women to leave, and they fled into the darkness. At that moment James appeared. He had been sleeping beside the two surviving grenadiers in one of the sheds where the indigo used to be processed, and when he started to complain about the racket, face to face with my father, she told him to get out as well. Her orders, delivered in such a charming voice, with gestures like those of a schoolteacher, were observed respectfully. On the contrary, when my father ordered his escort in turn to leave, the soldiers waited for a signal from their leader, a captain with straight hair, holding back deliberately and looking over at my mother with lascivious eyes. My father's power remained so fragile and diminished that those men would have tied him up and set him on his horse as a prisoner if General Muñoz had ordered them to.

And when the escort finally went out of the room, he picked up the candle the servant had left on the floor and advanced with it in his hand, the fumes burning his nostrils.

Then, as he approached my mother, who was staring at him with eyes curiously perplexed, he again felt himself vile and wretched. Once more that child at the Iron House was in the half-shadows, her eyes were feline, not yet bereft of defiance, at one moment reflecting the vacillating light from the candle, and at the next directed toward her feet that had been hurt by the rough stones and thorns as a result of having had to flee so many times while trying to find some refuge from the roadside attackers in hidden niches in the forest.

The woman facing him was not the one that his covetousness, plus a prolonged abstinence, had helped him to imagine, but an emaciated adolescent who seemed more like an apprentice seamstress tired after a day's work putting in basting stitches for hems, or even better, a servant raised up out of bed at midnight because someone was sick and she was needed in the kitchen to boil water. A body without excess, her breasts barely sketched underneath her bra, and her skinny hips seeming to have been compressed during her growing years by the weight of an outside pressure hovering over her shoulders.

The candle, nearly depleted, wavered for one final time, and in the darkness all that remained of it was the foul odor of petroleum. In the distance barked a solitary dog, and a gust of wind swept a rain of gravel sounds over the roof. The sudden darkness caused the cowardliness in my father's soul to disappear, and his arrogance returned, as if now he might be able to hide from himself. He couldn't see my mother, much less see into the darkness of her soul, where a bewildered struggle was being waged between the ingenuous chastity of the fiancée who was about to be sullied and the equally ingenuous ambition suddenly awakened in her with a frenzy: the ambition (so much the child of her ignorance) of sharing from that moment on—even though it might be as the consequence of rape—in the power of this man who had been enhanced and falsified by the praises of my uncle the King, she herself being a dreamer in the face of a power that her deluded imagination exaggerated.

My father dropped the extinguished candle to the floor and advanced on tiptoe, his hands held out before him. He heard the alert respiration of my mother and felt her smell receding away from him because as he kept moving toward her she kept backing up, until he heard her bump up against the wall, and when he felt around with his feet the first thing he touched was the burlap sacks dumped on the floor. Putting out his hand he found her arm and grasped it by the wrist, a wrist so small, so easy to get hold of, like a reed that he was afraid might break if he pressed too hard: and thus he felt around for the other arm and by grabbing at it in stages further and further along he managed to get hold of her other wrist until he was able to bend her over the sacks. There was only a very weak resistance on her part because she didn't want to give him too much opposition, and besides, if she had tried, her physical strength would have been so little as to be useless. Then he was tearing her clothing off with rapid jerks, covering her neck and cheeks with saliva, searching for her mouth which she barely turned aside, palpating her all over her body to confirm by touch what he had already decided, how poorly developed her flesh was, her meager breasts that he could scarcely even locate to caress, with her flanks that hurt him as they pressed into his groin while he struggled, her hard, cold knees that were so slow to open until, taking more pains with his tactics, he succeeded in undressing her completely, and, maneuvering so as to free himself from his pants, although they remained bunched around his knees, he came into her with such a degree of violence that even he himself was shocked, and she let out a scream, the howl of a small beast being wounded unto death.

7

Fleas on the roast chicken

Where should I go? To do what? I am like a solitary bird,
without a nest, perched in bewilderment on a dry, barren
branch...

Turgenev, *Poems in Prose*

In the year 1997 I spent the entire month of October in
Mallorca with my wife, determined to finish the final version of my novel, *Margarita, How Beautiful the Sea*, and
we stayed at C'an Murada, an estate from which one can
get to Pollensa on foot, as well as to Alcudia, walking along
a gridwork of paths squeezed in between the stone fences.
Peter Schultze-Kraft, with us once more, had come from
Hinterzarten in the Black Forest, and it was he who had
rented C'an Murada from a farmer who had formerly raised
sheep there but who now offers his modernized home to
the tourists, mostly Germans. He still keeps a few lambs
which make the sound of their bells heard every morning as
they gambol on the grass next to the windows, producing
the illusion of bucolic life.

In the Pollensa harbor the restaurants, bars, and hotels

are beginning to close down at the end of the season, for already there are almost no tourists left. José Victoriano, the Galician from Pontevedra, owner of La Gabarra and Peter's friend, is holding out until the last moment before he too goes off to his own land on vacation, and he hangs around talking with us until midnight in the salon decorated with fishing nets, while on the street side, in the bar, a few customers from the neighborhood are enjoying themselves drinking beer from glasses that the Moroccan bartender keeps filling up parsimoniously, knowing that with the low season looming, he has all the time in the world.

Nevertheless, not even in the low season does the Sunday market slacken its exuberance in the plaza of Pollensa where we go to have breakfast on the terrace of the Café Espanyol, with a roll of newspapers under my arm, and where I have agreed to meet at noon with Lourdes Durán, head of the Culture section of *El Diario de Mallorca*, for an interview in which besides *Margarita* we talk about this other one, the one you have in your hands at this moment, but which was then in its infancy. What is on a writer's mind when taking up the next novel before putting the finishing touches on the one in hand? That was Lourdes's first question, and I responded that to me the newer work comes up as a matter of recent, sudden urgencies disputing the territory of the previous ones, until they end by winning out over them when the latter are already in retreat.

We do the photo session in front of the Romanic church, on one side of which the Calvary staircase climbs up through the pines with its three hundred sixty-five steps, one for each day of the year. And on the other side is the museum devoted to the painter Anglada Camarassa. Then I mentioned the El Loro inn to Lourdes, the one next to the Pi de la Posada, where Rubén Darío began his phenomenal drunken spree at the time of his visit, and we go to look for it, but it no longer exists. As we take our leave of each other, since I'm interested in the *chuetas*, she removes from her purse a copy of the novel by Carme Riera, *The Final Blue*, which she is reading, but which she lets me have as a gift; she'll just look for another copy. The novel deals with the celebrated attempt at flight of a group of Mallorcan *chuetas* with the Inquisition in pursuit in the seventeenth century.

My interest in Castellón was reborn right here in Mallorca, after the figure had sunk into oblivion in my mind for several years, occupied as I was in political ventures, the last ones of my life, which it will not be of any use to tell about here, and in any case they are dealt with in my book of memoirs *Adios Muchachos*. I recalled that Professor Rodaskowski had gone so far as to believe Castellón to be a native of Mallorca, living in Palma as he had been during the years when the two of them were becoming acquainted. And later on, thanks to Vargas Vila's account, I found out that Castellón had lived with his daughter in the *chueta* barrio and also that he had been the one who had taken the photograph of Darío dressed as a Carthusian monk. Moreover, from reading his piece about the Archduke Luis Salvador, Darío also interested me as a character in the story line, and I was even intrigued by the Archduke himself. If I were to investigate Darío's last stay in the Palacio del Rey Sancho, I thought, perhaps it would be possible to get to Castellón that way.

The Palacio del Rey Sancho is part of the monastery of La Cartuja, and Peter, always the efficient one, got hold of the phone number of the museum and asked to speak to the curator. The situation is a little more complicated than it appears. There is no curator. This is not a question of a museum operated by the Balearic government, and the cells of the new monastery, among them the ones Chopin and George Sand had occupied, all have separate owners, just as the Palacio del Rey Sancho, which used to be the original monastery, had previously belonged to don Juan Sureda. But someone has offered to wait for us on the following morning at eleven by the side door of the new church, the point of entry for tourists.

Upon getting ready to leave for Valldemosa, the intense heat beneath the cloudy autumn sky seems strange to me. A vacuum has been created in the atmosphere, and the surroundings appear to have taken on something supernatural. At night, after we get back and turn on the television, we are informed about the storm that has been whipping the Balearic Islands all day, forcing navigation to be suspended and all the ports to be closed down, but it seems as though all this must have been taking place a long way distant from us. In Extremadura, floods have left many dead or missing.

We reach Valldemosa a little after ten. The highway from Palma ascends to the edge of a cliff that falls off toward the valley where the village's Arabian tile roofs are piled together with the blue mosaic cupola of the new church of La Cartuja. Beyond the slopes planted with vegetables, pine trees and olives, and the fields of oaks and carob beans, rise the buttresses of the Teix. This is the same panorama that Castellón contemplated while seated beside the driver when his vehicle was struggling to make it along the rocky path, forced to wade through the torrents that nowadays run confined in culverts. The boxes filled with his photographic equipment rode on the cart's bed, and the driver must surely have asked him to hold in his lap the wicker basket padded with wood shavings holding the three liters of McCullay whisky.

From the parking lot on the other side of the highway that leads to Deyá, filled with automobiles shining like they had just left the factory, you reach La Cartuja by way of the Via Blanquerna, shaded by linden trees, where the waves of Japanese and German tourists spill out of their buses on their way to visit Chopin's cell. Inevitably on the ground floor of each of the houses with its wrought iron balconies and Venetian shutters there is some kind of retail store open, cafés with canvas awnings, pastry shops, bars, souvenir places with racks of postcards set up outdoors next to strings of purses, belts, scarves; and on not a few thresholds a tile plaque is set with the protective image of Santa Catalina Thomas, *pregau per nostaltres*. With her back to the green curtain behind which one of the cells is being renovated, a Japanese tourist, dressed in a leather skirt that looks like a steel worker's apron, is taking a picture of the street, her camera held rather away from her face, while her companion, adorned with a pigtail like a samurai, waits patiently by her side.

In the middle of the Plaza de La Cartuja, between the new church and the Los Tilos bar, is the bust of Chopin donated by the Polish government and unveiled by Queen Sofía on September 21, 1997. The bust, by the sculptress Zofia Wolska, shows Chopin with his head tilted downward, his eyelids lowered as if he were reflecting on the keyboard of a piano, his page-cut hair covering his ears, and his nose even more prominent.

The one who is waiting for us very punctually at the side door of the new church is the Marqués don Álvaro Bauzá de Mirabo, now the owner of the Palacio del Rey Sancho, since his grandfather purchased it at the time of don Juan Sureda's bankruptcy. It was the Marqués with whom Peter had spoken on the telephone. He is a man of average stature, somewhat past seventy, quite affable, and wearing a baggy gray sweater. When I tell him at the beginning of our tour that it surprises me to find that La Cartuja has been divided among several owners, he explains that Mendizábal's law of disentailment put the monastery into the public domain in 1835, upon which the monks had to abandon it. The cells were first given as leases to wealthy families from Palma, who used them for summer living, and later on the whole batch of them were sold and passed into private hands. This Mendizábal, a freemason and sworn enemy of the Carlists, was the one who convinced George Sand, a liberal positivist and follower of the socialist "new religion" of Saint Simon, to come from Paris to Mallorca, or so don Álvaro tells us.

At that time there were no longer any monks in the monastery, which made it possible for the fourth cell of the new monastery, which now belongs to the Ferrá family, to be occupied during the winter of 1839 by Chopin and George Sand. According to the passenger list, they reached Palma on the steamship *Mallorquín*, arriving from Barcelona at eleven-thirty on the morning of Thursday, November 8, 1838, and embarked for the return trip on Wednesday, February 13, 1839, at three in the afternoon, on the same ship, which was also carrying its usual load of hogs. The cargo manifest on that day lists: *197 pigs consigned by the señor Miquel Moll, priest and dealer in small stock animals, all of them having been weighed on the scales one by one, according to the appended list, destined for the La Estrella sausage factory in Barcelona.*

The Archduke Luis Salvador would visit the factory years later and describe for us the way the hogs were processed at the time:

> ...they are placed on a moving conveyor made of wood, from which they are gradually lifted up by some infallible steel hooks at the nape of the neck and remain there at the mercy of the butcher's sure hand, which, armed with a shining, broad-bladed knife, plunges into the uvula. When completely drained of blood, they are subjected to the power of some jets of hot steam, after which combs rake vigorously through their fur, and thus they are finally slit from top to bottom, cut into pieces, and salted.

That same afternoon he also visited the steamer *Amerique*, then in the harbor, and made them show him the stateroom, sheathed in a flat red color, that belonged to Sarah Bernhardt. At the time she was on an outing to Madrid.

George Sand, registered under the name Aurore Dudevant, using her husband's name, was accompanied by her two children as well: Maurice, about thirteen, "weak and delicate, spoke very little and preferred to sketch in his album everything that moved him" (the local edition of *A Winter in Mallorca* that I have bought at one of the tourist shops along the Via Blanquerna, and which is sold also in English and German translations, contains some of the sketches); and Solange, "younger than Maurice, a blond girl filled with life and energy, avid for movement and noise; you would have taken her for a boy without those luxuriant curls, when she was dressed in men's clothing like her mother." Darío offers these and other facts about George Sand in his unfinished novels *The Island of Gold* and *Mallorca's Gold*, both mentioned by Vargas Vila.

Now that we are already in Chopin's cell, which is reached by going through the gallery alongside the Patio of the Myrtles, I can see at the entrance the portrait that Dubufe made of George Sand in 1845. She seems neither intelligent nor pretty, and her gaze, directed toward some distant point, lacks perspicacity. Her nose is too long and all her features remind you rather more of a Roman matron. This one is a long way from that portrait by Delacroix that hangs on one of the walls at Zelazowa Wola in which she looks like a vaudeville singer or perhaps a milliner with pretentious airs, but with life. A milliner, as was her mother.

The Mallorquín's registry of passengers contains this notation: *M. Chopin, artist.* In *A Winter in Mallorca*, George Sand calls him simply "our sick man" or "our friend," always hiding his name from the gaze of the curious. It is not difficult to imagine him in this cell. Dressed in funeral black, his long, hairy hands seem strange, like those of a cadaver, beneath the shirt cuffs turned the color of ivory by the starch. He is always coughing into his cambric kerchief which, with something like a serious indulgence, he then examines for signs of blood, eyes feverish, pale of aspect, advancing toward the final image he will have in the photograph taken by Bisson in the same year as his death, thrust inside a heavy, dark overcoat, his gaze disconsolate, seemingly waiting for the final journey seated on a bench in a railway station where there is no other passenger.

In the cell, comprising three rooms, a terrace, and a garden, there are now two pianos in sight of the tourists, far too much furniture, as in a bazaar, and a huge number of commemorative plaques and photos of famous visitors on the walls. From the terrace there appears once more the valley at the far end of the landscape, the slopes bordered with stone walls gradually climbing up toward the rocky promontories, and the pine trees, royal palms, and almond trees, just the way Pilar Montaner used to paint them.

The lovers had arrived in the midst of a spell of bad weather, scarcely aware that the Balearic winter is sometimes harsh, and sometimes even the fall season, like this one in which it is my fate to live, with its squalls and flurries like those in Nicaragua. They spent the first week in Palma, in a boarding house on the Calle de la Marina, and then they managed to rent a villa, So'n Vent, in Establiments. Maurice made a sketch of it, and it doesn't look as unpleasant as it seemed to George Sand, with its little garden in front, flower pots on the balustrade, a stone stairway, and its windows protected by wooden shutters like those along the Via Blanquerna.

The smell from the braziers constantly smoldering in the mansion's rooms made Chopin cough incessantly. In a short while the owner, a certain Gómez, urged them to leave, afraid of the dangers of contagion from "our friend's" disease. Sand refused to accept the notion that Chopin was tubercular and attributed his indisposition to bronchitis aggravated by nervous excitement; she would never permit the doctors of Palma to bleed him since that, according to her declaration, would more than likely bring about his death. Since childhood he had been given applications of leeches that left him anemic, and he was subjected to a diet of toasted acorns and oats. "I drink emetics and they feed me oats just like the horses," he wrote from the thermal baths at Reinerz in 1823. And, desperate for a cure, he would consult allopathic physicians and he even subjected himself to treatments by magnetism.

When they left So'n Vent the owner ordered the furniture and bedclothes in the sick man's room to be thrown into the middle of the street for burning, an action that was legal under the edict of Fernando VI of 1755. Gómez himself, in the presence of several neighbors, tossed on top of the calamitous array of shattered wood, cushions, curtains, and bed linens the oil lamp that his own hand had taken from the nightstand in the bedroom, after having wrapped his hands in a towel that also went into the flames. The lamp shattered into a thousand pieces and spilled its black oil. One of the neighbors felt around in the pockets of his jacket for his steel and flint and ignited the pyre. Far into the afternoon the fire burned, dispersing its infectious smoke toward the slate-colored sky.

During his first trip to Mallorca in the fall of 1906, Darío wrote the long poem *Epístola* in rhymed alexandrines dedicated to Juana de Lugones, the wife of the Argentine poet Leopoldo Lugones, who committed suicide in 1938. Darío liked calling himself "Nebur" in those days, "el caballero Nebur," an anagram of Rubén, and he had succeeded once more in curing himself for a while of his alcoholic obsessions. In that poem he speaks for the first time about La Cartuja, about George Sand and Chopin:

> La Cartuja was the setting where the famous
> Author Sand composed a book in Valldemosa.
> I'm not certain if she came there with Musset,
> And if it gave her joy or pain I cannot say.*

The asterisk on the last line leads to a note at the foot of the page, also in rhyme, in which the author corrects himself after having finally read *A Winter in Mallorca*, which the Mallorcan poet Felipe Alomar had lent him even while he was still writing the poem:

> Now I've read that volume by Aurore Dupin.
> Chopin it was, who was her lover. Poor Chopin!

Robert Graves, who spent many years of his life in Mallorca and is buried in the hilltop cemetery at Deyá, when mentioning George Sand speaks about the "well-known scandal of her honeymoon with Alfred de Musset, whom it was assumed she had seduced, betrayed, and abandoned." It is also Graves who ends up telling us that Solange was a perverse girl from the age of eight onward, stirring up hatreds and ill will among whoever was around her. She would drink her milk on the sly, knowing that the peasant children who brought it to her cell would be accused of it. Or she would search for fleas in the goat's fur to toss them onto the roast chicken that was waiting on the platter to be put on the table.

In *The Island of Gold*, Darío marvels over the great amount of space that George Sand devotes to the hogs in *A Winter in Mallorca*. Young pigs, the most beautiful in the country, that at the innocent age of a year and a half weigh twenty-four *arrobas* or about 600 pounds (as robust as that Hercules the champion hog she would admire so many

years later at the Agricultural Fair of Rouen): "The Mallor-
cans will name this century in future times 'The Age of the
Pig,' the way Muslims talk in their histories about 'The Year
of the Elephant.'"

And Darío is so taken by this theme that he comes back
to it in *Mallorcan Gold* and copies in his own introduction
what she describes about their experience on the return trip
on board *El Mallorquín*, which was loaded with hogs:

> When we returned from Mallorca to Barcelona in
> the month of March, it was suffocatingly hot, but
> nevertheless it was not possible for us to set foot on
> the deck. Even when we might have risked the danger
> that a bad-humored hog might nibble on our legs,
> the ship's captain doubtless would not have permit-
> ted us to bother his clients with our presence. They
> were very quiet during the first hours, but at midnight
> the pilot remarked that they were having a bad dream
> and looking like victims of black melancholia. Then he
> put the whip to them, and regularly every quarter of
> an hour, we were awakened by shouting and screams.
> These noises, produced partly by the pain and rage
> of the beaten pigs, and partly by the captain's incite-
> ments of his crew and the oaths inspired by their
> emulating him, were so frightful that we sometimes
> thought the herd was devouring the crew...

But during his first stay in Mallorca in 1906, Darío
himself had had something to do with another ship
loaded with pigs and passengers which was also headed
for Barcelona on a stormy night. This time he had come
to Palma accompanied by Francisca and also María, his
sister-in-law. They took a chalet, El Torrero, on Calle 2 de
Mayo, in El Terreno, at the time a brand new suburb situ-
ated between the ocean and the hill on top of which Bell-
ver Castle rises up, where Jovellanos was also imprisoned
after Godoy's underlings decided that the monks of the

Palacio del Rey Sancho had been treating him too well.

The Guatemalan writer Enrique Gómez Carrillo, who was dedicated to tormenting Darío (out of the incurable jealousy he felt for him, much like that of Vargas Vila), appeared at El Torrero on the way back from one of his trips to the Orient and describes the place:

> My poor Darío is curing his neurasthenia here, occupied with enemies both apparent and real. The chalet has a small garden with one tall cypress, and a terrace that invites contemplation of the sea. María, who is now a lovely adolescent, is at the window in a pose of indolent abandon. She lets Darío know about the stranger's presence and the poet comes to open the door . . . He has written nothing under the influence of the Mallorcan landscape; instead it seems as though his scenery has only come from inside his own head.

In December Darío received the ominous announcement that his wife Rosario Murillo had appeared in Paris, ready to garnishee his consul's salary and also to seize the furniture in his apartment in the Rue Marivaux, including his Pleyel piano, the one which later on he—abandoned by his government—would be forced to sell in order to support himself as Nicaragua's minister in Madrid. (His companion in misfortune, Chopin, during his winter on Mallorca, had suffered the seizure of his own Pleyel piano by the customs officers, and it had been held in custody for weeks because of bureaucratic idiocies.)

Furious, Darío made Francisca go to Paris to straighten out those matters—a rather odd measure given the fact that she was the illiterate one and he the one who understood how to read—while he stayed in El Torrero in the sole company of María. This forced absence of Francisca was to last until the end of January, 1907.

On December 13th, he and María went with Francisca when she boarded the steamship *Cataluña*, leaving at five in the afternoon. The ship was berthed near the four-towered stone building La Llotja, its chimney stack adorned with a huge C decorated with arabesques that was visible above the brass rooftops of the warehouses. Before the passengers were allowed to board, the crew had to finish loading the usual herd of hogs. As the animals were pushed along with much shouting, their hooves kept slipping on the iron plank placed between the dock and the gunwale. The last of the hogs to be shipped burst through the bars of the pigpen alongside some barrels of flour and fell into the water, only to drown shrieking, after which the captain angrily lowered the gangplank and was ready to beat the crew members.

Just then the painter Santiago Rusiñol came up in his carriage, intent on boarding the steamer, but after observing the strange calm that hung over the water, which had become sluggish as if it were thick oil, and also taking note of the close proximity of the black sky, he warned Darío that a groundswell awaited the ship and decided not to go aboard.

Francisca, wrapped in a silk shawl, was wearing a little hat adorned with a spray of artificial geraniums, a percale dress printed with tiny daisies, and kid leather boots with eyelets up to the ankle. The paper bag in her hand let the grease show through from the sausage sandwich that would be her supper. She gazed at Darío with a distressed look, but not lacking in docility, and he, gripping his cane part way down its length, made dismissive gestures and pointed toward the sea as if he knew something about it, saying that this period of calm was really a good sign.

The sound of the bell announcing the departure seemed remote. The moorings were loosed and the steamship left the bay sluggishly, as if it were difficult to make way through this water that was now like ink. Rusiñol departed in his carriage, and at a distance María followed Darío's steps back to the trolley stop to board the vehicle that was going to return them to Terreno. The horses trotted along unhurriedly on the cobbled pavement, so slowly that as they went through the Santa Catalina barrio María was able to purchase a handful of onions from a strolling vendor in a transaction accomplished through the little window.

They ate alone and in silence at the tiny kitchen table, while outside the wind was coming down out of the Tramuntana mountain range. Soon the rain began to whip at the window glass as if it wished to destroy it. María washed up the plates while Darío pretended to read the newspaper, standing all the while, without leaving the kitchen, and then when she passed by him on the way to her bedroom, carefully shielding the flame of the oil lamp that was breaking through the darkness in front of her face, he followed her with clumsy steps, like a thief entering someone else's house for the first time.

With her back turned to him, she finds herself bending over her bed to pull the covers back in the quivering light of the oil lamp when behind her she senses that tired breathing of an old animal whose nostrils are blocked. He is carrying the newspaper in his hand but he doesn't see what to do with it. She does not turn around. When he puts his arms around her and pulls her toward him, the newspaper rustles in the embrace and falls apart to the floor, and as he moves closer to her neck, his lips are still shining with the reddish traces of the sausage of the recent meal, the same sausage as in Francisca's sandwich, and then comes the onion smell and the scolding given him by the girl.

A little before that, at sea the storm had broken. The ship loaded with hogs moaned amid its violent rolling in the dense night. At dawn the rain was still falling when it was given up for lost, both in Palma and in Barcelona. Communications between both ports were shut down, and the radio-telegraph transmitter on board *El Cataluña* had not been used. Around noon Darío went to the harbor to inquire. Many people were gathered at the dock and rumors of shipwreck were passing about. A company employee, wearing a uniform but without stripes, was distributing copies of the passenger list, with the printer's ink still fresh. He took one and found Francisca's name at the end of the first column: Francisca Sànchez, Spain, 32 years old, unmarried, homemaker. Then he fled and went to take shelter in the Café Maturana where he sat in a corner drinking glass after glass of W & S. The waiters, who knew him, put him on the trolley car when the news came in that the ship had finally arrived in Barcelona, but he didn't realize that.

After drifting for a good many hours, *El Cataluña* had not shown itself in sight of the harbor until about four o'clock in the afternoon. For the most part the cargo of hogs had been swept overboard by the force of the waves, and the bloated, soaked bodies of the rest of them still remained on the deck. The next day Francisca was able to continue her trip to Paris on the train.

In *The Island of Gold*, where he himself appears as his own protagonist, he reports a conversation with an enigmatic English woman, Lady Perhaps, his alter ego and counterpart, about the fondness George Sand has for the pigs:

"And that dreadful George Sand," she said to me, "who couldn't find an animal more suitable to pay attention to during her *Winter on Mallorca* than that one which Monselet called '*mon auge*' and at which Parisian men and women alike gaze with singular concern."

"I do not find that so strange at all, my dear friend. An animal of that sort is a very curious one. In your prodigious Shakespeare his name is Falstaff, and in our own unparalleled Cervantes he is called Sancho. Someone has famously made the claim that every man has one of those animals within himself, one *'qui sommeille'*. . . and it was into the body of this tasty quadruped that the devils from out of the men's bodies were forced to go by the power of Our Lord Jesus Christ. Good night, Madame."

When Lady Perhaps chides him for his opinions about George Sand, he responds, "Yes, my Lady. I am not charitable toward children who mistreat birds nor with women who make martyrs out of poets." It was a strange obsession. He even complains that she dressed in pants and made Solange wear them too. He thinks her guilty of bad taste in disguising herself under a masculine nom de plume and thus getting herself called a "writer." "Would you have taken a fancy to her had she lived in your own time?" Lady Perhaps asks him. "I doubt it," he responds; "A literary female is almost not a woman; she is a colleague."

And Lady Perhaps covers her mouth, pretending she is trying to repress a scream, when she hears him affirm that Chopin's illness was aggravated, as with any man who had tuberculosis, by feminine proximity, and that this very illness in turn exacerbated his libido. A morbidity like that of a dog in heat biting its tail. A nervous arousal of the sexual instinct because of the feverish state of chronic inflammation of those tubercular lungs.

I can see Lady Perhaps laughing, her horse-like teeth showing the color of old bone, as she fingers the double row of her pearl necklace with stubborn fingers. Darío does not describe her but her jaw is somewhat sharp, and her blue eyes glitter in her mature face, which probably had been attractive once, at a much earlier age. There is a faint odor of lavender about her, and on her lip a light layer of sweat forms which she pats away with her embroidered handkerchief. Definitely, she thinks, this poet from the tropics, whose manners are sometimes so extravagant, and with whom she sits in the afternoon drinking vermouth, talks like a gossipy old woman energetically cooling herself off with her fan in an overheated salon.

And if Lady Perhaps could have heard Robert Graves! "A domineering woman, smoker of cigars, poorly dressed, irascible," her countryman would add many years later, his eyebrows frowning severely over a picture of George Sand. She and Chopin, he said, "must have seemed to the neighbors, and above all to the monks, as if possessed by the devil. And no wonder: visits to the cemetery on moonlit nights; mother and adolescent daughter both dressed like men; scenes hardly edifying..."

In a letter that George Sand wrote in 1846 to Count Gryzmala, a close friend of Chopin's, she confesses that her relationship with the composer had been "virginal" throughout the past seven years, the period that begins, if you start counting up, with the winter in Mallorca. That period in the monastery was one of abstinence, and Chopin had to have arranged it all to placate the unhealthy exacerbations of his libido.

Nonetheless, she always surrounded him with maternal affection, Darío recognizes, and Graves concedes that aside from serving as his cook and maid, it was because of him that she abandoned work on her novel *Spiridion* during those months. But one never hears music spoken of in *A Winter in Mallorca*, complains Darío, and in exchange, at every step there appears "the 'housewife,' the bourgeoise who does not neglect the pantry and makes a note of every time María Antonia the maid steals a cookie or a cutlet." Chopin had a better companion in his Pleyel piano than in George Sand, he adds, and her fondness for the sick man was nothing if not abnormal, "a whim on the part of someone who no longer wants to have a romantic life: she has a tubercular patient, an old monastery, monks, darkness, a cemetery, superstitious people around her, the clear moon above. . .she has her pale, pestilent lover. . . ." In short, Robert Graves agrees, she has everything in hand to fulfill her dream of becoming the queen of romanticism without the crown.

Our visit to Chopin's cell and La Cartuja monastery, guided by the hand of don Álvaro, has come to an end, and now we go toward the neighboring Palacio del Rey Sancho where Darío spent that stormy period hosted by the Sureda family in the company of the insidious Vargas Vila and—quite by accident—Castellón. The chapel alongside the monks' cemetery these days serves for folkloric concerts slanted toward the tourists. When we appear on the scene a company is trying out a Mallorcan dance, and as we go out we leave the clacking of their castanets behind us. Behind the stone portal that serves as the entryway into the Palacio there is a bust of Darío in the garden, and in the bend of the Ave María stairway that leads to the upper galleries, a wax figure shows him wearing a monk's habit, hood above the face, seated at a desk in the act of writing, with a goose quill pen in his hand. His bedroom on the floor above is preserved exactly as Vargas Vila describes it.

Now back in his office, don Álvaro informs me that no archive exists related to the Sureda family, and consequently there is not much to discover, what a pity!, about Darío's stay in the Palacio, nor about Castellón.

"The only thing left is the photograph in the monk's habit," he says nonetheless, and from a drawer in his desk he takes out an envelope and hands it to me.

There are four pictures of postcard size glued to a piece of cardboard. The one that is so familiar, of Darío by himself in the Carthusian habit. Two others, the ones Vargas Vila describes in his account: Darío with the Sureda couple, and Darío with Vargas Vila himself. And another one, new for me: Darío and Castellón, whom I recognize from his self-portrait.

"Castellón," I say.

"He took it himself, with a squeeze-bulb shutter release adapted with several lengths of rubber tubing, the kind used for enemas," don Álvaro says.

"Then you are quite familiar with Castellón," I ask.

"Not really," says don Álvaro. "But I know he was a real character."

"As a photographer?" I ask further.

"Especially because he was a member of the Archduke Luis Salvador's retinue," don Álvaro smiles.

As he remembers Vargas Vila's insistent claim, made to Castellón himself, in this very Palacio, he is the photographer who was tagging along behind the group in Darío's story. How is it that up until this very moment I have felt the relevance of that fact?

"Do you know any of the stories about that entourage?" asks don Álvaro. "Strange people, wanderers, hapless adventurers the Archduke would pick up wherever he went, depending on how they struck him, and above all, on whether they knew how to keep quiet. Talkative folk bothered him a lot. And he required exact obedience."

"And how did Castellón come to run into that crowd?" I wonder. "As a photographer?"

"That is most likely," don Álvaro agrees. "There are a good many photographs in existence of the figures in that retinue, taken by Castellón."

"There must be an archive," I say.

"Of course, in Son Marroig. Wouldn't you like to visit it?" Don Álvaro goes on. "I can call Dominik Vyborny right now, the curator there."

"I knew someone by that name in Warsaw some time ago," I say.

"Then it must be the same person," don Álvaro says. "He moved to Mallorca six months ago, when he retired. He requested the curator's post because he is very interested in a great uncle of his who was the Archduke's secretary, and he wants to write a book about him."

"Then it *is* the same one," I say, casting a glance at Peter and Tulita.

On our departure, the wax mannequin of Darío, with its shining, marble eyes in the parchment face, and the lock of artificial hair that peeks out from beneath the hood of the monk's habit, seems to have come from a circus gone bankrupt. And I think then that when Darío left the Palacio del Rey Sancho that Christmastime, never to return to Mallorca—just like Turgenev, who before his death no longer knew of anywhere to fly—there was nothing left for him but to come to rest in bewilderment on the same dry, barren branch.

8

The naked nymphs

AFTER THAT FIRST NIGHT, my mother Catherine realized she had no other alternative than to wait patiently, since now she had no control over anything, so equivocal and vague did the image of her destiny appear, and indolence was filling her to the point of overflowing. A fiancée suddenly become a concubine for the night. Hidden in a ravaged mansion on an indigo plantation, subjected to uncertainties, one of them that of love, she could only hope.

Because my father never returned to Palmyra. But she lacked for nothing in the way of provisions for the house, and he even had a chest sent to her with the lingerie and dresses belonging to his deceased sister, and ordered, besides, that his own room—which contained his riding equipment hung on the walls alongside his starched shirtfronts, and his top hats in the wardrobes—be opened for her. More than anything else she allowed herself to be moved there to try to feel herself in possession of something that belonged to him, because the rest was slipping away from her into the shadows. Meanwhile, my father had determined to sleep on a camp cot at his office in the Casa del Cabildo, as if he were doing penance. "I have lowered myself to the most inconceivable level, God have mercy on my soul," was all that he wrote in his bookkeeping ledger in the entry corresponding to the encounter with my mother, and I still do not know what he thought he had lowered himself to, whether it was the act of rape or else the attempt at an illicit love relationship with a *zambo* girl whose physical attractions were poor indeed.

When James suggested to my mother that they should return to my uncle the King Frederick to inform him of the outrage, she put forward good reasons against the idea, first of all, that they didn't have even one centavo. The last occasion on which he went to press her on this, each time angrier, more filled with impotence, he saw her merely smile, with an expression somewhat between submissive and haughty, upon which he decided it would be better to steal a horse that very night from the corral and himself undertake the return trip to fulfill that mission. When James finally managed to reach Bluefields, my uncle the King Frederick had already been buried, and the Kingdom's council kept putting off the matter of that calamitous report because they saw my mother Catherine's disgrace as the fruit of a piece of recklessness that was better to bury as well.

My father would not be long in dying. The plague presented itself to him in the form of an uncontrollable vomiting that seemed to be tearing out his guts and that spilled over his frugal plate of jerked meat, beans, and boiled plantain that he was sharing in the Casa del Cabildo with the General Máximo Jerez, the new chief of the army since Muñoz had been assassinated by a Reserve Guard who raised his rifle while presenting arms, an event in which many saw the hidden hand of Walker. Faced with that signal of the vomit he realized that the end was near, and close to nightfall, when he no longer even had the strength to sit on the chamber pot, he requested from Jerez to be taken to Palmyra because he wanted to die in his own bed. I don't know if he could have remembered that he had ceded it to my mother.

They laid him on a makeshift bed in a cart pulled by oxen, wrapped in a striped blanket because he was shaking with cold despite the fact that the day was hot like no other, and he never ceased defecating along the way. The captain leading the escort kept himself and his men at a distance for fear of the contagion, but also to get away from the stench. They had scarcely gotten a glimpse of the lights of the house when he ordered them to drop the reins, at which moment the cowherd in charge of the oxen chose to flee, so that the oxen went on by themselves with a lighted candle set on the yoke, until they encountered the cobbled pavement of the patio and tamely came to a halt in front of the steps to the corridor.

From the kitchen my mother heard the rough noise of the oxcart's wooden wheels against the flat stones, and because the terrified servants took flight, she herself went to take charge of the dying man followed by her ladies-in-waiting. Those women, having been trained in hospital duties by the Moravian missionaries, lifted him by catching the corners of his excrement-soaked blanket and transported him to the bedroom, where he expired in a few hours.

General Jerez presented himself on the morning of the following day to take the body away because they needed to render him state honors in León. He never got down off his horse, and while the box of unplaned lumber, placed in full sunlight in the patio, was being filled with shovelfuls of lime in order to counter the contagiousness, he was looking out of the corner of his eye at my mother with the disguised smile of a man well experienced in passing love affairs, while she, standing on the corridor steps, refused to show any signs of grief. There was a very lengthy roll on a drum. Four soldiers lifted the box from the ground in order to carry it to the cart waiting for the yoke, and General Jerez glanced at her on the sly for the last time before suddenly heading out the gate, his head with its prominent, rounded brow bobbing between his shoulders to the rhythm of the trot as if about to come loose entirely.

Forgotten by everyone, she was able to go on living in that house which seemed more wasted each day, abandoned now by its staff of servants. Her ladies-in-waiting went at dawn every morning to sell the surplus fruit of the hacienda—bananas, cassava, star apples, and guavas—in the market at León, and two of them ended up remaining in the city, one of them seduced by a cart driver, and the other by an assistant in a ropemaker's shop. Only Mrs. Maureen, the eldest of them, remained faithfully at my mother Catherine's side, and it was she who served as the midwife at my birth, April 9, 1856.

When Walker's filibusterers were pushed out and General Jerez negotiated a peace agreement with General Tomás Martínez, the leader of the conservatives, a distant relative of my father, with the assistance of the judges, ended up inheriting Palmyra. My mother didn't dare put in a claim in my favor. The legal heir, Juan de Dios Castellón, had no difficulty accepting her as a servant, charged now together with Mrs. Maureen with cooking for the laborers who returned in great bands to work in the indigo workshops, and he allowed her to continue living in the house.

That relative knew about my mother's story, and he favored her with a cordial and easygoing way of dealing which bordered on mockery, because he would often address her as "my Princess" when he came into the kitchen where the huge pots full of beans were boiling, destined for the troop of laborers in the workshops; and as for me, always hanging on her hip, he always referred to me as "the Dauphin." They began making repairs to the house, and then he warned her she would have to be moved to the servants' quarters the moment they finished the work. Although at the same time, constant in his playful games, he was putting it into her head, every time he encountered her next to the pots, that better she should look for a man with whom she could get together, because a princess should not remain the servant of laborers. Further, that he himself was going to take it on himself to find her a good partner.

Thus it was that one day he brought Terencio Catín into her presence. He was the overseer for the carpenters on the job, and lived in the Zaragoza barrio. He was more than forty years old, and he had lost an arm in the war. Nevertheless, his being one-armed never stopped him from climbing up agilely to the ridgeline and with his mouth full of nails, along with his one good hand, hammering them into the intersections where the crosspieces joined. Or from setting a door on its hinges by pushing with his shoulder, to say nothing of using a chisel to shape the roses for a cornucopia in relief decorating a wardrobe, or to work the funeral wreaths on the sides of a coffin. He was never gentle, and not a few times he was seen in the midst of quarrels in the cantina, but he began to pay court to my mother with the astuteness of a captive animal, to the point where in the afternoons after work he would sit beside her to help clean the beans of twigs and pebbles before they were put in to soak. They soon became lovers and he took us to live in León, while Mrs. Maureen, tired of all this running about, remained in Palmyra as the head cook.

What my mother didn't know was that Catín had another woman at home, with a child of her own, and his object was to have the two of them living together under one roof, something that neither of them had guessed, and my mother, who still had not reached the age of twenty but had learned from the Moravian missionaries about modesty of speech and therefore was altogether averse to any shouting or screaming, preferred to resolve the matter in another way. From the teachings of the *sukias*, the healers, she was familiar with the dangers and the benefits that come from plants, and so she prepared her rival a concoction containing seeds from the dragon's blood tree and leaves from a *leche de María* tree that causes *bienteveo*, the loss of skin pigmentation in blotches around the body. That was how she managed in the end to frighten her out of the house for good. With her skin now discolored by a scrofulous condition at the base of her breasts, her neck and chin, she screamed and hollered standing in the middle of the street the day she left, taking her offspring along, and accusing my mother Catherine of Negro witchcraft, creating a racket that brought all the neighbors to their front doors. Meanwhile, Catín was in the middle of planing a cedar plank on his carpenter's bench with his one arm, waiting for some lunch, true to his rule of eating whichever soup that one of his two wives at midday would be the first to set before him on his bench, because in a harem as mixed up as this one, there was double the cooking.

When a letter from the Emperor Napoleon III addressed to my father finally reached León, he was already deceased, and without delay it was put in the hands of General Jerez, the only one authorized to open it post mortem, considering where it had come from. In the letter the Emperor invited my father to travel to Paris, "for the purpose of demonstrating his eternal gratitude." Once it was opened, Jerez ordered it printed up on flyers as a way of getting some advantage in the negotiations with General Martínez, convinced—though who knows why—that this letter would help to turn the political balance in his favor. On the back side of the flyer was printed the reply that had been allowed to be sent to the Emperor, informing him of my father's death, a protomartyr of the liberal cause.

Catín was working one morning in the carpenter's shop, adjusting the span of a wardrobe, when someone handed him the sheet of paper, which was being delivered from door to door. He put it on the bench and bent over with the intention of reading it, holding it down with the aid of his sweat-dampened stump. He read it twice, haltingly, sputtering the words to himself, but still without fully understanding it, and then the third time out loud so my mother in the kitchen could hear it, running some words together and dropping the accents from others. If the Emperor of France wanted to show his gratitude to the father, he remarked at the end, he would also be interested in showing it to his son, and it would only be necessary to let him know that this son existed, by way of a letter that it would fall to my mother to write, since she would know how to word it and she could write with a clear hand.

She came from the kitchen with a ladle in her hand, disheveled and with her housecoat hanging loosely over her hips, which were now quite broad since she was beginning to put on weight, and she laughed in Catín's face, which made him so mad he wanted to slap her. But the fact that the letter was going to be written was already decided, precisely because that laughter did nothing more than to expose the dreams in my mother's breast that had been pushed aside; she was suddenly forced to think about my future. Catín, certain that he had won the battle, went out to buy paper and a pen, and she, now having lost the urge to laugh, sat herself down that night to compose the letter which my stepfather signed in his capacity as an honorable citizen of the city of León, while she, once more inclined to laughter (though now it had acquired a tinge of fury) insisted vehemently that she would never expose herself to the ridicule that her name would have if she were exhibited as something strange at the French court. But perhaps, as I think now, her recalcitrance stemmed out from fear of being ridiculed but from pride: her nuptial journey had been thwarted, she was raped by her fiancé, turned into a cook for the laborers, and now living in sin with a one-armed carpenter, but despite this chain of misfortunes and losses, she knew that never would my uncle the King Frederick have permitted her to lower herself to beg for favors.

Nearly a year later another letter with the imperial stamps of France reached León. And although it came addressed to Catín, the administrator of the mails determined once again that it could only be handed over to General Jerez, who was preparing at that time to embark on a trip to Washington as the Minister of the diplomatic legation of Nicaragua, his consolation prize after the triumph of General Martínez, first at the negotiating table and then at the ballot boxes, with which thirty years of Conservative government got under way.

The news that Napoleon III had written to the one-armed carpenter in the Zaragoza barrio caught on over the whole city, and when Jerez, followed by his escort of horsemen, arrived at the house bearing the letter, a huge crowd had gathered outside. Catín and my mother had been warned about the visit, and the patio was duly swept and the sawdust watered down to reduce the dust. To one side, in the shed where he operated the carpenter's shop, a stack of coffins still lacking their coats of varnish rose up against the wall.

Since quite early in the morning Catín had been dressed

in the campaign uniform of the liberal army, washed and ironed by my mother, and he strolled along the sidewalk in front of the troop of curious individuals that was expanding every minute, proudly showing off the flaccid sleeve over the arm he had lost, tucked in the waistband of his pants. He had lost that arm in the siege of Granada, when a shell from a cannon pierced through the roof and spread shrapnel throughout the house in the Jalteva barrio where the retinue of ladies of the night who always accompanied Jerez on his campaigns was camping out, and for whose safety a flying squad of riflemen was responsible. Though he could scarcely bear the pain and was on the verge of fainting, it was only when the last of the women had been moved out of harm's way, together with their trunks filled with rebozos, wigs, and petticoats (which were their combat trappings), their mandolins, guitars, and vihuelas, that he would allow them to take him to the central nave of the church where the battle surgeon amputated his now useless arm at the elbow and cauterized the stump with a hot branding iron.

General Jerez got down off his mount and walked with a stiff air and sluggish step, his shoulders raised, toward the rocking chair that had been set up for him in the patio beneath the sparse shade of the coco plum trees, as if he were making a great effort to maintain his distended head upon his shoulders and keep it from rolling on the ground. Dandruff sprinkled the epaulets of his black frock coat. And when he was seated, Catín had to remain standing at his side, blending in with the rest of the military entourage. They were all moving about nervously as if they were supposed to be taking care of a host of unfinished affairs from which the time spent at the carpenter's house was holding them back, although they had really very little to occupy themselves with any longer. For on his departure to Washington, Jerez would leave behind all those faithful followers as orphans who would then have to take off their campaign uniforms and go back to their old jobs as barbers, tailors, or saddle makers.

My mother, meanwhile, had brought in a tray with a single glass of muscatel wine on it, along with a bowl of aniseed cookies. Jerez took a sip and set the glass and the bowl on the little table in order to pull from the pocket of his frock coat the letter that he handed to Catín with a solemn gesture, as if it were still intact, even though he had taken it upon himself to break into the envelope, heating the imperial seals with a candle and afterward patching them up as best he could. So he already knew the letter contained nothing of interest to his political future or that might block his path to exile, although at some moments, heaven knows why, he still preserved that vain hope.

Catín yielded the honor of opening the letter to Jerez and requested that he read it aloud. The Emperor ordered that his offer be conveyed clearly, that the son of his well-remembered friend, the deceased Francisco Castellón, be educated in France in the name of the State, once he had reached the age of fifteen. That letter—stripped of any sentimental consideration, the work of some secretary of the Empress Eugenia, since it was written in a very pure and ceremonial Spanish—was what decided my fate.

Every year that went by, Catín had my mother write a new letter which he once more signed, informing the Emperor of my health and my scholarly progress, since I was being given private instruction by the Polish émigré don José Leonard, the esteemed Master of Freemasonry, to whose care Jerez had recommended my education before leaving, since both had belonged to the senate of hermetic philosophers of the 35th degree in the León Masonic lodge.

Master Leonard, a widower living on Calle de Espejo, in the San Felipe barrio, taught me Mathematics, Philosophy, the History of Humanity, and French, plus Esoteric Sciences. With the recommendation to never show them to anyone else and to read them when alone, he loaned me books that fired my boy's heart with enthusiasm. *Isis Unveiled* by Madame Blavatski, the great Russian seer, *The Seven Lamps of Architecture* by John Ruskin, and *The Spiritist Flame* by Alan Cardec. And when I left for France, he handed me a letter of introduction for Madame Blavatski.

It was he who showed me the first daguerreotype that I ever saw in my life, the portrait of his compatriot Chopin done by Alexis Gouin, a stereoscopic miniature highlighted in color by hand, the twin images mounted before a viewer with a handle decorated like a Carnaval mask, as well as another portrait, in ambrotype, also the first one of these I ever saw, of the national poet of Poland, Stefan Witwicki, kept in a music box which when opened played with the sonority of handbells the first phrase of the melody for his song *Le Guerrier*, composed by Chopin himself.

Answers were received from Paris eventually, after a long wait, but they always came, and by means of the same Spanish secretary the Emperor would ask for more news, until that whole annual correspondence passed into my hands at the age of twelve, when—with the help of Master Leonard—I began to respond in French. In one of those letters I read that it was the desire of Emperor Napoleon III that I enter the School of Medicine at the Sorbonne "to serve ailing humanity." Leonard became worried. He had always believed that the Emperor would accept me for engineering studies in order to put me at the service of the Napoleonic Canal project which was to divide the city of León in two.

Master Leonard had also made those visionary dreams his own, and just as if a magic lantern were projecting images of the future within his head, he would describe to me the steamships that as they approached the Pacific waters heading into the setting sun would leave behind the active volcanoes of the Maribios range, like the backdrop behind a glorious performance on a stage set by history. However, from this letter he was able to conclude that after the disastrous defeat of the Imperial troops in Mexico which had cost the life of Maximilian of Austria, Napoleon III wanted nothing more to do with American adventures.

That is the way Leonard explained it to me in his disappointment, but at the same time he was seized by the hope that once there in Paris I might be able to ignite again in the Emperor's heart the passion for the canal. I would have understood nothing about the interweaving of the threads that were forming my destiny at the time, nor of that web of motives by which this destiny was carrying me ineluctably to France, if it hadn't been for Master Leonard's continuous concern for explaining them to me, as if he were the tutor of a prince who one day was expected to receive a crown, a notion which, though cast in the light of a mirage, he could not seem to get out of his head. And at the same time, he tried to dissuade me from any idea that my father's reputation as a traitor, his murky relationship with my mother, and that dynasty of the Mosquito Kings on my mother's side, none of these were obstacles that might prevent me from fulfilling that destiny. But the truth is that my head never managed to get remotely close to any crown, except that of the vine leaves of my saturnalian nights.

The learned Leonard undertook on his own to persuade Napoleon III, himself a Masonic Master, in the high-level 60th degree of Sublime Guardian of the Three Fires, that he should renew his interest in the canal, but for a reply he obtained only silence. He was in the habit of maintaining disciplined, stern dialogues with him, because something like that was possible through the magnetic powers of the mind when it would fly out toward astral planes, but only if one dealt with high themes, because neither banalities nor matters of personal import, such as my journey, were able to be conveyed in these conversations. By the same means he had reproached him for the invasion of Mexico and the establishing there of that whimsical empire which so soon was sunk in failure, though being pained at the same time by the fatal destiny that had befallen Maximilian, the tragic naïf grabbing at a frivolous throne, and his poor wife Carlota, remembered now only in the laments of the *corridos*. And when they were about to execute him in Querétero, he had also communicated mentally with Benito Juárez, another Mason (49th Degree of the Great Luminary of the Pyramids), who responded to him politely but firmly that it was not in his power to do anything for the life of the prisoner, and that he had already given the same answer to the astral petitions of two other brothers, Victor Hugo and Garibaldi. So that when the news of Maximilian's execution arrived, carried some weeks later by mule drivers coming from Soconusco, and was proclaimed in León with rockets bursting and quarrels in the streets, Master Leonard, who already was aware of it, shut his door to whomever might come to let him know.

When in the month of January 1870 I finally started my journey to France, following the route taken so many years before by my father, reaching the Caribbean by passing through the Gran Lago and down the San Juan river, Master Leonard took leave of me with some uneasiness but without daring to declare his certain belief that the Second Empire was drawing near its end, since he knew the bad vibrations about Napoleon III's destiny that were now circulating among the sidereal spheres like an infinite myriad of electric flies.

Neither did he ever tell me about something he actually

knew about for certain, and that is that Catín had sought out someone to write a letter to the Emperor that he didn't want my mother to know about, in which he asked for money for my upkeep ever since I was a child at her breast, a goodly sum in gold louis which the new French ambassador for Central America brought with him, Monsieur Félix Belly, who also had the mission of handing me the emoluments for my voyage.

Catín was unable to enjoy his prize, nevertheless, because shortly after my departure he died of tetanus after running a rusty nail through the palm of his only hand as he was trying to pull it out of a door frame in the baptistery of the cathedral. Then my mother, now the owner of that bag of gold louis, whose possession her husband confessed to her only *in articulo mortis*, undertook a journey of return to the Kingdom of Mosquitia, also by way of the San Juan River. After reading the only letter I received from her in Paris, it still wasn't clear to me if she had a real intention of going on to Bluefields, the seat of the old court of the kings of her family, but the truth is she stayed in Greytown, the old San Juan del Norte, from where she wrote me.

There, making use of her sudden fortune, she established a boarding house which she named The Pond of the Merry Nymphs of the Forest, a name which surely derived from her former excursions through the library of my uncle the King, where Coleridge and Swinburne were not lacking, and which her clients, principally coarse and vulgar sailors, with no concern for Parnassian subtleties, abbreviated and altered to The Naked Nymphs, according to the complaints in her letter.

It was *in articulo mortis* as well that Catín admitted that with the money he had received he planned to flee to Greytown himself in the company of his stepdaughter, the daughter of that former lover of his, blemished by the *bien-*

teveo through my mother's arts, the girl by that time having reached the same age as I, fifteen years. He also hoped to have a new mechanical arm moved by pulleys and springs implanted, the invention of Doctor Claude Fell, a French émigré who had established himself in the port with re-nown success as a manufacturer of prostheses because the cases of sailors and fishermen losing their limbs to sharks were quite numerous.

The first thing that occurred to my mother Catherine the moment she got out of the bongo that brought her to Greytown was to look for Doctor Fell's office on the turbulent Shepherd Street, and she asked the shop assistant to take out of the showcase—where examples of legs, arms, feet and hands in various styles, sizes, and colors were exhibited—an arm of the sort that Catín wanted, in order to weigh it, caress the rubber skin, bend its elbow. Her resentment, though it had lost much of its remorseless perfume, was still strong enough to make her smile with malicious deliberation.

9

The beloved young man

The virgin of virgins is constant and pure.
No one shall tarnish her sacrosanct shape
Nor hear from her lips the whispered concession,
Sweeping her brow of the the rose of esteem.

Rubén Darío, *The Colloquy of the Centaurs*

T HE HUGE GATE OF Son Marroig, to the side of a tight curve
on the highway that runs from Valldemosa toward Deyá,
close to the abyss above which scarcely protrude the whis-
pering tops of pine trees stretching in waves toward the sea,
is always open for those visitors who can get their vehicles
down to the haven of the parking lot at the end of the ramp,
and they will not be bothered by any caretaker or guard.

We said our adieus to Peter quite early on the Palma
pier, since he was off to Barcelona by way of the ferry, and
thence to Hinterartzten. For the few days that remained to
us on Mallorca Tulita and I were going to settle in at C'an
Blau Vell, the home of Claribel Alegría in Deyá, long empty
since her husband Bud Flakoll's death, and only a short way
from the one where Robert Graves always lived. I had come
from there just now for my interview with Dominik, who

had been alerted by the Marqués Bauzá de Mirabo that I would arrive to meet with him that morning, the third day after my visit to La Cartuja.

I spied him standing against the balustrade on the second floor, surely waiting for me, and the moment he caught sight of me he came down and received me on the esplanade, always ceremonious in his greeting, and quite as if it had not been ten long years since our first encounter. This time he was wearing a short-sleeved shirt printed with vegetal themes in bright colors hanging loose over the belt, wrinkled linen pants, and tennis shoes without socks, as if sporting the disguise of a happy summer tourist, like the ones pictured in the excursion pamphlets put out by the travel agencies for people of the third world.

Once upstairs, we went directly to the library, whose tall windows open out on the balustrade. It is filled with sunlight, silence, and the smell of old paper. Many of the books and bound manuscripts were to be found off the shelves, in piles placed on the floor, or atop the reading tables, a sign that Dominik had not slackened his energies.

"No one ever comes here anyway," he says by way of an excuse for the visible disorderliness.

A bust of the Archduke is on a pedestal. And to one side, in a cage with gilded copper bars and a tin cupola in the form of a bell, very Victorian, a stuffed vulture clutches an old branch from a carob tree.

"Do you recall that vulture that Darío mentions in his story?" he asks. "Here it is."

"In the same cage?" I wonder, going over to it. The vulture's faded plumage is musty and sad, and its artificial eyes, burning red like tiny embers, give it a sinister appearance.

"No, this is a replica of the original, but smaller," he says. "The one in the garden was so big you could put a Bengal tiger in it. Sometimes the vulture's keeper, Ibrahim Achmet, had to sleep in it, on a straw pad, as punishment for his drunken sprees. But according to the Archduke in his diary, that was something that in any event never really bothered the recluse."

"The Archduke kept a diary?" I ask, with repressed covetousness.

"It is not only in novels that a character keeps a diary which turns out to be very useful at the right moment," he says, opening a drawer and showing it to me, from a distance. "He tells here how he came into possession of the vulture. Teresa, the daughter of that compatriot of yours, Castellón, took it out of the nest, risking her life, scaling a very steep cliff, to give it to him on his name day, on San Luis day."

"Teresa..." I turn back toward Dominik, casually. "You mean the girl with the ribbons on her hat who according to Darío was frolicking around the feet of the photographer in the parade, that was Teresa?"

"And later the wife of Baltasar Bonnin, the butcher, and the mother of Rubén, the little boy in the snapshot on Szeroki Dunaj Street," he adds, rubbing his hands together with the delight of someone who is at the outset of a much desired exercise.

"And I suppose the Turk wearing the fez and the embroidered slippers, who looks like an executioner according to that story by Darío, is the very same keeper of the vulture."

"You are not mistaken," he says. "Achmet was a Turk from Bitlis, boatswain on board the *Nixe II*. In 1908 he beat a Cypriot seaman over the head with a chair leg in Piraeus, and the Archduke himself handed him over to the law, with tears in his eyes. It was not enough any longer to make him sleep inside the bird cage."

Dominik had his work table in a corner, loaded down

with folders, and that is where we went to sit now, he in a Florentine armchair and I on the footstool facing him.

"Did you find out all that for your book?" I ask.

"That and much, much more," he responds with a bit of a smile, holding out to me the Archduke's diary which, bound in red kid leather with a strap to keep the place while the book is shut, looks like a missal. "I see that your interest in Castellón has not lessened."

"He never stops fascinating me, like a character who should be in a novel," I say, with a diffident smile, as if I were responding to an unwelcome question.

"You should not be ashamed of the apparent banality of the object of your search," he says. "A spring with a hidden mechanism always moves us to investigate what seems superfluous, and then it turns out not to be so. Who is this photographer Castellón that you should become so interested in him? And what use will it be to humanity if I write a book about Wenceslas Vyborny?"

As I listen to him speaking, I've begun to leaf through the diary, filled with inscriptions in German, French, and Latin, in a hand that is difficult to puzzle out.

"Is there something there on Castellón?" I ask.

"And why would there not be!" he exclaims, as he rises from his armchair, takes the diary from my hands, looks for a page, and shows me an entry in German, which much later we will photocopy:

Sunday, August 6, 1876.

Summer heat. The thermometer measures 36 degrees on the Réumar scale. I went out to take a walk before dinner and the sight of nature is more splendid than ever. The strawberries are showing off their purple fruits, the Scotch broom lights the way with its blazing brilliance, the cytisus is opening its pink blossoms as delicate as butterfly wings. When I return,

The beloved young man

Wenceslas announces a visit by a young man bringing a letter from Count Giuseppe Primoli, and I ask him to invite the visitor to the table. We sit together, the three of us. The letter is to introduce this fellow, who is from South America. He proposes that I take him into my employ as a photographer. He was born in 1856, so he must be about 20 years of age. The young man shows me an album of his work, and I am quite impressed, as is Wenceslas. I decide to hire him.

"You might say that the arrival of Castellón here in Miramar turned everything upside down," Dominik says, shaking his head sadly.

"Is it that Wenceslas and Castellón became lovers?" I ask, taking care not to seem puerile.

"Those relationships, they were so stormy, they truly tormented the Archduke," he says, "but the situation is still more complicated."

The Archduke had taken Wenceslas Vyborny into his service in the autumn of 1871, after meeting him in Prague during a formal visit to the Imperial Military Academy. He was captivated by the figure of that well-set-up cadet who, in his capacity as corporal of the company of Dragoons assembled in the practice hall, came forward with delicate grace but also true martial bearing to present the required salute, raising his unsheathed sword which divided his face into two parts. By means of court intrigues, the Archduke arranged to let him resign and brought him to Mallorca, with the consent of his parents, whom he visited in Kuttenberg loaded down with gifts, as if this were a proposal.

Wenceslas, who possessed all the selfish arrogance that went with his early youthfulness, which was exacerbated by that singular beauty which he knew how to use like a sharp-edged blade, was not an easy lover for the defenseless Archduke. He humiliated the latter continuously, and by sulking and pretending to be angry, obtained from him anything he wanted. And when he wasn't doing that, he would threaten to leave him, driving the Archduke to tears. They shared bedrooms at Son Moragues and the stateroom on the *Nixe II*, and despite the trials his friend foisted on him, the Archduke seemed happy. Up until Castellón arrived.

Dominik returns to the diary to show me another entry:

Friday, July 6, 1877

What is he looking for that he doesn't have in the company of my solitude? Are we not one and the same, one flesh? Who can say which amongst us is Thirsis and which is Coridon?
Ambo florentes aetatibus, Arcades ambo.

"That was when Wenceslas became entangled with Castellón," I say.

"And the Archduke had also become entangled with Castellón," he returns, with something of a sly rancorousness. "If Wenceslas attracted him with the classic features of his beauty, with Castellón instead it was his primitive characteristics he was enamored of—prince of jungles unknown, he calls him in his diary. But Castellón represented only a passing fancy in his life, while his true love, if you can say that about men, was Wenceslas."

"But Castellón was ill with asthma, he was nearly an invalid," I say.

"That's the most ridiculous thing you could say," he responds, not noticing how rude his words were. "Was he going to let a respiratory illness get in the way of his role as a two-way lover? Didn't George Sand love Chopin even though he had tuberculosis, and didn't he let himself be loved by her to the point of turning himself into her rag doll?"

"A triangle closed on all sides then," I turn aside his insolent remark.

"Which would not be long before it was exchanged for another," he is smiling now. "Soon Wenceslas began to escape in a small boat to meet in Palma with another lover, female this time, as we already know. Something that cost him his life, we already know that, too."

"A lover whose identity was secret, according to Darío," I observe.

"Because he never tried to find out!" he jumps out, euphoric. "Her name was Catalina."

"The same as the Catalina who became infected by leprosy in Palestine," I say.

"It was a question of the same person," Dominik laughs outright.

"Who was she then?" I ask, trying to screen my confusion.

"A *chueta* from Can Menor in Palma, Catalina Segura, the very one who later on was Castellón's wife, and the mother of Teresa, the little girl with the beribboned hat," he studies my reaction unashamed; and now, of course, his show of delight seems offensive to me.

"Did you know all this when we met in Warsaw?"

"About Castellón I only knew what was in the document by Professor Rodaskowski that I translated for you," he responds, recovering his solemnity. "Today I know so much more. I have been at work here half a year now, going through everything in this house, rummaging through books, turning archives upside down."

"An embarrassment of pleasures, this situation in which your relative Wenceslas found himself involved," I say, because I am tempted to provoke him.

"If it is promiscuity we are speaking of, there was no one like the Archduke," he remaines imperturbable. "Remember that according to what our Rubén Darío felt, he had, and I quote from memory, 'a great and extraordinary capacity for love that embraced women and men, animals and plants.'"

"How did Catalina Segura get into this?" I ask then.

"Her father, the jeweler Melchor Segura, had his workshop and his showroom on La Calle de la Argentería," he says. "The Archduke took Wenceslas there because he wanted to present him with a ring, and so they met Catalina, who was fifteen. I have that ring."

He goes over to the table and from another drawer he takes out a small box. He opens it, raises the ring before his eyes, and then hands it to me.

"The Archduke removed it from Wenceslas's finger after he died in the C'an Frances boarding house, where he often went to be with Catalina, and he himself wore the ring from then on, covered by a piece of black cloth."

"It lacks the stone," I observe.

"The Archduke took the ring off on his visits to Austria so as not to irritate the Court," he says. "At the end, after the Great War broke out, he took refuge in Brandeis Castle in Prague, where he was to die a little later. But he had entrusted it to Elise Winkelhöfer, the seamstress belonging to his retinue. I bought it from descendents of that woman, already missing its stone, which was an alexandrite, according to my investigations."

At first they were looking for a corundum, perhaps a sapphire, or ruby. But Catalina, who was attending to them because her father was working with the stamping press in the workshop behind the store, set out on the fabric, between the others that they had asked to see, the piece of alexandrite with its yellow highlights. It fascinated Wenceslas and he changed his mind. She showed them the catalogue then, and after the choice of design, they went on to the string of sizing rings to get the proper fit on Wenceslas's finger. The Archduke, who was pretending to look out the window, realized very quickly that he had lost him, not because of anything they said or even how they kept looking at each other, but by the play of their hands on the iron rings, as if they were getting engaged, and even worse, because he had already heard, while they were still in the street before coming in, how Catalina remarked to her father, "How ugly the Archduke is! My God!"

And later on the Turk, Ibrahim Achmet, the vulture's keeper, more loyal to Wenceslas than he was to the Archduke, would borrow a donkey from the stable on Sundays to carry letters from him to Catalina and bring back notes arranging their clandestine meetings at C'an Frances.

"And Castellón in the meantime?" I ask.

"He continued in the Archduke's employ but there was nothing between them," he says. "When the Archduke was told that Wenceslas was dying of sunstroke in Palma and hurried to his side, Castellón went with him. This is what the diary says:

Wednesday, July 25, 1877

How full of apprehension I was mounting these squalid stairways after making my way through a rear patio where stray cats are numerous, busy poring over trash in the smelly garbage cans. Wenceslas is lying on a metal bed. A table with a washbasin, a leprous mirror, and two chairs with thatched seats are all the furnishings in that room. The *chueta* woman is not there with him. According to the landlord, Wenceslas came here all by himself, dragging himself along, almost unconscious, and that odious woman, may heaven curse her, ran off when she saw him so ill. Doctor Moix, whom I had sent for beforehand, is standing by the bed, sending despairing signals to me with his head when he sees me come in. He has tried to keep him covered with pieces of ice wrapped in blankets, he tells me, but without success. The whole floor next to the bed is covered in sawdust and flooded with the water from the ice packs.

Castellón had brought his portable camera, but I have forbidden him to take any shots inside the bedroom. This business of wanting to take a picture of a friend so beloved of both of us, right at the point of death, is that not a cruel thing? The artist seems like a wild animal for whom nothing else matters when he is seeking his prey. I would call him a born marauder.

Night falls and the final moment arrives. Wenceslas's congealed gaze, intensely blue, fixed upon the void, will remain forever in my brain. With my tremulous hand drawing close to his eyelids, I shut his eyes. I take the ring from off his finger. It is my most highly prized possession.

"It is natural that she would have felt terrified at the idea of a scandal if the police appeared looking for a body in that pigsty," I say. "But from what he writes about her, the jealousy that he felt must have been something awful."

"And then without wasting a moment he chose her to fill the void that Wenceslas left," he replies disgustedly.

Once the funeral services were over and done with and Wenceslas's body had been sent back to Bohemia, where he personally turned it over to the parents, the Archduke visited the jeweler and convinced the father to let him have custody of Catalina under the promise that he personally would assume the responsibility for her education, with the help of an English governess.

"Did he load him down with gifts the same as he had the parents of Wenceslas?" I say.

"Melchor Segura was not a rich man, and the idea that a nobleman could ask for his daughter in order to give her an education filled him with pretentious airs. What better gift?" he says. "Besides, he was a widower."

"Then he took her to Miramar and made her his lover."

"And she in turn made him the lover of Castellón. There you have the new triangle I told you about," he says.

"And everyone lived happily ever after, as happened with Pauline Viardot, her husband, and Turgenev," I say. "How admirable."

"There was harmony for a while," he says, "until Castellón and Catalina decided to get married."

In an irate letter sent from Venice in September, 1878, the same day as the wedding, the Archduke tells Castellón, "If you wish to bring on my death take her with you, but you will have on your conscience all the people who might be injured by my demise, now that you have married the one I loved most in all the world."

They had slipped out to celebrate their marriage secretly in La Salute, accompanied by the whole entourage, while the Archduke was taking his afternoon siesta in the Palazzo Pisani, which he rented year round but was so huge and had so many bedrooms, many of then in ruinous condition, with puddles on the steps and the frescoes on the ceiling now almost faded away, that he would only open up about half of it. When he awakened and found the rooms deserted where the members of his retinue habitually stayed in order to muffle their gossip and laughter so as not to bother him, he descended the staircases as rapidly as his swollen legs would allowed and found out from the porter what had happened. He was already at the door of the church when he realized that the ceremony was about to reach its consummation, and he started to beat at the pilasters of the façade with his umbrella. It was with the permission of the parish priest that the Archduke's own chaplain had officiated at the wedding. Determined to beat him, too, he followed Father De la Bruyère as far as La Dogana, the Customs House.

In the end, after much arguing, the Archduke allowed Castellón that he would agree to accept the marriage as long as they did not desert the entourage. And also as long as Catalina continued using her last name Segura as if she remained unmarried. Castellón respected this last clause of the agreement to the point that Teresa, the couple's daughter, was always Teresa Segura. On returning to Mallorca, Catalina began to occupy Sa Estaca, a kind of wedding gift, if you want to look at it that way.

"Without Castellón," I say.

"Of course it was without Castellón," he responds. "He stayed in the rooms assigned to the retinue as if he were still a bachelor, and in order for them to meet alone as husband and wife, they had to arrange a date in Palma, the same as Wenceslas had done."

"In the same room at the C'an Frances," I say.

"You are not going to believe me if I tell you that, yes, it was in the same room," he says, "but with something more luxurious in the way of new furniture that the innkeeper ordered put in. He had sold the first set at a good price."

Many were the years they spent in this shared arrangement, with the Archduke visiting her on the sly at Sa Estaca and Castellón seeing her, also furtively, in the boarding house in Palma. When Catalina died, both men were in their fifties and were in a sorry state physically, Castellón's asthma having been aggravated by the constant changes of climate (and Venice was not among the best), and the Archduke was suffering from ulcers and chafed skin on his legs as a consequence of diabetes mellitus. Not a few times did he have to be lifted off the *Nixe II* on a stretcher.

"But at some point," I say, "Castellón deserted. When he took those pictures of Turgenev after he died, he was working in Paris for the *Revue des Deux Mondes*."

"Year of 1883," he offers, without consulting any of his papers. "They fought, but it was about a problem that had nothing to do with Catalina, who remained in Sa Estaca the two years that Castellón lived in Paris, half dead from hunger, until the Archduke allowed him to return because of her constant begging."

"What problem?" I ask him.

"The Archduke would not tolerate drunks," he says.

The worst of it was that Castellón was inciting the other members of the retinue to drink, and above all, Achmet the Turk. The drop that overflowed the glass was when the two of them, both drunk, took the vulture out of the cage and carried it to the cliff so it could fly away and escape. But the vulture refused, as it found itself quite comfortable in captivity. Castellón went on drinking just the same after his return from Paris, but the Archduke declared him clinically ill, *pathologisch trunksüchtig,* and that was the kind way he found to cease blaming him and to pity him instead.

"Very tactful on his part," I say.

"That may be, but at the time of the Archduke's death Castellón did not show any at all," he is unyielding. "Just another vulture, like any of the others of the entourage that tried to open the belly of the cadaver by pecking at it. Better for me to read you a page of the declaration he presented in 1915 to the executor of the will, Baron Adolf Edler von Bachrach, through the Austrian consul in Palma, claiming compensation:

> I base my just claim on the fact that His Highness always treated my deceased wife Catalina as a very close member of his family, and she received her alimentation, fully and luxuriously, at his own table, where she occupied the place of honor; he conceded her the use of the residence Sa Estaca on his estate at Miramar, on Mallorca, and the rooms of all His Highness's residences were at her total disposition, not only to live in but also for social receptions, and the same goes for a private stateroom on board the *Nixe II,* where the crew obeyed her in everything and satisfied her desires and necessities; she herself had the same use

of His Highness's carriages, and while on voyages to foreign ports, of the rented vehicles such as might be needed, and he always provided her with a complete wardrobe and shoes as her pleasure dictated.

And of greater value than everything I have mentioned, he bequeathed to her during her life the jewels that His Highness inherited from his mother, the Grand Duchess María Antonia, Princess of Two Sicilies, and that figure in the attached inventory; and there should be added an emerald bracelet acquired by His Highness in the auction of the goods of his brother Juan, lost on the high seas; jewels that must be held apart from the compensations herewith solicited...

I raise this claim, not for my personal benefit, although it is true that His Highness only rarely paid me a proper salary, and I was forced to live in the greatest poverty beside him while I was a member of his retinue, but for the well-being of my daughter Teresa, who is now at a needy age, and whom His Highness honored and loved as his own daughter.

"Whose daughter was Teresa, really?" I ask.

"Who knows?" Dominik sighed.

"Castellón must have accepted the jewels that the Archduke gave to Catalina," I say. "What did he do with them?"

"Those jewels never came into Catalina's possession. That must have been nothing more than a promise."

They had been deposited by the Archduke in a safety box at the Länderbank, the Imperial family's bank, and every time he found himself at Brandeis Castle with his retinue, he would go to Vienna to show them to Catalina, as a way of renewing the promise. But then later on, without anyone knowing it, he took them out of the Länderbank and carried them to a broker in the Dorotheum, Vienna's famous pawnshop. Because he was always in need of money, for his eccentricities were expensive; he never bought clothes, but he did purchase archeological treasures that cost a fortune, every one of them. And on Sundays he often sat no less than two hundred at his table, in batches, anyone who wanted to come. And that is not to mention the cost of his trips aboard the *Nixe II*, with its crazy-quilt itinerary. No one knew anything about the fate of those jewels until Baron Von Bachrach came across the receipt from the Dorotheum among the Archduke's papers, and he informed the Emperor.

"I would bet that Castellón never received a reply to his petition," I say.

"The Crown was never going to open any correspondence about a request for compensation that brought such an insult with it, the legacy of the Grand Duchess having been promised to a housekeeper, who was also Jewish," he says. "And it drew a heavy curtain over the other insult, the fact that a member of the Imperial family had gone to the pawnbrokers, just like any shopkeeper in a tight spot. The Emperor ordered them to recover the jewels secretly."

"Castellón lost a second opportunity to become rich," I say. "Because if Napoleon III had not fallen, he probably would have become the top doctor in the Empire."

"He went on being a luckless artist, as he had been up until then, still sluggish, if you wish to call it that, in whatever concerned his daily affairs, lacking any tact or any consideration involving himself—but that in no way cheapens the quality of his photographs. I have some of those other gems here for you—" he says, holding out to me a folder with accordion pleats, tied with a ribbon.

Several are of the Archduke's entourage, and the first one pertains to the voyage to Palestine they undertook together in 1899, when Catalina became infected with leprosy. They are posing in front of the Dome of the Rock Mosque in Jerusalem, and with the help of the shipping manifest of the *Nixe II*, Dominik had succeeded in identifying them, according to the list paper-clipped to the snapshot:

Juan Singala, captain of the yacht, age 45.
Ibrahim Achmet, boatswain, age 38.
Bartolomé Calafat, maritime agent, age 23.
Abate Louis de la Bruyère, chaplain, age 50.
Catalina Segura, housekeeper, age 38.
Antonio Vives Colom, private secretary (replacing
Wenceslas Vyborny), native of Binisalem, Mallorca, age 49.
Ana Rapoll, native of Valldemosa, wife of Vives, age 40.
Antonietta Lanzerotto, native of Venice, maid, age 23.
Francesco La Escola, native of Brindisi, interpreter of
Arabic languages, age 38.
Gabriele Angelo Abdalla Brevino, native of Alexandria,
cook, age 40.
Elise Winkerhöfer, native of Munich, seamstress, age 52.
Jeanne Billing, native of Liverpool, governess for Catalina
Segura, age 23.

The Archduke is missing, for he despised being photographed in a group. Also missing is the Hindu with the turban who looked like a fakir as described by Darío, but Dominik tells me that a curious figure like that never existed in the entourage, neither before nor after that photograph, although there were more than enough with the specimens we had before our eyes. Neither did the Archduke ever have a monkey, which Darío's imagination had also supplied.

"It's strange that this Jean Billing, the English governess, should be younger than her pupil," I say. "A girl teaching a mature woman."

"She was not the only one through the years," he responds. "In accordance with his whims, the Archduke never ceased educating Catalina so that she would shine before the Austrian Court, something that he himself knew to be impossible."

"Twenty years with private teachers," I say.

"They taught her natural sciences, numbers, table manners, formal customs of the Court," he explains. "Don't you recall that he had presented her to his cousin Sissi, the Empress, by way of proof, and he was very pleased by that *entreteint* between the two, exactly as Darío describes it?"

Catalina's fervent desire to visit the Holy Land now fulfilled, the *Nixe II* made its way through the Adriatic to end up at Trieste, from which the full group continued on to Venice, and there the Archduke bade them all goodbye, since he was going on to Görz, determined to find some solitude in order to complete his philological book, *Tender Expressions and Affectionate Words in the Friulian Language*, which was published posthumously by the Crown in Prague. In his diary, the Archduke describes his farewell to Catalina, which would be the final one:

Friday, October 26, 1900

Last night, when she left, La Salute, covered with gray, showed from my window a pale glow from the light of the moon. I still believe I feel the last squeeze of her hand. And in that sad moment I recalled, as if under a spell, the time when I discovered myself truly in love with her, there in Miramar, months after I had asked her father to let her come live at my side and allow me to mold her with my own hands, like Pygmalion with Galatea: it was a December afternoon, nearing Christmas. As I was approaching, hidden by a turn in the path that climbs up to Sa Estaca from the bay, I heard her singing. She was singing the following verse in the peasant dialect:

Christmas Eve is coming,
Christmas Eve is gone,
We too shall go away
And not return again.

I remained standing there quietly, waiting to see her appear. When she took note of me she ceased singing and with a smile came to where I was. She had come to collect the salt in the clefts of the rocks the ocean leaves on stormy days, something she had learned from the peasants in my employ.

"Only a squeeze of the hand to say goodbye," I remark.

"A goodbye forever," he goes on. "Catalina died in 1905, and during those five years they never saw each other again."

"She was finally leaving him for Castellón," I am confident.

"It is odd, but that was not the way it was," he corrects me. "Castellón stayed with the Archduke in Venice, and he went with him to Görz. Catalina returned alone to Mallorca, now pregnant."

"A late pregnancy, when she must have been going on forty," I say. "When did Castellón return to be with her?"

"When her father, Melchor Segura, wrote him that her illness had become worse," he has the details. "That letter, which remained in the Archduke's archive, has a date of March, 1904, on it, one year before Catalina's death."

"Then Teresa was born in Castellón's absence," I say.

"Castellón stayed in Görz, with the Archduke," he assents. "Teresa came into the world in Sa Estaca, but Melchor Segura came for the mother and daughter and moved them to his house, above his business."

"But in Sa Estaca they would have been better attended," I object.

"False," he responds. "In the absence of the Archduke, the disorder became widespread, and nothing was done. Although they might suddenly be able to bring from the harbor at Palma crates filled with costly relics or antiques, things that he himself had consigned from some distant port, here in Miramar there weren't even any garbanzos for the pot. The doctor's charges for his attendance at Catalina's birth were never resolved. Doctor Juan Cruz."

"I imagine life would have been difficult for Catalina in Palma, with all the fears about leprosy going around," I say.

"It is possible that Catalina's illness was not leprosy," he says. "It could have been a matter of *dermatitis sifilitica*. At least that was the opinion of Gerhard Hansen, that learned Norwegian (nothing less than the discoverer of the leprosy bacterium), according to a consultation the Archduke had with him from Görz, describing her symptoms to him."

"A long distance diagnosis," I exclaim.

"In any event he recommended that the sick woman be taken to the Leprosy Hospital at Bergen, which he directed, in order to confirm that opinion, a matter that the Archduke never took the proper steps to attend to," he says.

"Occupied as he was with his book on tender expressions and affectionate words," I note the irony.

"He left the case in the hands of Doctor Cruz," he says.

"A male midwife!"

"Well, what sort of specialist could have been found on Mallorca in those days? Remember the difficulties George Sand went through looking for someone who could take care of Chopin. They prescribed an infusion of marshmallow for his tuberculosis! Doctor Cruz limited himself to giving Catalina oil of ginocardio mixed with milk and applied by rubbing on the spots where there were ulcers."

"And if it was syphilis, which of the two would have been the most promiscuous so as to infect her?" I ask. "Castellón or the Archduke?"

"You keep talking like a cloistered nun," he remarks, looking at me in distress. "Flaubert and Schubert were syphilitics. It was the illness of the century, the century of the pale spirochete. And also the century of tuberculosis, Chopin's century."

"How did Melchor Segura arrange things so that his daughter wouldn't be sent to a leper's colony?" I ask.

"He knew how to hide it so well that few people were ever aware that she had returned to live with him," he says. "Only the doctor had access to the house, and so as not to raise suspicions, Melchor took the child to the home of his sister, Manuela Segura, who took care of breast-feeding her; fortunately, she was bringing up her fifth child at the time."

Catalina ended up becoming an alcoholic. She would get drunk on a rum from Jamaica called "Cabeza de Indio," terrible stuff, that her father would go out to purchase at a nearby bar. She would vomit and defecate in the bed and the poor old fellow had to wash her, clean her wounds, and replace her bandages all by himself.

When Castellón appeared again at last, she refused to receive him. She didn't want to show herself in that way, her body lacerated by the leprosy ulcers, her face deformed by what is called clinically "lion's face," her brow bulging and her nose eaten away. Until her father convinced her to cover herself with a dense widow's veil. That was the only way she accepted this final interview, she in her bed, and he standing at the door to the bedroom, saying the saddest things, almost shouting, as if they were arguing.

"When did Castellón return to live at Miramar with the child?"

"Never. Perhaps it was that he didn't want any dispute with the Archduke about the paternity," he says. "He stayed with her in Call Menor, in his father-in-law's house; but it wasn't long before Melchor died as well. Number 17 Calle de la Argentería."

"How did it come about then that they appear in Darío's story bringing up the rear of the parade?" I ask.

"That was just a matter of an occasional visit," he says. "And this was a special day, the traditional ceremony in homage to Wenceslas Vyborny."

In the premises where the former jewelry store used to

be, which closed down with the death of his father-in-law, Castellón set up his photography studio and dedicated himself to raising Teresa. And for that reason, from his remaining so long in the neighborhood, he acquired the reputation of himself being a *chueta*, which he never denied.

Dominik offers me coffee, and I tell him that I prefer mineral water. And while he is gone to look for it in some other room of that desolate house, in which you can hear the footsteps resounding, I spend the time going through the other photos in the pockets of the folder, and I pause before the portrait that Castellón did of Catalina Segura.

She must have been about thirty then, and there is something about her that interferes with her beauty in a subtle way. It might be her cheeks that are slightly overfull, or her short wavy hair that was too dense, like her eyebrows, which notwithstanding embellish her lively black eyes with their eager and at the same time frightened gleam; while her nose—which later on the leprosy would consume—does not spoil the effect, but neither does it do anything for it. Below the diminutive earrings hanging from the lobes of her delicate ears is suspended a light veil in two layers that covers her neck and descends in a point to the décolletage of her close-fitting black dress, and underneath the veil is a necklace with two strands of dark beads, one that encloses her throat and the other that reaches the point of the veil. Meanwhile she appears to be in a pensive mode, though somewhat distracted or maybe perplexed when faced with her own thoughts.

And here is a photograph in small format that Castellón took of the Archduke, surely without his knowing, in the bedroom of the Palazzo Zindis, in Trieste. It shows him seated on a Tudor chair, barely covered with a damask robe thrown over his shoulders which would look like a cape if it were not for the flaccid sleeves hanging, and which showed his belly and hairy chest uncovered, his swollen legs up on a footstool, and at the feet of the chair a glazed earthenware urinal with its neck cocked like that of a duck. His little eyes, almost hidden in that bearded face, just the way Darío saw them, seem to be contemplating something in the mirror that fills him with admiration and horror at the same time. On his bare lap he holds a palm frond, like those associated with martyrdom, and behind his own bust there is another bust, but a marble one, placed in a niche.

"The marble head behind him is that of Antinuous, the beloved of the Emperor Hadrian," Dominik says, returning with a bottle of "Solán de Cabras" water. "The Archduke had it rescued from the sea after the first *Nixe* went down off the reefs at Cape Caxine on the Algerian coast."

"And that palm frond?"

"It was blessed in a sanctuary on Lipari, in the Aeolian Islands, on Palm Sunday, 1897," he responds.

And that was all. Dominik's investigations didn't go much further than what concerned Wenceslas Vyborny. He left me to find out by myself that when the Archduke died at Brandeis Castle at five in the afternoon on Thursday, October 21, 1915, the members of the strange entourage remained stranded there, deprived of any means of returning to their places of origin, and without anyone to pay them their back wages. Baron Von Bachrach, feeling sorry for them, had taken an affidavit from each of them and sent their dossiers to Vienna, with the recommendation that they be lent some pecuniary assistance. The Archduke, to the general surprise, had left all his goods to Antonio Vives Colom, the private secretary who took Wenceslas Vyborny's place, and who by this time was getting close to seventy.

But then came the upheavals provoked by the Great War, initiated the previous year after the assassination of Franz Ferdinand, the heir to the Imperial throne and the

Archduke's cousin, and those dossiers never got anyone's attention and became forgotten in some office in the Hofburg. Later on several of the members of the entourage took to pointless schemes and unscrupulous behavior, strolling around every day, returning at night to sleep in the castle rooms that had been allotted to them while the Archduke was alive. When winter made its presence known—and that year it was harsher than any—no one had the foresight to order coal to keep the castle warm, and Antonio Vives, who never received a penny of the fortune he had inherited, died of pneumonia. That is, he died from the cold.

"I don't believe I know anything more that might be useful for you," Dominik says. "Would a photocopy of the Archduke's diary interest you?"

"I think I have enough now."

"The advantage novelists have is that they can always invent things," he says.

"For example, Castellon's death."

"On that point you have no need to invent anything," he says, and with a flourish like that of a magician on stage, he places on top of the pile of folders a post card.

"More surprises."

"The last of them, I promise you," he says. "And a surprise for which you will be grateful."

The post card shows the Merlini Pavilion amid the green fronds of the Royal Lazienki Park, underneath a summer sun. On the back is a typewritten note signed by Professor Rodaskowski, the letters imprinted in red and black at the strike of the keys, depending on the bi-colored ribbon on the ancient machine. And since the note is written in French, the cedillas and circumflex accents lacking on the keyboard appeared added by hand.

"It is dated a long time back."

"He gave it to me to send on to you, almost immediately

Sergio Ramírez

after your departure from Warsaw," he says. "But since I thought my duty to you had ended, I wasn't really interested in sending it. Besides, you didn't even leave me your address."

"You could have gone to the Nicaraguan Embassy," I say.

"The world of offices makes me sick," he defends himself. "And moreover, you were a high official, I was merely a translator. What rank did you have then?"

"Vice-President. But why did you keep this card and bring it with you then, without knowing we would meet here?"

"I also brought the rough copy of the translation I made of that long letter of Professor Rodaskowski for you, together with this card, and anything else I thought might be useful to me in my research on Wenceslas Vyborny," he says. "But what is written on the card goes far beyond my mission. Instead, it draws closer to yours."

I started reading the note now while listening to his last words: "My dear friend Ramírez: In my previous communication I forgot to tell you that Von Dengler took Castellón with him when he became commander of the Mauthausen Concentration Camp. This must have been in his capacity as a personal photographer. I remain always at your service."

"This information only opens a new path for me to follow," I say. "The true and final end of Castellón, this doesn't tell me anything about that."

"Well, at least you have enough now to invent the rest."

"Invention never is gratuitous." I get to my feet.

"I would not be able to give you an opinion on that matter because I am not a novelist," he raises his hands with a rapid movement by way of apology, as if he wanted to rid himself of a bothersome, extravagant notion.

"Would Professor Rodaskowski have known whether Castellón left for Mauthausen together with his grandson?" I ask him as we leave the library together.

"Professor Rodaskowski died years ago," he says. "You would have to find that out in the archives which surely must be preserved at the concentration camp itself."

"Rubén is the key witness," I take another tack. "If only he is still alive and I am able to find him."

"To me it still seems much easier for you to invent what you discover missing," he says, shrugging his shoulders.

"Calle de la Argentería, number 17, in the Call Menor," I say, looking at the notes in my little book, standing now at the foot of the staircase. "Correct?"

"Very close to the Santa Eulalia church," he acknowledges. "Are you going now to look for that address?"

"Before that I am supposed to have a bite to eat with a journalist friend of mine in Palma."

"What makes you assume you will uncover something about Rubén there?" he asks. "The most probable thing is that the boy perished at Mauthausen, or if he survived, he never returned."

"You can't lose anything by trying."

Before saying goodbye on the esplanade, Dominik stands thinking awhile, his brow furrowed in the dazzling sun.

"Will I be a character in your novel?" he suddenly bursts out.

"You already are. You're in it," I respond.

10

Dorsal decubitus

PRINCESS MATILDE'S COACHMAN, a fat, good-natured soul with a nose reddened from the abuse of wine, came to the Saint-Lazare station to take me to the accommodations they had gotten me in the Rue de Malebranche, near the Sorbonne, since it was already known that the Emperor's plan for me was to study medicine and surgery. It was this fellow, nick-named *Le Tonneau*, who put in my hands the letter my mother had mailed in Greytown.

I wrote her repeatedly in reply but without any luck. In one of my letters I told her what she would never have been able to imagine, that instead of enrolling at the School of Medicine I found myself engaged in learning the art of photography. And in the last of these I declared my wish to have her pose for me sometime to make a heliograph of her, the process I found the most attractive in my improvised apprenticeship to Count Primoli: an image fixed on a glass plate covered with bitumen of Judea, washed with oil of lavender or turpentine, and then treated with gallic acid to give it the appearance of a watercolor.

I succeeded in seeing the Emperor only once, and not because it was arranged, since several times the audiences planned by Princess Matilde for me personally to show him my gratitude had fallen through, and the occasion I'm talking about was not the most propitious for that. I don't believe he was even able to take notice of my presence because of the serious nature of the events immediately following.

He had been suffering from an illness, hidden from the public, that caused him to urinate blood, and the pain was such that it prevented him from holding himself erect in the saddle of his horse, an appalling situation for someone who was about to begin a war which in France was already being heralded as a triumph; for not only would he need to review his victorious troops ceremonially in the grand farewell parade at Long Champs, to which the populace was invited, but even more significantly he would be expected to set himself before them as their leading horseman.

His chief physician, Baron Lucien Corvisart, was unable to discover the cause of the illness, which he attributed mostly to glucemia (and tried to prove it by placing ants close to the basin into which the Emperor urinated every morning to see if they got sick). Princess Matilde, believing that groping in the dark this way would end in the death of the patient, used all her persuasive powers and succeeded in convincing him to let himself be examined by Professor Bernard Gran, an active Republican and ferocious antagonist of Bonapartism, but reputed to be the most eminent physician in Paris; and once she got his permission she stealthily arranged the consultation in absolute secret, something that not even Empress Eugenia became aware of.

I am able to tell about this in detail because I was part of the conspiracy. Since it was a case of introducing an enemy into the Palace de Saint Cloud, which if it became known would have provoked a political earthquake, there was no one better to assist in the plan than an adolescent recently arrived from distant tropical lands without knowing anyone at Court, and totally unknown to the secret police, where there were always leaks and, moreover, where the Empress had installed her own paid agents.

One Monday in June, 1870, the Princess charged me to pick up Professor Gran before midnight, at his home in Faubourg Sainte-Honoré, from which place we drove in his own carriage to the Suresnes bridge, and there we changed vehicles to a coach whose windows were darkened with a coating of tar, driven by *Le Tonneau*, to be taken to the palace stables where they already had orders to allow us to pass. We went through a gate hidden by some brushwood thickets, and *Le Tonneau* even accompanied us that far. The Princess was waiting for us on the other side, wrapped in a dark velvet hooded cape, and ready with a lantern that shed a light as gold as honey over her aging face. Thus it was that, after traversing a private corridor, I suddenly found myself inside the imperial bedroom, which was blocked off at that moment from any connection to the Palace, without the Princess— whose footsteps I was following—much less the physician in her charge, remembering to forbid my presence.

Professor Gran quickly solved the mystery of the illness. After his auscultation and the routine questions, he said to the Emperor that he ought to perform a rectal probing, and as he spoke he began putting on a vulcanized rubber glove which he then spread with simple vaseline, upon which the patient had to lift up his fine cotton bedshirt and place himself docilely on the bed in the dorsal decubitus position.

In this simple way, burrowing rapidly and diligently

with his finger, he was able to verify that the Emperor had a stone the size of a pigeon's egg in his bladder, and he proposed to remove it with a procedure that consisted of filling the bladder with oat water injected by means of a uretheral catheter in order to cause the stone to push itself up above the rim of the pelvic bone, and then, through an incision in the perineum no larger than a button hole on his shirt, to introduce into it a metallic instrument of his own invention which he called *Le Sauterelle*, and which he showed the Emperor after removing it from his medical bag, where he kept it wrapped in a piece of flannel.

In truth it did resemble a grasshopper with long, thin front legs and a set of levers for the hind feet and a screw for its head. The front legs were fitted with some tongs designed to enter the bladder in a closed position and, when manipulated by means of the levers, to trap the stone in order for it then to be crushed *in situ* when the screw is turned; in this way the Emperor should be able to expel the resulting sand with the flow of his urine. The duration of the operation, from the moment of opening the buttonhole to its closure with two tiny stitches of goat hair, would not go beyond three minutes, he said, looking at the dial on his pocket watch.

After listening attentively and patiently, the Emperor refused, at first with a categorical shaking of his head, and then his hoarse, agitated voice. It was not a case of being afraid of an adversary's hand armed with a scalpel while he himself was defenseless from the effects of the chloroform, he said with a smile, nor was it his distrust of the effectiveness of *Le Sauterelle*, but the fact that the news alone of the operation would turn out to be harmful to public opinion at a time when a war involving the mother country was imminent. Princess Matilde, having followed the progress of the examination from a few steps away, understood that it would be even more damaging if the Emperor weren't able to mount his horse, and she tried to convince him of this, but it was futile. "I will have the operation in September," he conceded, "when I have returned from the battlefield, and the surgeon will be Professor Gran."

But by the beginning of September, his army defeated, he found himself imprisoned in the summer palace of King Wilhelm I of Prussia in Wilhelmshöhe, and the moment they learned of his defeat, the populace gave themselves over to wiping out any vestige of the Second Empire. Princess Matilde, whom I never saw again, left for good to take up exile in Belgium, and there was no one left to pay for my room and board in the Rue de Malebranche. It was then, when all hope of entering the School of Medicine had vanished, that I took shelter in Count Primoli's offer to live in his house and work as his helper and apprentice.

Primoli's flat in the tiny Rue de Ste.-Beuve, near Notre-Dame-des-Champs, was furnished with divans and ottomans, and adorned with paintings of his friends lining the walls up to the ceiling, a portrait of him by Dubufe, and landscapes by Giraud and Bezzuoli (these last two names forgotten now, like so many others), and every night it attracted gatherings of all sorts of artists and writers, opera singers, *cocottes*, bohemians from the aristocracy, and exiled political figures from America and Eastern Europe. These were private parties that the host called "saturnalias," where they smoked hashish in Turkish pipes and drank absinthe until dawn, parties which were never missed by one gloomy writer from the Argentine Republic, with eyebrows that met each other, and so tall that he never seemed to stop growing; he always carried with him a *bombilla* straw for *mate* that he would suck on with religious verve.

The photography laboratory occupied the same rooms, and despite the fact that myrrh was kept burning constantly in copper incense burners during those saturnalias, there was always a much stronger smell in the air than its perfumed aroma, a smell which came from the corrosive odors of substances kept around in decanters and gallon cans, like gallic acid and silver nitrate. And there were other persistent smells. One was an odor similar to that of dishes smeared with egg that remained unwashed after breakfast, for the glass plates were prepared with the albumin from egg whites, and you walked around on a carpet of egg shells that crackled beneath your soles with the dry sound of disemboweled insects. Another was the gentle fragrance of beeswax purchased in one-pound pots from the apiaries of the L'Avonne valley; when it was melted it was used to coat the printing paper. And then there was the smell of spilled milk, because after treating the paper with wax, it was left immersed in a bath of rice water, vinegar, or milk. There were some kitchen smells, and also those of "the scene of the crime," because the nitric acid, which was used for the collodion plates when diluted in alcohol, smelled like gunpowder from a newly fired pistol.

Primoli, a member of the Saint-Germain Lodge, admired Madame Blavatsky enthusiastically, and even more so when he heard her lecture before the Theosophical Society of Paris, which we attended with the intention on my part of delivering Master Leonard's letter to her. She declared the necessity of a process of electro-magnetic optics, something that, according to her, modern science would not be long in discovering, for the purpose of photographing the spiritual aura of a person by separating the crust from the bodily matter and thus exposing the luminous spectrum formed by its sensory fluctuations, now freed from any wrappings. To photograph the soul! How strange, I thought to myself, as I listened to that woman dressed in mourning expounding her thesis, who, as she read on, kept waving her eyeglasses on their handle with unsteady pulse

and allowing the sheets of paper simply to drop to the floor
after she had read them. The *zambos* of my blood line think
that if you let someone draw or paint your portrait, you are
exposing your soul and will lose it forever.

I wasn't able to hand the letter to Madame Blavatsky
because she disappeared too quickly from the platform
after finishing her lecture, surrounded by a squad of faithful followers; but it was received by her assistant, Madame
Kandó, a Hungarian widow acclaimed in the newspapers as
a medium of formidable powers, and she promised me a reply from London, but it never arrived. Nor was I interested
in it except as something to forward to Master Leonard, for
it would cheer him up. The truth is that for Primoli, and
consequently for me as well, the greater attraction was the
saturnalias, being incompatible in every way with Theo-
sophic beliefs, which, according to Leonard's preachings,
called for one's conduct to exhibit the same symmetry as
the Temple of Solomon.

Our friendship ended badly because early one morning,
when only the leftovers from the saturnalia remained, I was
unable to resist the urge to take a shot of him while he was
lying still asleep on a divan, next to Igor, a Russian from
the Crimea who painted landscapes for the stage settings
at the Opera Comique, both of them naked and with arms
and legs intertwined, the same position in which sleep had
overtaken them. Still on Primoli's head was the pointed red
pileus cap that he always put on to start the party, faithful to
the ancient ritual, and which, in contrast to the chalky color
of their two bodies that was just beginning to become noticeable with the growing light, looked like spilled blood.

While the glass plate prepared with the collodion was
drying, in a fury he went over to smash it with a hammer
and accused me in a trembling fit of hysteria of trying to
humiliate him because of my jealousy. The truth is that Igor

Sorokin didn't attract me, and this was so because he looked like a portrait of me, while love is an affair between opposites. The same height, same figure, eyes the same (those of a wild animal), except that he had a scarcely visible flaw on his right cheek, like a delta of violet colored waters calmly spreading.

We separated then, but Primoli had the generosity to offer me a letter of recommendation to the Archduke Luis Salvador, and so I left for Mallorca, less and less concerned about my return to Nicaragua, that country which was gradually turning into a bothersome memory. On the other hand, I left him my notebooks where my experiments for developing a portable camera were recorded, and also the first model that I had constructed of oak, an invention that he patented in his own name but without perfecting it, because his talent little by little was drying up from all the hashish smoke, and also from allowing himself to be carried away by the perverted flattery of passing love affairs.

If the one who persists in seeking me out were to ask me what sort of relation I had with Primoli, I would say: That of a master with his assistant, one who passed for an apprentice, throughout a number of situations of trust and a great deal of intimacy, for this certainly existed between us, although always by chance whenever it took place. And if anything placed us on an even footing, it's the fact that we were both mediocre photographers, far from being admitted into the hallowed number of the "twenty-eight immortals" commissioned by the *Galerie Contemporaine* to execute a series of portraits of the most celebrated figures of the Second Empire and the Third Republic. My photograph of Turgenev's naked body was never going to be allowed to enter that gallery, but nonetheless there is one there done by Nadal. And although Primoli did photograph Rossini on the steps of the Opera Comique, it's the one by Carjat that was granted a presence in the Gallery.

That fellow who keeps searching for me will have probably been able to throw light on some of the meanders around the bizarre map that my life must appear to him, and perhaps he may manage to find out enough about me to satisfy the most burning needs of his curiosity. I have to think, however, that when these memoirs get into his hands he will wonder about the reasons I have had for spending so much space on the stories of my father Francisco Castellón, my mother Catherine, and my uncle the King Frederick.

This is perhaps because the lives of those relatives of mine have always seemed notable because of their misfortunes, although the truth is they paid the price according to how they themselves set the terms. They were unable to reach the culminating point of the destiny they imposed upon themselves, and their failures made their frustrations poignant, although it would be unjust to call them ambitious, and that's why I prefer to see them as dreamers. Ambition is a sickness of one's conscious self, while dreaming is a sickness of one's lack of awareness, if my pursuer will allow me a little philosophy.

All three of them raised their stakes against the disdainful, mocking dealer of cards, which were marked beforehand with that subtle art known only to depraved cardsharks; and all three must have felt, in the last moments of their lives, the all-consuming terror that not only had they lost everything they had bet but that death would appear before them dressed in an odious manner. My father drowning in his own excrement, my uncle the King having to hold his guts in his own hands before collapsing in the dust of the street, and my mother, whom I never saw again, finishing out her days running a brothel in Greytown, the port that soon fell into ruin when the railroad got built across the Isthmus of Panama.

I know that my own life has not been any the less tragic,

if it is suitable to use a term which is sometimes applied all too smugly—for complaining about one's bad luck can sometimes also be a form of boasting about one's self. And lifting your shirttails to show off your wounds never ceases to be a shameless act. But neither did I ever play my cards against a crooked croupier with the stakes being power in a country such as Nicaragua, that is more worthy of compassion than of dreams. The second-rate cards dealt me—which gave me some downright painful permutations, occasionally even sinister ones, though now and then brought me a little happiness—these are just what any player gets.

My life after being abandoned in Paris when Princess Matilde fled into exile and I had to eat from the hand of Count Primoli, who was more generous with me than with Maxime du Camp; my journey to Mallorca and those years in the entourage of the Archduke Luis Salvador, a petty and arrogant being; my fitful life with the unforgettable and unfortunate Catalina Segura; my emigration to Warsaw with my daughter Teresa and her husband, a butcher whom nature had denied any intelligence and consequently any sensitivity; the unfortunate destiny of my daughter, her attempted suicide and imprisonment after being accused of adultery by that same Baltasar Bonnin, and the later murder of the couple in the middle of the street; the difficulties I had surviving in the ghetto, doing my best at any price, even that of sordidness, to put some bread in the mouth of my orphaned grandson Rubén. . .and something else that I don't know whether my pursuer is even aware of yet, my move to the Mauthausen concentration camp—all these are episodes that fate dealt me without my ever contriving an entrance with fanfares upon the stage of dreams, which is the setting for catastrophes. And if I never wished for anything more than what destiny allotted me, it was on its own account that destiny decided to make me one of its unfortunates, with me knowing all along that in any event to bow my head before each blow wasn't going to earn me any compassion and thereby permit me to receive better cards in the next round.

Through this trade that Count Primoli dedicated himself to teaching me, I learned that the visible aspects of people, which are in each one of their photographs, are inhabited by the invisible ones, which reside in the assumptions that connect those photographs. This is what he called boastfully a "recomposition of interrupted identity," and it is what anyone experiences who sits down to go through the pages of an album where the same figure, now dead, appears in different poses, different situations, with different companions, and at different stages of life. We bear the surprise then of discovering that this person, whom we never knew and who lived in a past that does not belong to us, seems to be a different person in each photo, so that it becomes difficult to achieve a recomposition of his definitive identity. The fact is that such an identity doesn't exist, because this person in reality never was always the same, although he might seem so before the eyes of his close contemporaries, for whom familiarity has created before their eyes a false single image, unchanging even despite the passing of the years.

Aging, for the living eye, is merely to see someone changing disguises from one to the next, gradually, until he is left with the most ridiculous one of all, that is, the disguise of decrepitude. But the dead eye of the camera, more reliable than the living eye because it does not lend itself to illusions but simply portrays someone by directing as much light as it needs to the plate or to the celluloid film, knows how to see the differences, knows how to separate even as it determines those different persons that exist in a single being and that never did look like each other. This is the best

of the mysteries that death leaves behind, and one that begins to work its ways from the moment we start comparing
the photographs in the album after having examined them
one by one: How many people were within that one? How
many were there, and who were they?

Primoli showed me the well-known procedure of divid-
ing a face photographed close up into two hemispheres by
covering one of the two halves with a piece of cardboard,
which allows you to realize that in that face there are two
people emerging at the same time, not only different but
contrary. I tried it out on myself when I did my first self-
portrait, with which I discovered that even at the early age
at which I had recently arrived in Paris, one of the hemispheres of my face, the right one, was sinister and gloomy,
and the other revealed the docile, mild smoothness of innocence. All of these commentaries, however, are those of
an idle mind tortured by asthma and even more so by the
evil of old age.

The one who has been so long on my trail will probably
have discovered already that I was a mediocre photographer, an apprentice all my life. I am not saying this out of
modesty, for I was never troubled by any of that, though
at times it may have seemed as though I was. What always
bothered me was fear, the fear that is often covered up beneath the false mask that also serves to hide one's mediocrity, as well as one's frustrations.

When I made what might be called my key photographs
because they revealed intimacies veiled to others, such as
the photo of the naked body of Turgenev, or else because
they revealed something about myself to me, like the one of
my daughter Teresa and her husband cut down by gunfire,
I was motivated by fear, which at other times has stayed
hidden beneath the mask of curiosity. It was like pressing
the shutter release and then running away or hiding after

pulling off a piece of mischief that deserves punishment.

The snapshot of Turgenev's dead body was rejected by every single editorial office where I tried to sell it. Nobody was willing to publish a disrespectful obscenity like that, which could bring considerable legal consequences down on my head, so I was warned; and worse, that picture made it so that never again would the *Revue des Deux Mondes* give me an assignment. And as far as the other one goes, that one should never have left my hands, even though I was brave enough to have sent it through clandestine channels for publication abroad. That photograph existed only for myself, the old man who, trembling with fear, had to descend the stairs to the street with his suitcase, walk past the bodies of his daughter and his son-in-law, trying not to flinch, in order to get to his grandson to take the boy's hand, and with him silently join the continuous procession that was being fed into at every intersection, moving on foot toward the ghetto.

There are others that I took in fear and that got me into disgrace, such as happened with the nudes I took of Frau Christina von Dengler, the wife of Sturmführer Nikolaus von Dengler, my protector, the commander of the Gestapo in Warsaw; I previously had taken her picture once in the costume of Cleopatra.

She was going on forty and was a very white-skinned woman, nearly albino, quite tall and with huge feet, who had to work just to keep herself erect when walking, but inevitably looked like a broken doll. And when she posed nude for me, she seemed then like a broken doll soaked in milk, milk that is beginning to go sour and touches your nose with an aroma that may not be repugnant but is the harbinger of imminent decay.

When she determined that I would take those pictures of her, surely she took into consideration that I was more than eighty years old, with which she could free herself from any danger of finding herself observed with lecherous eyes. Her loathing of carnal sin, a Lutheran trait, had moved her on one occasion to order a punishment of fifty lashes (and her orders were obeyed the same as if her husband himself had given them) to be administered to her delivery boy for the house provisions and to a girl working as kitchen help, both of them Polish Jews, who had been discovered fornicating underneath a piece of canvas in the back of the truck in which the malefactor made his trips to the market.

The afternoon when they brought me to the house in a military vehicle, I was under the impression this was simply a matter of taking pictures of the birthday party of one of the couple's eight children, and only when I was brought into the kitchen through the service door, where they gave me a snack, did I become aware that Von Dengler was actually absent, having been called to Berlin to receive his new commission as commander of the Mauthausen concentration camp.

A good while passed before the electric bell sounded in the kitchen. One of the housemaids answered the call, and she returned with the order to take me to the foot of the stairs, where I arrived with my suitcase full of equipment. When the girl had retired, Frau Von Dengler appeared at the balustrade, wrapped in a robe with vertical stripes, a man's bathrobe, and she signaled me to come up and invited me to come into her bedroom. Once the camera was ready she let the robe fall to her feet, immediately seizing it again by the neck with a modest gesture. Certainly she would have preferred a photographer who was blind, if such a thing were possible, somewhat like the dancer Kuchiuk-Hanem did when she blocked the contemplation of her delicate nudity by the eyes of her musicians, a young boy and an old man who was already blind in one eye. They both played violin-like instruments with sheep-gut strings, the healthy eye of the old man being covered over by a flap from his own turban and the child's eyes with a black veil, according to Maxime du Camp when he started talking about his trip to the Middle East with Flaubert.

When I presented her the following day with the enlarged copies of the takes, she insisted that I give her the negatives. I couldn't imagine why she would have wanted the pictures. Neither did I find out how they got into her husband's hands, unless it was she who showed them to him in order to excite his passion by trying to imitate the model on the French playing card that had been confiscated from that delivery boy and that she promised to burn the moment it was handed over to her. But what her nude pictures had the least of was the element of lasciviousness. Despite my efforts to give them an erotic flavor, they had fallen without redemption into the abyss of ridicule where there is neither eroticism nor pornography. That woman had consumed all her juices like a fruit that is long past ripeness, with her swollen pubis in a thicket of surly hairs like an armpit, her breasts inflated like rubber balls in prodigal excess suitable for nursing, and the provocative poses that she herself had chosen—sitting astraddle a chair with her husband's kepi cocked on her head, lying on her back in bed with one leg bent while she pretended to be reading, embracing a clothes rack which she was licking with her tongue, crouching on her knees to show her buttocks, head down and face turned back toward the camera with an idiotic simper on it—all these did nothing but make matters even worse.

Then, when Von Dengler returned, contrary to his promise to take me with him to Mauthausen as a photographer, a promise made when he had gotten the first news of his coming transfer, he determined that because of those pictures my punishment would be to be loaded onto one of those cattle wagons of the phantom trains, which departed Warsaw hitched up to the rear of his own train with a consignment of prisoners taken from the ghetto.

My pursuer will already have seen perhaps the nudes that I did at a very early age in Paris. They lack skill, but they are truly nudes, while those of Frau Von Dengler don't even deserve such a name. With true nudes the camera never ceases to insinuate something of mystery, and in these, on the contrary, they only show a jumble of flesh that is already beginning to smell bad, and all because there is nothing there that transcends the body when it is free from ridicule, or that transcends any face or even an inanimate object when it manages to reveal to us something of what is hidden beneath the spell of the acids in the pale light of the darkroom phantoms.

I pursued the revelation of that mystery from the moment Primoli had me take a brief look through the lens, with the world in reverse before my eyes, and I began to close in around it like someone who moves about the object being photographed with a hand camera. But in the end, like Robin, that ancestor of mine who inspired Defoe's character Robinson, and the one my uncle the King was so proud of, I did nothing but go around my desert island in circles without finding anything but my own tracks, while the mystery remained safe. To have lost my battle against an impossible objective that offered me nothing more than hints—that's what I would have to call mediocrity. Or failure.

This fellow who is seeking me would do well to avail himself of what a belated enemy of my father wrote about me, surely to mock him even after his death. That man, named Crisanto Medina, Minister Plenipotenciary of Nicaragua in France, also an enemy of Rubén Darío, whose life in Paris he made supremely bitter by stealing his salary as Consul, wrote in his libelous article, "Chip Off the Old Block," that I had scarcely set foot on the platform in the Saint-Lazare station when I sank into a dissolute life, requesting that the aide-de-camp sent to meet me take me that same night to the *Divan Japonaise* in Montmartre, a brothel whose name he claimed must have been given me by a sophisticated Mexican writer whose eyes and imagination were equally feverish, the author, moreover, of a licentious novel in which he told about his love affair with a legendary French actress and according to Medina's story had traveled with me on the boat from New York.

In keeping with the tone of that opening, based on a so-called investigation conducted by the author himself, I established my general headquarters in the Moulin de la Galette, from where I was able to have all the brothels in Montmartre close at hand, and that was how I spent the moneys that were given me in the name of Napoleon III, whose subordinates were unable to bother themselves with me because the responsibilities of the imminent war against Prussia were overwhelming the bureaucracy of the Second Empire. And I continued along this same path until the final debacle, when I was repatriated to Nicaragua to finish out my days stabbed to death in a cantina in León, still an adolescent, "an adolescent wasted by his asthma but filled with haughtiness and always dissolute, who went to take refuge in the ruins of what had been his childhood home, toppled by an earthquake, where the only thing that remained standing was the shed that had served as the carpenter shop of his stepfather, a one-armed fellow named Terencio Catín."

Would it not have been better to rely on this version offered by an individual who was so rotten and all his life envious of anyone else's sparkling brilliance, who was scorched by Darío's glory, since he had it so close by, and who in the sum of the details of the vicious itinerary that he grants me believes himself successful in the legitimacy of his inventions? Why not believe him, everything considered? Isn't it simpler for my pursuer to have me die the victim of a motiveless murder in the prostitutes' barrio of the Ermita de Dolores in León? Isn't it better to have ended up in a pauper's grave at the edge of the Panteón de Guadalupe?

But then it may be that I myself remember the smoky walls of that brothel, the fishbait stench of the candle burning on the table of ill-matched boards next to a cloudy-looking glass filled with half a quart of brandy that the madame whose cheeks were firey with rouge had just served me, and also remember the strings of paper ribbons of rice paper hanging from the ceiling because this is the night of the seventh of November, when even in the whore-house they have been singing to the Virgin Mary trimmed with berry-shaped tassels on an altar, and further remember the stranger drawing nearer with that knife hidden under his hat and squeezed against my chest in order to slash me under the ribs.

One can manage to have a thousand deaths, or none. When my pursuer finally catches up to me, I could also be buried—and why not?—in the tiny cemetery of Deyá, on a hill from which one glimpses the Mediterranean on one side and the massive hulk of the Teix on the other—if it turns out that I return to Mallorca to die.

I return? The day of the liberation has arrived, the American troops enter without firing a shot because Mauthausen has remained in charge of a squad of municipal guards who would rather throw their old rifles to the ground and line themselves up in the square where the gallows is with their hands in the air, to wait for the advance guard. And then later on, one afternoon the Asturian De Mieres, who is nothing but ribs and a head, comes to ask me to take a memorial picture of all the Spanish Republican prisoners before the train takes them to Vincennes early tomorrow morning. Have you any plates? They pose happily in front of the monumental stone gate from which, with the help of some ropes, they have removed the eagle with the swastika in its claws, they never cease making jokes, the penis of the most rowdy among them, the Valencian Manolo Vincent, is thicker than their thighs are now, and they laugh, but when the group breaks up and I go into the coal bunker that I use as the darkroom to develop the plate, the very same Asturian has gone off to denounce me to a Captain of Intelligence named Frank Goldberg, who right then begins taking declarations from some of the survivors in one of the barracks converted to an office, the Captain comes to look for me in the coal bunker, and behind him, at a distance, the Asturian; they search, but they find, hanging from the clothes press, only the photograph of the Spanish Republican prisoners that I have just removed from the washbasin.

I have to explain, the Captain orders me. What do I have to explain? The whereabouts of the pictures. What pictures? The photos of the bodies of the prisoners sacrificed in the gas chambers, of those who died beneath the weight of the granite blocks on the Stairway of Death, of the ones who were tossed into the ravine at the quarry, of those in the parade of condemned prisoners marching toward the gallows square accompanied by a band made up of musician prisoners, of the ones in the executions on the gallows scaffolding. I came here by force, I'm a prisoner too. That's a lie! says the Asturian, he's a fraud. Shut up, the Captain orders him. They forced me to take the pictures. Where are the negatives? I handed them all to the commander, Von Dengler. And the copies? Yes, the copies too. The Captain is quiet. He looks at me a moment. Where did you come from, grampa, what nationality are you? From Central America.

I'm a Nicaraguan. What? he exclaims in English. And then: I'm gonna turn you loose. You know why? My mother is Central American, she's a neighbor of yours, from Guatemala. I reckon you're lucky.

11

A suckling pig

What happens is always what must happen.

Turgenev, *To Cut It Very Fine*

THE SAME DAY AS MY meeting with Dominik there appeared in *El Diario de Mallorca* the interview that Lourdes Durán did with me in Pollensa, and as a way of celebrating the event, I told her by telephone before leaving Deyá that morning that I was inviting her for lunch. We agreed to meet at the Bosch, a bar that is one of the emblematic meeting spots in Palma, where I arrived late because, after having lost the way several times I preferred to leave the car in a parking lot close to the Plaza de las Cortes and take a taxi, only to discover that I could have made the trip on foot in just a few minutes.

Now that I read Lourdes's interview again, years later, I realize that in speaking to her about this novel, then still in the making, not a few of the ideas about narrative that I had in those days have gradually been placed within its pages. But there are others that remain buried in the original plan, and still others again that, even though they are yet outstanding, will not form part of any other book, because when I close out my accounts with this one, some different themes will be lying in wait for me which will not have anything to do with what I've written here or with what has escaped forever from between my fingers. "A novel is only what survives the intentions of the author," I had also told Lourdes.

"His intentions or his obsessions?" she asked.

"Both."

That hour at mid-day in the Bosch, when all the offices and businesses along the Paseo de la Borne and Avenida Jaume III empty out for the daily recess, was the noisiest and most boisterous of any during the day, and since after a lot of difficulty we only managed to find a spot at the end of the bar, where we felt terribly crowded, it was better to get out of there quickly and head toward El Parlament, the restaurant she had chosen on the Carrer del Conquistador, a quiet place devoid of the uproar.

Castellón's story, with the many snares and different solutions which at that period it offered, was flitting around more than ever inside my head after my long talk with Dominik, and during the meal, in that ambience of companionable silences ideal for confessions, Lourdes had to suffer through an exhaustive report about my investigations and frustrations, especially concerning my character's life on Mallorca. So many loose ends to tie up, and just as many blank spots still to fill in, I told her, something that sounded like a call for help, as if she might be able to reveal, once and for all, the answers I wanted to hear in the worst way.

I assume that at bottom I was expecting once more to enjoy the indulgence of fate. The glass door of a deserted pavilion that only needed a little push, the arrow-shaped sign pointing toward an unexpected path among the ash trees that only required to be followed, the album that fell to the ground when it slid off from among an armload of books and fairly calls out to be picked up, a manila envelope or an accordion-pleated folder with photographs that someone takes out of a desk drawer and hands me . . .

The meal was finished at last, and I can recall everything we ordered, as often happens with anything to do with decisive moments: carpaccio of shrimp and *arroz ciego*, plus a *crianza*, a youngish red wine, from Binissalem, everything chosen by Lourdes, who remained quiet, ready to listen to me.

"What did you say Castellón's grandson's name was?" she asked while prodding around in her purse looking for the mobile phone that had begun to ring with the notes to *Für Elise*.

"Rubén."

"And you say that Castellón's photography studio used to be located on the Calle de la Argentería?" she asked again, returning the telephone to her purse after pushing the button to interrupt the call.

"At number 17," I responded.

"There's a little shop there at number 17," she said.

"What kind of shop?" My hands held still on the table cloth as if moving them would turn my luck bad.

"A shop for esoterica," she said. "Among other things they sell mandalas. Do you know what a mandala is?"

"No idea."

"A mandala is an imaginary palace that you construct in your mind while meditating."

"And how can they sell imaginary palaces then in a shop?" I was smiling.

"Because you can also make them out of wood, or with colored sand, but they must be destroyed once they are finished," she said.

"How old is the man running the store?"

"I wouldn't know what to tell you, but he's not a young-ster."

"And do you remember what his name is?"

"To be truthful, I don't know."

"The street, do you think it's nearby?" I asked, leaving the tip in the little tray.

"Oh, very near, you just have to walk back a ways toward the Plaza de las Cortes, the same direction you came from where you left your car," she said, picking up her purse.

"You have to come with me. To introduce me to him."

"Introducing you is out of the question," she said. "I've probably seen him only a couple of times behind the counter. You already saw that I can't even remember his name."

"All right then, just point him out to me. That way you'll have made the favor complete, and you'll have a spot in the novel."

"Don't I have one already?" she laughed.

"Well, you'll have an even better spot."

"I would love to, really, but I have to get back to the newspaper. Those pictures we did of Carme Riera at her house didn't turn out very well—this is for an interview that comes out tomorrow. The photographer had to go back and retake them, and I have to choose some that will go with it."

"I learned a lot about the *chuetas* in that novel by Carme Rieta," I told her as we were walking out the door. "Thanks again for the gift."

I walked her to the taxi stand in the Paseo del Borne, and when she had gotten settled in the back seat I made signs to her so she would roll down the window.

"I am going to imagine a virtual palace like those," I said.

"Take special care with the doors," she responded.

When her taxi was gone I started walking in the direction of Call Menor, and as I was about to emerge onto a small plaza adorned with a solitary fir tree, there, rising up opposite me, was the church of Santa Eulalia. Walking along one of its sides I discovered the Calle de la Argentería, deprived of all street sounds in the afternoon and now rather deep in shadow because, with the street being so narrow, shade from the old buildings enveloped it all day long. A tangle of television antennas, like skeletons of umbrellas, covered the rooftops, and from the balconies and windows of the upper floors various pieces of clothing had been hung out to dry. A woman with hands outstretched took in a nightgown and a pair of jeans and then turned toward the street with the air of a prisoner envious of the world outside, only to disappear at length behind the curtains.

The Calle de la Argentería had fallen off because the prosperous businesses of the Call Menor were to be found these days on the Carrer San Miguel and Carrer del Sindicato, and it was only the secondary *botigas* that remained here, although the names of the jewelry stores were the very same ones as when the Archduke had come here with Wenceslas Vyborny to choose the ring that he wished to bestow on him.

JOYERÍA SANTIAGO
Engagement rings
JOYERÍA DE LA VIUDA DE GASPAR PIÑA
Watches by installments
JOSÉ Y MARCOS FOSHER
Silver and silver polish

It was time for them to close up, and nearly all of the metallic curtains had been lowered to the half-way point in order to let the shop attendants leave, as well as the owners, who surely must have still been going over their accounts within.

A suckling pig

It didn't take me long to find number 17. The dying light was burning on the glass windows of the balconies tucked in above the premises of the shop, which was marked by a brass sign in black hanging from a spike in the wall, with the name MANDALA SHOP in English painted in strokes looking very much like the ones seen in Chinese writing. From the third floor of the building under renovation next door, the sleeve of a chute descended to open out above a dumpster placed on the sidewalk. Next door to the shop there was a pharmacy, now closed, as you could see by the empty shelves, a balance for weighing coins standing in a corner with its face turned away, and the posters advertising remedies and vitamins that were simply leaning against the walls.

But the Mandala Shop was still open, and in the doorway hung a curtain of glass beads. Placed on the sidewalk was a sandwich-board sign like the ones designed to advertise restaurant menus for the benefit of the tourists:

Salt from the Dead Sea
Candles for reiki therapy sessions
Oils and spices for perfuming with incense and
    traditional depuration: Benzoin, bergamot, lavender,
    neroli oil, myrrh, sweet marjoram
Nippon Kodo Incense for aromatherapy of Feng Shui
Guidebook by the Monks of the Gaden Shartse
    Monastery for constructing mandalas
Courses in Sanskrit (book and cassettes)
All the publications of the School of the Renaissance
    of Conscious Peace

In the window that looked toward the street, on a wrinkled fabric of pink-colored silk, there was a mandala palace, made in Taiwan, constructed out of colored wooden cubes for assembling like a child's toy, and beside it the box it had been packed in, on which the palace was reproduced in a photograph.

At my step the curtain swished with a murmuring like dry leaves. There was no customer within, no one to attend to me. On top of some planks mounted on sawhorses and covered with more of that same pink fabric as in the window, little bottles and tubes of oils and powders were displayed piled up in small wicker baskets, candles in geometric shapes, little bars of incense mounted in concentric circles, along with the brochures and manuals promised on the blackboard outside, which were opened out to fill the otherwise empty space. Floral fragrances filled the air. From the back of the shop a radio receiver allowed the sound of Chopin's Étude No. 12 for piano to be heard, newly announced by the commentator.

I put my hand out to run it over the glossy cover of one of the brochures, and even with this pressure the board seemed to jiggle slightly, as fragile as the eight-petaled lotus flower pictured on the cover under the title *The Crystalline Purity of the Palace of the Vajrasattva Buddha.*

I picked it up and opened it to the first page:

> The palace of death can only be built four times, and those are the four forms of dying that we have during the course of each one of our lives. Its doors are four, just as four is the number of opportunities to construct it. Each one of the four doors appears at each one of the four corners of the earth. We will never know when we have truly come before each door, after each lengthy voyage.

"Are you interested in the mandala?" I heard this from behind me.

I turned. I had not felt him approaching because he moved across the floor on rubber-soled sandals that showed his toenails painted dark red like drops of blood falling from a broken nose. His floppy hemp pants would fill out like a sail with even a slight breeze, as did his shirt, made of some sheer material, also white, hanging loosely over the belt and unbuttoned halfway up his hairless chest, an exhausted garment that seemed to envelope him like a peplos, because had he been fat, he would now look like a wineskin that as it gradually has become more empty shows the loosened folds of its skin instead of an engaging sign of vitality. Around his neck were two strands of a thick silver chain that seemed to fulfill the function of securing his head (crowned by a scanty tuft of hair of a reddish tint leaning toward saffron yellow) to his trunk. His blue eyes beneath his crinkled eyebrows would have to be called artificial, like those of a doll.

Suddenly he spread out a fan that showed on a black background two thick-waisted women wearing mantillas and clacking their castanets with hands raised high, like those on the wrapper of a bar of Myrurgía soap, and began fanning himself rapidly.

"A friend got me interested," I said.

"Lourdes," he asserted.

"Do you know Lourdes Durán?"

"That depends on her," he replied. "Sometimes she doesn't want to appear connected with the head of an esoteric group and prefers to keep it hidden."

"An esoteric group?" I ask.

"The School of the Renaissance of Conscious Peace," he said. "Is there any in Nicaragua?"

"I don't know," I was puzzled.

"There can't be," he laughed. "It was created by me, and there are no affiliates."

"You are Castellón's grandson, Rubén," I say, like someone with the roulette wheel already in motion betting everything he has.

"And you are Sergio, the writer. I was waiting for you."

"You waiting for me?"

"Don't think I'm any Madame Blavatski," he said, and

now he was striking his thigh with the fan that he had suddenly folded up. "I read your interview in the *Diario* and Lourdes told me you were coming."

"We just parted," I said. "Did she call you just now on the phone?"

"No, no, she warned me this morning, after you invited her to lunch." He didn't stop whipping his leg. "She was certain it would all end with you visiting my Mandala Shop. And don't keep referring to me as *Usted*. Use the *tú*."

"Whatever you like," I switched to the familiar form.

"I'll close up then and let's sit down to talk in my cave, there in back. The flat that's just above us, I sold it in order to set up this business, which isn't much of a business at all, as you already noticed."

He went out to the sidewalk and came back in carrying the folded-up sandwich board, and then lowered the metallic curtain by turning a crank, upon which it immediately became quite dark. He gave a turn to the ancient light switch, and the little shop was bathed in the calcinated light of the fluorescent tubes. The cash register embedded in the back of the establishment now seemed monumental. I went over to it. It had a keyboard like that of a harmonium, and the information about its maker figured on a small brass plate screwed beneath the cylinder for the paper: *William F. Graham and Sons, Cash Register Manufacturers, Wolverhampton, 1900.*

"It's the same one," he says.

"Same what?" I ask.

"The same cash register that opened with a short ding of the bell when Melchor Segura went to put the bank bills in the drawer that the Archduke had given him in payment for the engagement ring for Wenceslas Vyborny," he explains.

"I assume that Castellón continued using it when he opened his photography studio here," I say.

"It probably didn't ring very frequently then," he pulls back the curtain toward the room behind the shop so that I can go through first. "In this place he could only do pictures of the first communions of *chueta* children, and photos of *chueta* couples, because no one who wasn't a *chueta* would ever come to this street to have their pictures made."

A screen in three sections divides the room behind the shop itself, and on each section is a nude picture of one of the Olympic goddesses painted on an oval panel. Hera is offering the milk from her breast stuffed into the mouth of a little boy armed for battle, Aphrodite is flying amid the clouds in a car pulled by doves, Artemis is carrying a wounded fawn in her arms. On the other side of the screen can be seen a bed with tangled bedclothes from which emanates a strong odor of camphor, and on this side too there is a pair of armchairs with vinyl upholstery, as if they belonged in an office. On a small bamboo table placed between them is a cluttered pile of books.

"King Frederick displayed a pile of books like this one so don Francisco Castellón would understand that despite his kingdom being simply a sort of exercise in pantomime he himself was a man of culture," he says, while sitting down in one of the chairs and gesturing me toward the other.

"Which books?"

"You'll find out in due time," he responds, leaning back as if exhausted after a long trip.

On the table I find the edition of *A Trip To Mallorca* that is sold in the tourist shops in Valldemosa; the volume of Chopin's letters edited by Henryk Opienski; *The Unsettled Passions of Ivan Turguéniev* by Juan Eduardo Zúñiga; the biography of Napoleon III written by Fenston Bresler; *Luis Salvador, King Without a Crown* by Horst Kleinmann; Flaubert's *Cartas del viaje a Oriente* and *Madame Bovary;* and, moreover, Roberto Ibáñez's collection of *Páginas desconocidas de Rubén Darío*, a difficult book to obtain, in which the article "El Príncipe Nómada" appears; and a very used copy of *Conversaciones de sobremesa* by Vargas Vila.

"I don't want to show off my erudition like King Frederick, but just enough for you to see I am quite familiar with the themes of interest in your future novel," he says.

"So what is *Madame Bovary* doing here?" I ask.

"I don't know, there's a bookish mode in literature these days, and probably it will occur to you to re-create the drama of the woman so disappointed in everything that she poisons herself by shoving her mouth full of tartar emetic," he replies.

"That is also the story with Teresa Segura, your mother," I say. "But she was saved."

"Oh yes, of course, they saved her life with a stomach pump at the Hospital of the Good Samaritan, where she was taken in the car belonging to the pharmacist, a Russian bachelor (and probably gay) named Serge Pestov."

"Is that not true?" I ask.

"It will be true if you and I want it to be true," he says.

Behind me the packages of printed materials of the School of the Renaissance of Conscious Peace reach to the ceiling. Above the last stretch of a shelf fixed to the lateral wall at the back, very handy to his chair, there is a hotplate with a coffeepot, a portable typewriter, and also the radio receiver that had been playing the Chopin étude; in the second section there is a jar filled with small chocolate bars, and down below it a pile of folders and more books.

On the same wall the open gap of a doorway reveals a pull-chain toilet, a heater and some utensils facing the toilet, and a net bag dangling from the ceiling with some cabbages, radishes, garlic, peppers, and onions, like a still life by Juan Sánchez Cotán. Next to the doorway are four photographs fixed to the wall. Three of them I recognize from a distance: the shot of the champion pig at the Agricultural Fair in Rouen, the one of Turgenev's naked body, and the one of Szeroki Dunaj Street on the day the Gestapo murdered Baltasar Bonnin and Teresa Segura.

The fourth one I have never seen, and I come closer. Some musicians, specters with huge eyes and shaven heads, in prisoners' uniforms and with their feet wrapped in rags, are marching while playing their instruments in front of a flat-bedded vehicle on which a small group of prisoners are standing, three adults, two men and a woman, and two boys, their hands all tied together with a single rope. There are seven musicians: three violins, a trombone, a clarinet, a small trumpet, and a transverse flute.

"That is one of the last photos Castellón took in Mauthausen. The prisoners on the cart had tried to escape, and they're now on the way to the gallows."

"Why did Castellón emigrate to Poland?" I ask, going back to sit down again.

"Because Baltasar Bonnin had to leave, and he took Teresa with him," he responds. "You already know that through Professor Rodaskowski."

"Were they persecuting *chuetas* in Palma again?"

"The dictatorship of Primo de Rivera had actually established a law of protection for Jews so that they could return to Spain and set up new businesses," he says. "But in Mallorca the new governing principle actually stimulated persecution. They began marking the doors where *chuetas* lived with a red circle within another yellow one. Like in the Middle Ages."

Baltasar Bonnin had recently inherited the butcher shop in the Carrer del Fiol from his father, and he had decided to marry Teresa on the second Sunday in December, 1928, at the Santa Eulalia church. But at the end of November he stabbed a furrier's apprentice with the knife he was using to skin a hare. Every afternoon, urged on by a Dominican preacher, workers from the Calatrava barrio gathered in a mob to set up, by turns, a siege of the shops on the Call Menor. On the day when it was the butcher shop's turn to suffer the annoyance, Bonnin went out to confront them, they splashed a bladder full of urine all over him, he went for his knife, and they fled in disorder when the saw him armed, but he caught up with one of them who was lame from birth, knocked him down and stabbed him in the abdomen.

A friend of the pair, who was a fireman on a steamship on the Barcelona line, managed to hide them in the hold where they were transporting hogs. Castellón reached them there a week later. They were married in the Sant Jordi church, in Sabadell, the very day they had already chosen, and the following year they went to Warsaw.

"Those famous pigs of George Sand again," I say.

"And Rubén Darío's pigs as well, when he dispatched his wife so he could stay with her sister," he says.

"You owe him your name," I remark.

"It was easy for Castellón to meddle in that business of my name," he responds. "Bonnin had allowed Teresa back into his house again by that time, but he didn't know if I was his son or Lieutenant Kumelski's. Teresa never revealed the truth to him. Do you know the truth?"

"How am I supposed to know?"

He looks at me, amused, and raises his hand to take the jar of chocolates off the shelf. "Sometimes I don't know what is worse, being the son of a rotten ladies' man or of a cuckhold butcher," he says, as he quickly tears the wrappers off of two or three of the chocolate bars and pops them in his mouth. "Care for any?"

"Thank you, no. I never eat candy," I respond. "My brother Rogelio died of diabetes."

"As far as diabetes goes, that's what I inherited from the Archduke," he says, and contemptuously points to a cardboard box on the floor, at the foot of the shelf, where I can see doses of insulin, packages of cotton, a bottle of alcohol, and some disposable syringes. "When the sugar gets too low, you have to eat candy, and when it goes through the roof you have to inject yourself."

"The Archduke? Why the Archduke?"

"If my grandfather had been Castellón, I would have been an asthmatic, but asthma—I've never had any problem there," he says, and takes another handful of chocolate. "Don't you think I look like the Archduke somewhat? Don't I have the right snout as if searching for acorns on the ground?"

"Frankly, no," I respond.

"I really believe I'm a Hapsburg, from the bad side," he insists. "Because every time I look at myself in the mirror to try to figure out who I look like most, I never come across a single face from among the natives of the jungles."

"I would say you look more like your great-grandfather don Francisco Castellón," I tell him.

"The traitor?" He puts his hand into the chocolate jar once again. Around him on the floor the wrappers with their vivid colors are mounting up.

"Do you know his story well enough to make that judgment?" I ask.

"Through his own son, who felt pity for him, but also a little bit of embarrassment, and disgust."

"He must have told you a lot about him then," I say.

"He was delighted by that story of how he got Napoleon III out of that prison in the castle at Ham, but there's no such wild yarn in the biography written by Bresler, nor in any other."

"Without that story of the escape from the castle the Emperor would not have had to pay him back for the favor, Castellón would never have come to Europe, and you would not exist," I say.

"Assuming that the masterful photographer is my grand-father and not the Archduke."

"Trust in me," I tell him.

"Now I'm supposed to trust you, but not when it comes to whether I am the son of that Lieutenant Ladies' Man or of the butcher with the horns," he says.

"There are things that I do know, and others that I do not."

"You invent them and then you believe what you've invented," he complains.

"Did you feel afraid there in the street?" I am looking at the photo on the wall.

"Just a great emptiness, something more like loneliness."

"And you remember nothing more?" I ask.

"The bark of that officer ordering me to put my hands in the air," he says. "And that this officer was cross-eyed. You won't believe it if I tell you that just then I felt like laughing when I saw the confusion in his eyes, with one that was trying to look at me, the other that was looking over at the pharmacy's sign."

"You were only masking your fear," I tell him.

"I would have laughed even if I found him strolling along the pathways at the zoo on a quiet Sunday morning."

"But you were not enjoying a Sunday at the zoo. Your parents were lying in the street, murdered on the order of that cross-eyed officer," I was insistent.

"They just seemed to me a couple of bodies, as if some-body had wanted to dump them in front of the door of the butcher's shop," he says.

"And now?"

"Worse than it was then. Now they're just that picture on the wall."

"It would not have mattered to you either if they had killed Castellón," I say, accusing him.

"I saw him come to the doorway with a little suitcase, set it on the ground, and put his hands above his head just like me but without anyone ordering him to," he says. "Then I realized that if they killed him too, I would be alone in the world. And from that perspective, I felt happy."

"Because you had never felt any affection for him," I say.

"That wasn't the problem. Of course I felt what you call affection for all three of them, but what dominated me at this new moment was the feeling of absolute freedom, of a future without any shackles that I couldn't measure in capacity or importance, but one in which I could only envision surprises. The felicity of at last leaning out over the void."

"That is a lot for a child."

"You're mistaken," he says. "Innocence is capable of anything."

"If Castellón had not taken that picture, you would not exist for me," I tell him.

"In spite of those other two on the wall, the champion hog and Turgenev's naked body?"

"That would not have been enough."

"Aren't his eccentricities sufficient to turn him into a good character for a novel?" he asks.

"No," I am firm. "Without that picture he would not exist for me, and you wouldn't either."

"And now look how that fabulous, forsaken kid in the middle of the street has ended up. Aren't you disappointed? Aren't you sorry now for having come looking for me?"

"I came in order to finish off the final chapter," I say. "To take away with me what I need to know about Castellón."

"So you're only interested in me as a witness."

"But you also interest me as a character."

"Just a walk-on, then," he says drily.

"That depends on what you tell me about your grandfather, because there is still much I need to find out."

"Not again that business about my grandfather," he says wearily. "It's better to accept that I had two maternal grandfathers and two undependable fathers."

"All right then, one of your two maternal grandfathers," I give in. "Where do we begin?"

"What did Vyborny tell you this morning that's new?" he gazes with repugnance at the jar of chocolate bars before replacing it on the shelf.

"Does Vyborny belong to the School of the Renaissance of Universal Peace too?" I exclaim.

"Universal Peace my fucking foot!" he returns. "I went down that path just to make a living, but you can see I didn't get very far."

"How did you come to meet him?" I ask.

"He came here because he was looking for material about Wenceslas Vyborny, his ancestor, well, you know all about that," he says. "But I couldn't help him much."

"And how did you know I saw him this morning?"

"Because Lourdes told me. You must have said something about interviewing him when you invited her to lunch."

"Dominik hid it from me that he knew you, just like Lourdes," I say. "Perhaps the Marqués de Bauzá de Mirabo is also a member of your sect?"

"No one was hiding anything from you, and this Marqués Bauzá de Mirabo I wouldn't know from a telephone pole," he says. "What's the end of your novel look like? Are you writing something like Ellery Queen or what?"

"If what you have in mind is mysteries, all the threads of the plot lead right here to this back room."

"Maybe the only thing they wanted was to make your search more interesting," he says. "Think how mean it would have been to send you directly here and that's it. It wouldn't have been good for your novel."

"These Jewish things are always mysterious," I tell him.

"The truth is that there's not a shred of any mystery left in this barrio any longer. There are prosperous shopkeepers, perhaps, and others like myself, that give a little start any time the cash register bell rings because it's been so long since the last time."

"Well, all mystery aside, there must be something attractive for you to be a *chueta*."

"I don't know anything about attractions, but just about the only thing I'm sure of is that I'm not one of those *can retallats*, those 'dogs with hoods,' there are still some of those around the Call Menor. And besides being a hooded dog, gay. And if you want to go all the way, a hermaphrodite as well. Imagine it."

"I am imagining it," I respond.

"No, you can't imagine what that is," he says. "A loneliness as huge as the time in the middle of the street with my hands above my head waiting for them to gun me down."

Now he closes his eyes, leans back, and allows his hand to come to rest on the pile of folders.

"And what about those folders?" I asked.

"You are curious," he said.

"It's part of my job," I responded.

He shook his head as if his patience was beginning to wear out, opened his eyes, and picked out one of the folders from the stack. "Enjoy yourself with this one. It's the story of Catalina and Benito Tarongí, brother and sister, my *chueta* ancestors who lived in this same building."

"Your grandmother was named Catalina after that other one?"

"There was always a Catalina in the family, in memory of the one burned at the stake," he said. "They were all teetotalers. Except the last of them, my grandmother, who took to drinking and went so far that she used to have delirium tremens."

"And that was not the worst of it," I said.

"Yes. The Lazarus disease that leaves the skin like softened marble," he said. "Poor woman. You know that she died upstairs here, hidden from all eyes."

"I do know. Even from the eyes of Castellón, who was only able to see her one final time."

"It would seem that I have little to tell you," he says.

Catalina Tarongí was brought to trial for keeping the fast of Queen Esther, and Benito Tarongí for sacrificing a sheep on Good Friday, according to the records written in the hand of the Jesuit Reverend Father Francisco Garau, Examiner for the Holy Office. In those records too is a description of the auto-da-fé that both were subjected to on Sunday, May 6, 1691:

> Catalina, who earlier had boasted she was going to throw herself into the fire, when the flames began licking at her screamed for them to take her out of there, although she persisted in not wanting to invoke Jesus. Benito, when he only smelled the smoke, was a statue, but when the flames reached him, he fought them off, covered himself, and struggled as much as he could and until he could no more. He was fat, like a suckling pig, so that even when the flames had not touched him yet his flesh caught fire like a half-burnt log and when his belly split open his entrails fell out as happened to Judas. *Crepuit medius et difusa sunt omnia viscera cius.*

"Me they would have burned alive both for being a *chueta* and a sodomite," he laughs, covering his mouth with the fan he has opened out fully once more.

"How was it the Holy Office didn't confiscate this property?" I ask.

"They did confiscate it, but the family must have bought it back again through a third person," he says. "And did you notice that bit about the suckling pig? My blood, thanks to this diabetes mellitus, would have burned like caramel honey."

"The persecution by the Nazis was also an auto-da-fé," I say, "and you were a survivor. You do not take that so seriously?"

"I wouldn't call myself a survivor because my life was never in danger," he says.

"They could have killed you that day in the street."

"I'm talking about my time in the ghetto."

"Then was Castellón's life also not in danger in the ghetto?" I ask.

"He was protected by the commanding officer of the Gestapo, Nikolaus von Dengler, and he won the affection of his wife," he says. "You know the story about the nudes."

"I think not."

"It was the time that Castellón did a series of nudes of that well-stacked woman in her bedroom," he says. "I was with him that afternoon, but she sent me to the kitchen with the Jewish maid and they shut themselves up in the bedroom for something more than photography."

"But Castellón was an old man," I respond.

"In his studio in the ghetto I surprised him more than once fondling the Jewish girl models, kids of fifteen or less, that they sent him to do pictures for the series "*Buntes Paradies*" which was published in an illustrated magazine from Berlin," he says.

"Nazi propaganda photos."

"To show how well we ate and dressed, that we didn't have lice in our hair, and above all, that we were not being sent to the ovens," he says.

"And what happened when Von Dengler discovered the photos?" I ask. "Or did he never even find out?"

"He found out, yes, but nothing happened. They had an agreement between him and his wife about living freely."

"Then it is true that when he was transferred to Mauthausen as the commander there he took you both with him?" I ask.

"Castellón affirms something else," he says. "He says that when Von Dengler discovered the pictures, in revenge he put him on the ghost train to Mauthausen, like meat to dispose of."

"Where does he affirm that?"

"You'll find out pretty quickly, have patience," he says.

"All the patience in the world," I respond. "That is what I came for."

"It's absurd, he wouldn't have resisted the trip crowded together in a cattle car in the middle of winter."

"You are the only one who can contradict him," I say. "Or is it that you didn't go with him?"

"You see now? I'm your best witness. Of course I went with him."

"In Von Dengler's entourage?"

"In a special railway car that had leather seats, bathrooms with hot water and abundant towels, a movie projector, and a phonograph player," he says.

"You felt comfortable in that car."

Once again an expression of irritation crosses his face, and again he opens the fan out. "Why not? Von Dengler loved me like his own son."

"In spite of being Jewish," I say.

"Well, let us say that he loved me like a bastard son," he laughs and touches my knee with his fan.

"Tell me then how Castellón ended," I say. "In the gas chamber?"

"What makes you imagine that?" he says. "He walked around all over the concentration camp, wherever he wanted, taking pictures. Von Dengler even assigned a soldier assistant to carry his equipment for him."

"Pictures that Von Dengler wanted for himself," I suggest.

"Some. But he did others to suit his own artistic taste."

"So he died then in his own bed," I say.

"In March, 1944, of pneumonia, in the shed behind the Von Denglers' chalet where we both lived. Outside the barbed wire fences," he says.

"And what happened to you then?"

"Finally you're getting around to me," he says. "Nothing. I went on feeding Frau Von Dengler's geese."

"And you stayed in the chalet."

"Until the Americans came."

"And how did the Americans treat you?" I ask.

"When they entered the camp, Von Dengler had already shot himself and his wife had fled to Salzburg with everything, plus her legion of kids," he says.

It was not difficult for him to align himself with the prisoners because among them were many veterans of the Spanish Republic whom he used to supply with food he stole from the officers' stores, and he was taken to France together with them. The authorities there confined him to a vocational school of the Christian Brothers in Toulouse, where there were only war orphans, to give him a trade. He chose bookbinding, and when he had learned that, they turned him out on the streets. Then he decided to return to Spain. He presented himself at the Consulate in Perpignan, told them his true story, and they granted him a safe-conduct. The Red Cross repatriated him to Barcelona, and from there he took ship as a stowaway to Palma. Thus he returned to this shop which then was closed up and in need of repairs. With the help of some relatives he opened his bookbinding shop, at which he worked for years.

"Until I became caught up in the mandala fad, and I sold the flat upstairs to establish this school and open the shop," he said.

"At one time I thought that Castellón, at the end of it all, had died on Mallorca," I remarked.

"One of his deaths, that's possible."

"Four is the number of doors to the palace of death," I said. "I know that from one of your brochures."

"But only one of them is the door of physical death," he said. "The fourth."

"Mauthausen," I responded.

"In any event, that has no importance here," he said. "The four of them are in the same category, even though some of them open only in dreams. What is important is to complete the cycle, so as to rise to the higher plane and transcend into some other being. Metempsychosis."

"Therefore, Castellón is now roaming through the astral planes taking pictures of dead bodies until he succeeds in being reincarnated," I said.

"If you want to make fun..."

"I am not ridiculing anything," I said. "Trying to find out more about him, I read *Isis Unveiled* by Madame Blavatsky, and metempsychosis is discussed there."

"That book will explain everything better," he responded. "About his life and about his deaths."

"When do we meet on one of the astral planes?" I said. "It will probably be too late for my novel."

Taking no notice of my remark, he gets to his feet and goes toward the corner behind the screen where the bed is. I hear him digging around somewhere and then he returns bearing an embossed folder bound in Cordoban leather in order to present it to me as if were an offering.

"We have reached the end," he says. "He knew that someday you would come, looking for this."

He goes back to sit down again and meanwhile I hurriedly open the portfolio which contains a thick file of pages typed cleanly and correctly, organized into chapters. I start to look them over.

"I want to ask you a question," I say.

"However many you like," covering a yawn with the hand that is holding the now collapsed fan.

"Was it you who wrote this?"

I decide to pay close attention to the reactions on his face, convinced that he will hesitate in responding, but I am wrong.

"I have only been the amanuensis," he answers.

"Did Castellón dictate these memoirs in Mauthausen before dying?" I ask. "You were only eleven years old then."

"No, I have written them here in this back room."

"When did you begin?"

"The year before last."

"Then they are memoirs from beyond the grave," I remark.

"But very faithful," he responds.

"You have not required a medium?"

"Like Madame Kandó?" he is laughing. "No, I have worked by myself."

"But you heard Castellón's voice dictating them," I insist.

"Only the out and out paranoiacs hear voices," he says.

"Of course. You are right."

"Now you can take them with you, they're yours, they're what you came for," he says.

A glass of the waters of oblivion

THREE DISCONNECTED RECOLLECTIONS come to mind as I wrap up these pages, and I don't want to neglect noting them down, now that the one who has been seeking me has so little left to find out about me.

The first is connected to the night-long drunken romp at Christmas time in 1913 that I took part in with Rubén Darío, whose name always reminds me of a frightened animal, paralyzed by the fear of suffering more wounds than he already has, but also a persistently stubborn one. On that occasion I had taken him to the Call Menor because he had gotten terribly muddled, what with wild ideas from his imagination or odd things he had picked up from his reading. Among them was his eagerness to hear how I managed to get along among these wealthy Jews who, every night before going to bed, would take their bags of gold coins out of their hiding places beneath the bed to polish them one by one, and who, having been obliged while in public to eat blood sausage, bacon, and other unclean foods in order to keep up the pretense of having been converted to Christianity, would then run to the bathroom to vomit it all up.

It was close to sunrise when the car dropped us off in front of the Santa Eulalia church. He then got down on his knees and approached the still unopened doors, until he fell to banging on them, asking for confession. But the sacristan, who had been readying the interior of the church for the first mass of the day, rushed out in a fury and threatened to call the police. Rubén insisted that I take him to my house, but since I had nothing there to show him other than my poverty, plus my daughter Teresa who was of course asleep at this time of day, I tried to distract him.

We walked together arm in arm to the Carrer del Sindicato, stumbling over the smooth paving stones, and so we approached the slaughterhouse where they were sacrificing a batch of pigs that were squealing in fear and jostling violently against the sides of their cages and leaping up and falling back in a blind heap, hooves scraping on the pavement. On becoming aware of the dense odor of their dung as well as getting our feet wet in the blood that they were washing away and letting drain along a channel into the gutter, he abruptly threw his arms around me in horror because, so he said, those pigs must have been the ones possessed by demons that with the help of Jesus's power had hurled themselves into the Sea of Galilee; and then, somewhat calmer, he started reciting in Greek some lines that he afterward translated, informing me that these were couplets by Apollodorus about Hercules' fifth labor, which consisted in cleaning out the Augian stables with his hands.

After this we came to the Carrer del Olivero, and in front of a carpenter's shop where a pedal saw was already at work cutting boards of cedar, he invited me to smell the fragrance of the wood because, so he also said, it was the perfume of our infancy in Nicaragua, and he let the sawdust being blown through the open vent rain down over his head.

In the Carrer de la Argentería the silversmiths had set up their workbenches outside in front of their doorways because it was the custom to work in the open air until the sun began to shine, each one of them with an anvil between his legs, laboring over the fineness of their pieces, while their women would bring them their breakfast of garbanzo beans and slices of bacon. Rubén then went over to Pere Porcel, an uncle of my deceased wife and head of the guild, as if to admire the eleven-foot-long chain that he was busy pounding out, link by link, striking the head of the chisel with a boxwood hammer, but Rubén was really more interested in getting a whiff from the bowl waiting beside the old man on the bench, determined to prove to himself that the ornament floating in the garbanzos was really bacon.

Another one of my wife's uncles came to meet us with his hat held out before him. His name was Eloy Tarongí, and he was withered, skinny, and terribly rich, the owner of the umbrella shop on the Carrer de San Miguel. He spent his whole life dressed in the severest black, and as a penance he was committed to begging for alms to help feed the penniless residents of the Misericordia shelter. With an exaggerated gesture Rubén dropped his mite into the hat without my being able to prevent it. When the man had moved on I explained to Rubén that he had just given charity to a rich man, upon which he became very angry and shouted out that he felt he'd been deceived, and he came up with the mocking remark that his black suit looked as if it were made out of the same shiny material as an umbrella, for I had mentioned the fact that Tarongí was the owner of a shop where they made umbrellas. But when the umbrella maker heard Rubén's taunt he turned in his tracks, extremely offended, not with Rubén but with me, and announced that he would never again ask me for any photography work.

But the bells of Santa Eulalia had just begun to ring the morning angelus, and the silversmiths all left their hammers and their breakfast bowls, and together with others who were rushing toward the narrow stairways that only had room enough for one person at a time, started kneeling in the middle of the street, heads down, upon which Rubén began imitating them. Once the bells became silent he had the impertinence to observe, without caring whether anyone heard him or not, that all this was just the same old thing as ever, the *chuetas* hurrying to prostrate themselves where no one could help but see them, just as in the old days when it was worth their lives if they didn't openly show evidence of their Christian habits. Fortunately he forgot about coming to my house, said he was thirsty, and we went off in search of a car; what we were leaving behind were some smells well-known to me, the smell of coal and cast silver, of gold dust and menstrual remains lingering in the underskirts of the women who were now eating what was left in the bowls.

And now another recollection, which comes to me very close upon my own end. The snow that falls in dense swirls over the barracks, barbed wire, and watch towers at Mauthausen and that gradually erases the flights of stairs cut out of the stone going down into the quarry where the Emperor Franz Josef had ordered blocks of granite cut for paving Vienna's streets, according to a detailed account in a pamphlet by the Archduke Luis Salvador, and where now

A glass of the waters of oblivion

gangs of famished prisoners are prying loose those hundred pound blocks that other prisoners are forced to carry to the top, stair by stair, under threat, if they are unable to make it, of being tossed down from the so-called "paratrooper's trampoline," a precipice that juts out over the quarry and on whose ledges and thickets of brush the snow is also falling, softly, funerary.

But now I must take the picture. A photograph of the procession marching down the narrow, frozen street, like glass, headed for the square where the gallows is set up, a group of musicians in front of the flat-bedded vehicle carrying the prisoners captured in flight, three adults of a family of Hungarian gypsies assigned to amuse the children of the commanding officer Von Dengler with their juggling, and two children from the same family. They had managed to get quite far away, since they were found hidden on one of the barges transporting granite blocks up the Danube. The procession comes to a halt so I can take this picture better, without the musicians ceasing to play. And when I look through the viewfinder the prisoners are holding on to each other to brace themselves against the jostling of the cart; the driver, also dressed in the uniform of a prisoner, is pulling back on the reins; the horses are puffing and blowing, exhaling a fragile cloud of steam; and the seven musicians of the band are marking time with their feet, the flute player in the foreground holding his flute out with his hands wrapped in frayed rags and the three violinists passing their bows briskly back and forth over the strings.

These photos of the processions of the condemned and their executions as punishment for their attempts to escape are fastened by their corners to the pages of Von Dengler's album. According to my helper the soldier (because I am never told directly), behind my back the camp commander has praised my last previous photo of a partisan from Calanda transported from the Barcarés concentration camp in France who had become totally entangled among the snags of the barbed wire barrier, as if it were some kind of shroud. And now he will also get the photograph of this procession, and the one showing the five prisoners hanging from the gallows, three longer pendulums with bare feet and two shorter ones outlined against the gray sky in which some crows are cawing.

"I want good pictures," he has ordered. "This album is my best guarantee against my superiors." That is why this soldier from the SS who carries my equipment follows me around all the time, and now he has raised his hand to halt the parade, giving me time to set up the tripod in the middle of the street. Then, when I kneel down (so hard for me to do) to take out of its case the Goerz bellows camera they have furnished me, I see the reflection of my face in the congealed water as those spectral figures continue playing.

My face is that of an old man become too old. Sir, what do we do with this old guy? asks Von Dengler's aide-de-camp on the station platform in Linz when they inspect the shipment of prisoners on the ghost train from Warsaw. Around my neck I am wearing a sign around my neck, tied with a string, that says: BY ORDER OF STÜRMFUHRER NIKOLAUS VON DENGLER. He'll work on the rocks like the others. He can't do that, growls the aide brazenly. Von Dengler looks me up and down. A benzine injection is worth more than his hide, he says; let him make pictures for me, but he will sleep in the barracks with the others. I would like to see my grandson, sir, I ask. Even though I know I'm going to die, I want to see him again before that.

Because in Warsaw he had been pulled from my hands, kidnapped by Von Dengler's wife who wanted him in her service as a page, and so he traveled with them in a special car. Von Dengler doesn't respond at all to my petition, he just looks at me scornfully and turns his back to go off down the platform with his retinue of officers. I never saw Rubén again except once from a distance as he was watering the roses at the chalet, dressed in a gray SS uniform half a size too large for him, his temples shaved and a cap sunk down over his ears.

On the wrapping paper of the photography materials they supply me with, on the backs of unacceptable copies of photos, I have written these final pages of what remains for me to establish concerning my life, so that the soldier who helps me carry my equipment around can hand them to Rubén, to whom I have already entrusted the rest. This soldier, a peasant from Wittenberg, has promised to do this for me in exchange for a picture I did of him for his birthday that he wanted to send home to his mother. But I'll do this only when you are dead, he told me with a smile of complicity.

And my final recollection then is that of a dream. Last night I dreamt I had returned to Nicaragua in some future time, at the end of the century. I was getting into León at midnight in the midst of a terrible downpour, and I asked the driver, who in my dream looks like this soldier from Wittenberg, to take me to the Zaragoza barrio but to drive slowly, so I can find the house that had belonged to Terencio Catín.

There was no Napoleonic plan bisecting the New Constantinople, blessed by the line of the canal through Nicaragua, no swarms of sailors in the barrios of prostitutes on exhibit behind glass windows as in the Reeperbahn in Hamburg, no bellowing from the boats in the night breaking their way through the fogbanks, no sound of the bells on the buoys in response to those in the old churches, as my father the dreamer had envisioned, and behind the curtain of rain I only saw empty spaces of wasteland where weeds were growing, walls half tumbled down, and more weeds on top of the burned gateways, ruins of the most recent of the civil wars that appeared before my eyes in the glare of the vehicle's headlights and eventually sank back into the darkness.

I found Catín's house, and he was on the sidewalk. In spite of the rain that was whipping at his face, he never stopped planing with his only arm the boards for a coffin that was my coffin, as he told me smiling while measuring with his eye one of the boards and putting it with the others next to the wall, and my mother Catherine then appeared at the door bowed over from the weight of pregnancy, she seemed to expect someone but she didn't see me, and suddenly Master Leonard who was sitting beside me in the car took me by the arm, there was no need for me to be worried, what Catín was making for me was a cradle, and the person my mother was waiting for was the midwife. You'll come into the world in the midst of a hurricane, he was telling me, the most tremendous that has ever devastated this country.

A picture, you've got to take a picture, Leonard squeezed my hand gently, opened the door, and got out, only to be dissolved in the rain. Then the soldier from Wittenberg went on down the road, always at the wheel, and when it got light we had reached the foot of the *cordillera* of volcanoes that I had glimpsed so many times from the patio at Catín's house, always threatening, always bellowing, always casting out glowing rocks, always lifting up dense fumaroles that for fireworks rivaled the storms. A turbid current of knee-deep water hurled itself down from the heights of the least offensive of those volcanoes, one that had been inactive for the longest time, strewing rocks in its path, uprooting trees, flooding and destroying villages and corrals, drowning livestock, killing hundreds of families as they slept, now buried forever beneath the muddy flats that stretched way into the distance.

The smell of the bodies rotting made us ill and flocks of vultures weighed down the naked branches of the *jícaro* trees, the few that had not been swept away. In the corners of my jacket pockets were more than enough rolls of film, and in the suitcase two cameras, a Nikon F60 for color and a Canon 500 for black and white. Color wouldn't do well here because in this desolate landscape the contrasts had been erased. I took out the Canon and cocked the shutter release.

Then I saw him. On the dirty gray of the clay that defined the whole of the horizon was lying the naked body of a little boy about three years old. To his right, a lean, black hog was sniffing, drawing close. Pigs, children, naked bodies, this was like an everlasting repetition of my whole destiny, I said to myself as the hog kept moving closer and I am walking all around the child, shooting, with an infinite horizon of limestone and ash in the viewfinder, there is no sky in the field of vision, merely gray, the darker outline of the naked child and the still darker one of the oncoming hog, its coat all muddy, jaws half-open where tusks could be imagined, the groove for its little eyes, sharp-pointed ears alert, spiraled tail, muddy coat, half-open jaws now that the horizon is turning completely around and the world is retreating and the earth shakes under a new avalanche of rocks, mud, and broken tree trunks dragging me into the darkness together with the child's dead body and the hog.

Arlington, 2000. Managua 2000-2003.